BLOOD
PASSAGE

BLOOD DESTINY, BOOK 2

Connie Suttle

For Walter, because he made it possible
And for Joe and Dianne, whose help has been invaluable
Thank you

Blood Passage
Copyright © 2014 by Connie Suttle
All rights reserved

The Author's information may be found at the end of this book.

This book is a work of fiction. Names, characters and incidents portrayed within its pages are a product of the author's imagination. Any resemblance to actual persons (or vampires, werewolves, High Demons, Greater Demons, Lesser Demons, Larentii, shapeshifters, Ra'Ak, wizards, warlocks, witches, Avii, Saa Thalarr or gods) living or dead, is purely coincidental.

This book, whole or in part, MAY NOT be copied or reproduced by mechanical means (including photocopying or the implementation of any type of storage or retrieval system), without the express written permission of the author, except where permitted by law.

ISBN-13: 9781499794212
ISBN-10: 1499794215

Other books by Connie Suttle

Blood Destiny Series:

Blood Wager

Blood Passage

Blood Sense

Blood Domination

Blood Royal

Blood Queen

Blood Rebellion

Blood War

Blood Redemption

Blood Reunion

Legend of the Ir'Indicti Series:

Bumble

Shadowed

Target

Vendetta

Destroyer

High Demon Series:

Demon Lost

Demon Revealed

Demon's King

Demon's Quest

Demon's Revenge

Demon's Dream

The God Wars Series:

Blood Double

Blood Trouble

Blood Revolution

Blood Love

Blood Finale

The Saa Thalarr Series:

Hope and Vengeance

Wyvern and Company*

First Ordinance Series:

Finder

Keeper*

The R-D Series:

Cloud Dust

Cloud Invasion*

*Forthcoming

CHAPTER 1

"Lissa, this is Brock." My surrogate sire, Merrill (as handsome as the devil with ebon hair and piercing blue eyes), introduced me to a vampire who was perhaps an inch taller than his own six-three. I'd been called into Merrill's overly large kitchen for the introduction. Franklin stood at the stove nearby, preparing dinner for himself and Lena, Merrill's housekeeper.

Brock's scent told me immediately that Merrill had made him. That was my secret, now—knowing who'd sired whom. If I'd met the sire, that is. Perhaps I would tell Merrill of this particular ability someday. *Perhaps.*

He'd frowned slightly when I informed him that I could determine the age of any vampire by scent. Not their exact age, mind you, but I could certainly tell which ones were older and which younger.

Brock wasn't nearly as handsome and nowhere near as old as Merrill. I'd guessed the tall, brown-eyed vampire to be around a hundred years old. His scent was one of the lightest ones I'd encountered among vampires. Even Charles's was heavier and spicier.

"Hello," I held out my hand politely. Sometimes vampires frown on touching, so I was taking a chance. When Brock smiled and took my hand, I almost breathed a sigh of relief.

"Brock is here to teach you to take blood properly," Merrill said, motioning for us to follow him. Franklin turned from his cooking for a moment and winked at me before I followed obediently behind

Merrill and Brock. Our destination was Merrill's study, where most of my lessons took place.

"Remain standing," Merrill instructed, so I stood behind my favorite chair, which faced his hand-carved, cherry wood desk. My favorite chair was the wingback on the left. I don't know why I preferred it to the one on the right; both were spaced evenly before Merrill's desk and were identical as far as I could tell.

"I taught Brock how to take blood properly," Merrill went on, "so he will be taking from you, teaching you not only how to do it for yourself but what happens with the bite when it comes. This will enable you to take properly if you find it necessary and no bagged blood is available."

Merrill's words made me want to shrink away from Brock. I'd only been bitten once—to my knowledge anyway—and that resulted in my turning. I had no memory of it and just the thought of being bitten frightened me.

Merrill knew right away. I suppose he'd spent a very long time reading the reactions of others, vampires included. I was a new turn and most likely an open book. "Lissa, he will not harm you," Merrill scolded. I must have cringed enough to offend both Merrill and Brock. Drawing a steadying breath, I straightened up immediately.

"I really won't hurt you," Brock said gently, attempting to reassure. He was giving me a lop-sided grin but that didn't help much. I didn't know this man—or vampire. *At all.*

"Now," Merrill began, "if the donor seems reluctant, you must place compulsion."

Brock's eyes met mine as he took my hand and murmured, "I will not harm you. You have nothing to fear." His weak compulsion washed over me. I nodded at him, my eyes wide with fright. My terror was stronger than Brock's compulsion, but I wasn't going to point that out to him or to Merrill.

"Now, you must bring their body against yours and hold it securely," Merrill explained. Brock pulled my body against his with one hand while the other cupped the back of my neck. I shivered in his grasp.

"Next," Merrill continued while pointedly ignoring my silent alarm, "you may choose to place a kiss. Your saliva holds just a bit of natural anesthetic, so any initial pain may be muted."

Brock placed a careful kiss over the artery in my throat. I could feel his cool breath against my skin as he held my body firmly against his. The kiss, as careful as it was, did nothing to allay my fear. I knew what was coming, tightly embraced as I was against an unknown vampire. He held power over me—they all did. It terrified me.

"The bite comes next," Merrill said while Brock sank his fangs into my throat. I stiffened as I felt his teeth enter my skin, and whimpered while the most intense orgasm I'd ever experienced washed over me before blackness descended.

※ ※

"Lissa? Wake up, child," Merrill slapped my wrist. Franklin was there with Merrill; I could tell by the scent. He was also the one washing my face with a cold, wet cloth. My eyes blinked open and I stared at Merrill and Franklin both.

"I don't know why I wasn't expecting this, at least on some level," Merrill chastised himself. I was lying on a sofa in his bedroom—Merrill's suite was near his study, so they'd taken me there to bring me around.

"You haven't known her very long," Franklin attempted to calm Merrill down. "How would you know?"

I was listening to them with barely half an ear. I'd fainted only once since becoming vampire and remembered it vividly; Gavin kissed me, then blackness had come. Gavin was currently on assignment, but when he returned and called to see if I'd go out with him, he had some serious explaining to do.

"How do you feel?" Merrill patted my hand.

"All right," I sat up on the sofa and looked around. I'd never been inside Merrill's bedroom before and probably would never be there again. It was richly decorated in a masculine sort of way. There was only one photograph in the entire suite and it rested on Merrill's bedside table. I didn't linger long on the image.

"Maybe you should drink some of this," Brock walked in, offering a unit of blood. My cheeks might have flooded with color if I'd still been able to blush. I accepted the blood with my own version of embarrassment, shaking hands and all.

"This isn't embarrassing or anything," I muttered, biting the top off the bag to drink.

"We knew the climax would come, I just hadn't any idea how intense it would be," Merrill said. "For that, I apologize."

"Well, that's the first time I ever did that with two men in the room," I grumbled as I sipped blood. Franklin snickered.

"If it's any consolation, I'm gay," Brock said. "So, only one of the men was straight."

I met Brock's steady gaze, his clear, brown eyes revealing a bit of worry. "I don't think my body knew the difference," I shrugged.

"Tomorrow evening, we will take you out and you will do this for yourself," Merrill informed me. "We planned to go out tonight, but your faint has precluded that activity."

"If you could eat them, I'd make brownies for you," Franklin smiled as he took the bag of blood away. I'd only finished half of it.

"I remember chocolate," I heaved a shaky sigh. "Thanks for the thought." I smiled back at Franklin. We'd become good friends, he and I. He patted my shoulder.

"Come, we'll do other lessons tonight," Merrill helped me off the sofa. I followed him on unsteady legs as he walked toward his study. Brock and Franklin turned toward the stairs lying in the opposite direction.

"I know Gavin gave you rule four," Merrill began, once we were seated in our usual spots. "Rule five is this: You cannot attempt to turn anyone unless you are past your five-year apprenticeship. After that, you may only attempt ten turns throughout your lifetime. This rule played a large part in Edward and Sergio's death sentences; they'd turned nearly thirty between them. I think you were twenty-eight or twenty-nine. Another died while they hunted you. They'd also killed all your predecessors, playing their sick games. You were the only one who lived."

"Wow. I had no idea." I was shocked. No doubt, there were missing persons reports on many a detective's desk, and all because two fanged morons thought it was fun to play with people's lives.

"There are other stipulations as well," Merrill steepled his fingers and gazed across his desk at me. "First, it must be a viable candidate, in a place where the turn may be completed without interruption or observance by other humans. By viable candidate, we mean that they must be dying or near death, of good character and over the age of eighteen. If they are a criminal as a human, then they will be a criminal as a vampire. The commutative property taking effect as it were," the corner of Merrill's mouth curled into a slight smile.

"You will be considered rogue and subject to the death penalty if you ever drink from or attempt to turn a child. And once you do perform a turn, you must monitor that individual, watching over them every night until the transformation is complete. You are required to do this so they will not wake unsupervised and in confusion as to what they are. You will take responsibility for your child from the beginning, making sure he is carefully taught everything he should know to become a member of the vampire race. If your child disobeys, he must be punished. If he becomes unmanageable, then you are expected to notify the Council, who will order the child brought in for questioning. If the Council determines that the child is unfit, they will order the death of the child and that death will come swiftly."

"I don't think I'll be trying it," I whispered, stunned by Merrill's explanation. The thought of taking responsibility for an adult vampire gave me the shivers.

"I've only turned five and two of those are dead," Merrill informed me, the emotionless mask sliding into place across his features.

"I'm sorry," I said. Merrill inclined his head in silent acceptance.

※ ※

We parked several blocks away and walked to a popular nightclub in London—Merrill, Brock and I. Young people were everywhere outside the brick building, talking, laughing and standing in a long line. It was Friday night and the place was crowded, with loud music thumping through the air from a live band playing inside.

"I will select your target; you must get him alone and drink from him," Merrill instructed quietly as we approached the club and the spillover of humans outside it. He'd deliberately kept me from eating before we left the house. It was now past midnight and I was definitely feeling hungry. I'd had regularly scheduled meals since coming to live with Merrill.

"No," I whispered, as Merrill pointed out the one I was supposed to target. The young man had short, spiked hair, black roots with blond tips, piercings in every visible body part and additional piercings that I could make out beneath his thin shirt and low-riding jeans. What wasn't pierced was tattooed—everything from skulls to spider webs. I think he even had a gun and knife tattooed on each of his biceps.

"Lissa, you will not always have the luxury of picking and choosing. Go get that one and be done with it," Merrill ordered sternly when I shook my head and attempted to back away.

Disliking my surrogate sire for the first time ever, I squared my shoulders and stalked unwillingly toward my target. Merrill had instructed me to dress *casual chic*, as he termed it, and I'd found a sleeveless tank top in cranberry and my short, black skirt with sandals. I was overdressed for this crowd, I discovered.

"Hi, handsome," I said to the young man, a strong desire to gag making its presence known as I trailed a finger suggestively down his tank-top-covered chest. He was probably stoned along with being drunk; a faint scent of alcohol was on his breath.

With blue eyes unfocused and pupils merely pinpoints, he smiled at me. Since I didn't smell much alcohol on his breath, I figured it was drugs. And, as heroin or opioid addiction causes the pupils to contract, it was likely he wasn't new to his habit.

Resigning myself to impending and subsequent impairment, I placed the initial compulsion, suggesting that we walk toward a nearby alleyway. He agreed eagerly, draped an arm around my shoulders and tried to kiss me once before we reached a dark spot where we wouldn't be seen.

I took his blood quickly, following Merrill's instructions to the letter before placing compulsion to forget me and the act I'd just committed. Merrill was somehow behind me when I finished and he and I walked toward Brock, who now leaned against the car, waiting for our return. I was wobbling by the time I arrived.

"What's wrong with you?" Brock asked as I nearly fell into him. He managed to catch me with one hand while opening my door with the other.

"Lover boy was stoned," I giggled. It doesn't take much to get me drunk; *that's how I got vampirized to begin with*, I thought to myself. Is *vampirized* even a word? I giggled again.

"Let's get her out of here," Merrill muttered. He and Brock herded me into the back seat of the car. Brock drove while Merrill leaned over the back of the passenger seat, keeping a watchful eye on me as we made our way through the outskirts of London.

"I used to go through the drive-through window of my favorite donut shop and say 'gimme a half dozen, I want to commit a sin'," I threw a hand in the air and giggled at my own joke. Donuts were a favorite form of gluttony back then. Merrill remained watchful and silent, choosing to lift an eyebrow at my antics instead.

Brock pulled into valet at a popular London restaurant and Merrill ushered me inside, Brock following behind. I was still behaving erratically and wobbling as I walked.

Merrill's hand slipped beneath my elbow to steady me after only a few steps. "You must appear to be human and completely normal,"

Merrill hissed in my ear. I stared at him briefly before exploding with laughter.

"Lissa, do not force me tell you again," Merrill snapped. I straightened right up. The threat of compulsion had saturated his words and there wasn't any way I wanted more of *that*.

Forcing myself to eat a light meal after the drug-laced blood I'd ingested may be one of the hardest things I've ever done in my life. Merrill and Brock also ate a small plate of food. I was instructed to speak with the waiter and to make sense while I did it. I wanted to smack Merrill and Brock—when I asked them to excuse me so I could go to the ladies' room and eliminate what I'd eaten by coughing it up, Merrill wouldn't allow it.

Brock drove us home afterward, the motion of the automobile making me feel worse with each passing moment. The drugs were having a bad effect and the food was about to make me ill, if that were possible.

I couldn't help myself; the moment Brock parked inside Merrill's garage, I was out of the car and rushing through the still-open garage door. Dropping to my knees, I coughed up my toenails on the nicely manicured lawn outside. Merrill offered to help me stand afterward, but I slapped his hand away, got off my knees and wobbled into the house, wiping tears as I went. I may have slammed the door to my bedroom, too, while I was at it.

※ ※

"I can't say I liked that lesson much either," Brock muttered when he and Merrill heard Lissa's bedroom door slam shut. Merrill sighed.

"She won't speak to me for two days," he said, walking toward his study.

"Sounds about right," Brock agreed and went to find a book to read.

※ ※

Still furious when I woke the following evening, I ate, got my shower and dressed. Merrill would be holding class again at the usual time. I didn't speak to him or ask any questions the whole time he talked and he didn't force the issue.

My arms were crossed tightly against my body throughout the lesson and when Merrill dismissed me, I was out of his study so fast I was a blur. The rooftop was my place to sulk or think and I was there, sulking for the remainder of the night.

Rain fell two hours before dawn; therefore, I was soaked when I came inside. I wasn't worried about Merrill's expensive rugs, antique or otherwise, when I made sure not to track water and wet grass on the floors and carpets. I didn't want Franklin and Lena to be forced clean up after me. My shoes and socks were removed before I entered the house and I ran through the entryway so I wouldn't drip on anything.

The second night was just the same. Merrill talked; I listened and sulked. Once again, the roof was my place to hide. After the third and fourth nights of silence (on my part, at least), Merrill studied me from behind his desk. "I have to hand it to you," he said finally. "All the others were angry for two nights and then began talking again. You hold the record."

"I'm sure the world record people will come calling any minute now," I muttered sarcastically. I would have drawn my knees up to my chin but that would be rude and I might damage the furniture with my shoes.

"Lissa, you must behave as a human will, no matter the circumstances," Merrill scolded. "You may find yourself in the position of having taken bad or tainted blood and then having to behave normally. That was a test. If you hadn't passed it, we would have repeated it."

"Oh, God," I mumbled. I was feeling ill, just by thinking about it. I have no idea how that young man remained on his feet; I was completely under the influence by taking only a little of his blood.

"You look green," Merrill remarked as he rose and walked around his desk.

"I feel worse," I said. "I think I'm going to be sick again." I was out of his study and down the hall in a blink, then on my knees and dry heaving into a powder room toilet in less time than that.

"I don't know what's wrong," Merrill was suddenly beside me. Someone else was with him. *Someone not vampire.* I was too busy trying to heave up something that wasn't there when the second man knelt next to me. A warm, strong hand was placed on my forehead and he leaned me back, even as the urge to keep on vomiting faded away. It was a blessed relief, actually.

"What's wrong with our little girl?" the man crooned. I gazed helplessly at a tall, brown-haired man. He didn't appear old at all, but an endless depth of knowledge and experience flickered and shifted behind hazel eyes. So deep, in fact, was that abyss that it might take centuries for me to reach the bottom of it. And there was no scent—as if he were shielded somehow.

Only the smell of sunlight clinging to his clothing let me know he wasn't vampire. In my sickly state at that moment, I was too confused to attempt any explanation for it. Blinking back tears that had come with the dry heaves, I stared at him and tried to say something—ask him who he was—but he placed two fingers against my forehead and I was asleep.

※ ※

"Who can say what that youth had inside his body," Griffin told Merrill. "And she still had a bit of the werewolf poison in her system. It didn't mix well." He dried his hands after washing them in Lissa's bathroom. "I eliminated all of it," he went on.

"If I'd known that, I would have sent her after a drunk," Merrill grumbled.

"How were you to know?" Griffin said, tossing the towel onto the marble vanity. "Stop blaming yourself; she'll be fine."

※ ※

"Merrill is away," Franklin advised me when I made my way downstairs the following evening. It was Wednesday night and with Merrill's absence, I was left with nothing to do.

"I feel better, at least," I said. "I haven't felt good for days."

"I know. Merrill told me," Franklin said. "Come over here and give me a hug." He was sitting at the kitchen island, his empty plate beside him. He'd already eaten and Lena had gone home for the evening. Moving to his side, I put an arm around him, burying my head against his shoulder.

"Here, now, what's this about?" Franklin turned and placed both arms around me.

"I don't know if I can do five years of this," I sniffled against Franklin's shoulder.

"I know," Franklin rubbed my back gently. "Merrill's a fine teacher. We'll get you through this." I didn't say it, but if there were more lessons like the bite lesson, it was going to be a really long five years.

The roof was the first place I went, and then the hot tub and the library. I even watched television and that's something I don't do often. One of the articles I caught mentioned a display of tiaras which had been worn by Princess Diana—both the Cambridge Lover's Knot tiara and the Spencer family tiara. They'd been lent to the London Library and displayed in a special case. Guards were posted around them for a week, but someone managed to steal them anyway. The Royal Family and the Spencer family were quite upset over the whole thing.

Thursday night when I woke, I did my usual in addition to changing the sheets on my bed. Lena offered every time but I was able-bodied and bored. I did it myself, usually on Thursday because that was Lena's day off.

Clattering downstairs later so I wouldn't frighten Franklin by sneaking up on him, I found him in the kitchen as usual. Instead of his usual, cheery hello, I received a pain-filled glance. Franklin sat on a barstool, his skin gray and clammy. Merrill was still out of town (where, I had no idea—he never told me and I never asked).

"Franklin, what's wrong?" I asked, feeling his forehead. His skin felt hot and he was shaking.

"My side is killing me," he said, placing a hand on his right side.

"Oh, good lord," I said. "Honey, we have to get you to the hospital." Pulling my cell from the pocket of my jeans, I tried Merrill's numbers first—there were two of them. I got voice mail both times. Then I tried calling Charles. Same thing—voice mail. "Franklin, I hope you know where the hospital is," I told him, and lifting him easily in my arms, carried him toward the garage.

Merrill has a pegboard inside the garage where all the car keys are neatly labeled and hung. Figuring the Cadillac was the least expensive thing to replace if I wrecked it, I settled Franklin on the passenger seat. I had no experience whatsoever with driving on the left side of the road, so I got my trial by fire that night. I'm sure all those people honking and offering rude gestures meant well.

Franklin was giving me directions as best he could but I could tell he was in terrible pain. "Just hang on, honey, okay?" I kept telling him while trying to negotiate left turns. To me, all of it was backward.

When we pulled into the emergency room drive, I raced inside and placed compulsion on the first person in scrubs I could find. They brought out a wheel chair and we got Franklin settled into it and on his way inside. Thank goodness, Franklin had his wallet with him; I didn't even know his last name, which turned out to be Wright. He even had an insurance card since he was listed as a U.S. citizen. The nurse must have suspected the same thing I did because they took him in right away. Sure enough, it was his appendix.

The waiting room was as cold and cheerless as it could possibly be as I sat there, waiting for the surgeon to come and tell me how Frank was doing. "It wasn't abscessed or perforated, although that wouldn't have held true much longer," the doctor informed me when he appeared several hours later. "You got him here at a good time. We'll probably keep Mr. Wright for a couple of days; he's in good shape for someone his age."

"Thank God," I sighed. "Thank you, doctor, I was really worried."

He smiled at me. "No worries," the smile turned into a grin. "You could have coffee with me later, to show your appreciation."

"Well, we'll see about that," I said, putting him off. Just what I needed—an amorous human physician.

I was allowed to visit Franklin in his room a while after that, but he was asleep still, after coming out of recovery. Stroking his forehead, I dropped a kiss on his cheek and whispered quietly that I had to leave. It was nearing five in the morning and I wouldn't get home before daybreak if I didn't go soon. "Someone will be here later," I informed the nurse as I was leaving.

"We'll take good care of him," she promised. I gave her my thanks and headed toward the car.

Traffic had slowed significantly; I was in that dead space just before the morning rush began and I left the London area behind before it really started up again. My memory is much better now than it used to be—I found my way home, discovering that I'd left the garage door open when I'd driven the car out earlier.

After checking the entire house, I left yet another message for Merrill. This time I explained what had happened and where Franklin was, adding that I'd done the best I could. I also told him that the Cadillac was in one piece. I'm sure that was a minor miracle, considering my state of mind and my inexperienced driving on the wrong side of the road.

A note for Lena was the last thing I did, writing down Franklin's room number, along with the name of the hospital and leaving it for her on the kitchen island. I was a wreck when I went to bed at dawn.

Lena was in the kitchen when I hurried downstairs Friday evening. "Master Merrill is on his way to the hospital, Miss Lissa," she said. "I went to see Franklin the moment I got your note," she added, her pretty, brown eyes worried. "They told me he was doing fine, but how can you tell?"

Lena was a worrier, it appeared. "He'll be all right, I think," I reassured her. "The doctor was very nice and seemed quite competent." I didn't say what I really wanted—why hadn't Merrill waited for me to wake so I could visit Franklin, too? Now I was stuck there at the house. No way did I want to call Merrill on his cell phone, just so I could whine about being left behind. I'd go to the roof and pout instead.

I thought about Franklin and about Don while I sat dejectedly on Merrill's roof. The six-month anniversary of Don's death had come and gone; we were into August already. Franklin also came into my thoughts often, so I sent up a little prayer for him.

Does anybody listen to the prayers of vampires? I had no way of knowing. Merrill floated up and joined me on the roof an hour before dawn, sitting down beside me with a sigh. I didn't say anything as he settled himself in a comfortable position.

"Franklin's fine," he said right away. "I should have waited for you I know, little vampire," he waved away the words that threatened to spill from my lips. "He asked about you first thing and I felt ashamed of myself. If you hadn't gotten him to the hospital as quickly as you did, things might have turned out much worse. The surgeon said his appendix was on its way toward perforation and that might have caused peritonitis."

"I know," I said. "I had an uncle who died of that during World War II. The good news is that I didn't wreck the Cadillac. Not that I didn't try, inadvertently. All those people who honked and screamed obscenities did it in the nicest way possible."

Merrill chuckled and placed an arm around me. "Gavin said you asked about a vampire manual once. You could have taken the online course for all this and done just fine I think, but rules are rules."

"Yeah, well," I grumbled, deliberately holding back my opinion of vampire rules.

"Franklin may be home when you rise, Lissa. He'll need care for a few weeks. You may help with that if you want."

"Of course I want to," I grumped. "I don't have much else to do."

"I know," Merrill said. "We may have to do something about that. And we have to keep Franklin entertained too, while he's recuperating."

"We should get him an MP-3 player," I said. "He loves soundtracks and swing bands. Audio books, too, you know. All that stuff could be downloaded onto an MP-3 and Frank could read and listen without having to get up and change CDs, which is what he does now."

Merrill stared at me as if I'd grown another head for a moment. "Well, we'll see about getting him one, then. I trust you know how to work it?"

"I do. One of the law clerks showed me how. And believe me, if I can operate something like that, anybody can. Of course we'll have to get an online account or something so we can get the music he wants, but it's easy after that."

"Then we'll see about doing that," Merrill smiled. "Come, I'll take you off the roof tonight so you won't have to climb down."

Merrill can float easily, just as I'd seen Gavin do. Merrill drifted both of us to the lawn outside his manor. "That must come in handy," I said, straightening my clothes when we reached the ground. "If I float, I have to be mist."

"I've never been able to turn to mist," Merrill sighed regretfully, leading me into the house. "I've often wished I could, but it wasn't to be."

Franklin was listening to a new iPod the following evening when I checked in on him. "Want something to eat?" I asked, peeking into his bedroom. He had a huge suite with a separate sitting area, shelves for his current reads, a large flat screen on the wall and a tiny bar that held a fridge and a small sink.

"I want fried chicken," Franklin grinned at me, pulling the earphones from his ears and motioning me inside his suite.

"Are you supposed to be eating that?" I gave him a skeptical look, my hands on my hips.

"No, but you asked what I wanted." His color was definitely better and he offered a cheeky grin.

"You know what, I'll make some for you, just this once," I said, taking off for the kitchen. Franklin got his meal an hour and a half later, complete with his favorite mashed potatoes. I sat and talked with him while he ate.

"So, how long did the doctor say to stay off your feet and not do anything strenuous?" I asked.

"I'm not supposed to go back to work for four weeks," he said. "But I'll be bored to death by that time."

"Maybe we can get a laptop or something for you and you can play solitaire or one of those shoot-em-up video games. In between reading, of course," I said. "And I can cook, that's not a problem. The thing is, though, if I'm trying a new recipe, there's no way I can taste it to see how it turns out. If I try something new for you, you'll be the guinea pig."

"I'll be happy to," he said. "Can you make barbecue by any chance?"

"I don't make my own sauce," I said. "I've never tried; I only buy something already made. I can pull something off the internet, though, and we can try that out."

"Well, maybe we should do that," he smiled encouragingly. "I'm willing to try it."

"All right. Barbecued chicken or ribs?"

"How about both?"

"Okay. If it turns out all right, we can freeze some of it," I said. "But you have to be honest about how it tastes so I'll know if we need to try a different recipe."

"I'll let you know. Ask Lena to pick up anything you need."

"I'll leave her a list," I said. We talked for a while longer, Franklin finished his dinner and I took his dishes away. "Yell for me if you need something," I said before going through his bedroom door.

"Now, you don't want to help me into the bathroom," he replied a bit stiffly.

"Are you kidding? I once watched five hundred werewolves in human form take a whiz on the nearest trees. I'm used to it, now." I left him laughing and holding his side.

❧ ❦

"Honored One, here's another stack." Charles carried a pile of letters into Wlodek's study, setting them on the older vampire's antique desk.

"Would that there were ways to tell them to stop this already," Wlodek grumbled. "I thought we would have a year, at least, before they all learned of this and started requesting meetings."

"What are we going to do?" Charles watched Wlodek's face carefully as the Head of the Council leafed through one request after another.

"Many of these are much too young to be asking," Wlodek sighed, setting the stack aside. "All it will take is an older one placing compulsion or attempting murder—discreetly, of course."

"Of course," Charles nodded.

"We will have to bring her out in this year's meeting instead of next year," Wlodek grimaced. "She will not like this in the least, I am guessing."

Charles heartily agreed.

CHAPTER 2

"These are quite good," Franklin bit into the ribs I'd brought him. Lena had gone ahead and cooked the ribs for the most part, I'd just added the barbecue sauce I made and baked them a little longer while the chicken was cooking.

"It was a Kansas City barbecue sauce recipe I pulled off the internet on Merrill's computer," I said. "I think it's one of the sweet sauces; it has brown sugar and molasses in it."

"It's nice," he said. "Maybe not as good as barbecue I've gotten in Memphis, but still good."

"Well, there you go," I said. "Does anybody make barbecue like they do in Memphis?"

"Possibly not," Franklin smiled and took another bite.

"Now," I said, pulling out a pen and a pad of paper, "tell me what else you'd like to eat and we'll see what we can do about that." I had a list of potential meals when I took his plate away, including meatloaf, spaghetti, stuffed peppers, beef stew, chicken and noodles, all sorts of things. It worked out well, too, that I could leave a list of grocery items for Lena. She'd buy it during the day and leave the cooking with me. Cookies found their way into the menu, too—once a week.

"These are the best oatmeal cookies I've ever had," Franklin crunched into one.

"I use old-fashioned oats instead of the quick kind, which is what the original recipe called for. I liked these a lot better."

Franklin also got restless two weeks after he'd gotten home, so Merrill gave him permission to teach me how to drive in England. The Range Rover was the vehicle of choice; Merrill insisted we take that since it could take the abuse better (he has such a poor opinion of my driving). We drove all over the countryside. It was really nice, we didn't meet up with much traffic and I got to see a lot that I hadn't seen before. Franklin had a great time. We even stopped at a small café somewhere to get a cup of coffee and allow him to use the restroom.

We went out every night for four nights, after which Franklin pronounced me "fit to drive." We'd even gone into London the last night and wandered around. What I wasn't expecting on the fourth night, however, was to find Gavin at the house waiting for me when we returned.

"You look happy," he said, while giving me a brief hug. I still wasn't sure how I felt about him—or us, for that matter. Did I trust him? That answer was still a huge no.

"I feel better about driving around, now," I said. "I had to take Franklin to the hospital three weeks ago and probably scared the bejezus out of both of us getting him there. What about you? Clap anybody in irons, lately?" I was still pissed that he'd chained me up in the Council's jet while holding the harshest compulsion on me. I wasn't able to blink without his permission. And scared? If I'd still been able, I would have wet myself.

"You're not going to forget that, are you?" he winced.

"Not anytime soon," I said.

"Did you have anything planned for tonight?" he asked, changing the subject.

"I was thinking about getting in the hot tub, but that's something I can do another time. Why?"

Franklin sat at the island in the kitchen, having a cup of tea and listening to our conversation. Merrill was in his study, taking care of business. Anyway, that's what he'd told Gavin.

"I just want to see you. Talk to you," Gavin said.

"I want to talk to you, too, and it has to be in private," I said.

"Why don't you take him into the spa room; it's nice and soothing in there," Franklin suggested. "I'm going to bed." It was around midnight and Franklin was tired, I knew.

"Goodnight, then," I kissed Franklin on the cheek. He hugged me and went off toward the stairs.

"What did you wish to talk about?" Gavin asked as we walked toward the room Merrill had added onto the back of his manor house. It held a wide, heated pool and a hot tub, with a beautiful slate floor surrounding both and glass windows all around. Patio furniture was scattered in the corners, along with potted palms and other tropical plants. The pool itself had a waterfall that emptied into it and the sound it made really was soothing, whether you were human or vampire.

We sat down at a tiny table in one of the corners. I studied Gavin for a few moments before saying anything. He had the slightest beginnings of fuzz on his head; his hair would be slow to grow out.

He'd lost his hair when a rogue vampire aimed a flamethrower at him, burning not only the hair from his head but the entire front of his body as well. I was afraid he wouldn't live over it at the time. Without Radomir's help, he'd have died. Gavin was lucky to be among the living—as much as vampires can be living, I suppose.

"Merrill asked somebody to come and teach me how to bite," I said, looking Gavin straight in the eye. "He practiced on me so I'd know how it was done. I fainted. Now, I only know of one other time when that happened. Would you care to explain that to me?"

"Who bit you?" he demanded. Trust Gavin to skirt the issue and go straight to the one that triggered his jealousy.

"Somebody named Brock," I snapped. "And he told me he was gay. Now, answer my question."

"I know Brock; he's an Enforcer," Gavin said with a sigh. "Lissa, I did bite you. I couldn't help myself. I just couldn't handle your scent any longer. It was a moment of weakness and I told you afterward that it wouldn't happen again. Not while you were rogue and I was watching you."

"And there I thought I disappointed you somehow or messed the date up by fainting on you," I turned my head away.

"No, Lissa. I knew if I did it again, I wouldn't be able to stop myself. I almost didn't that night. I wanted to couple with you and that would have been unethical. Disappoint me?" he snorted.

"What was I supposed to think?" I tossed up a hand in confusion. "You placed compulsion; I know that, now. Jerk."

"Lissa, you may call me anything you like over that." Gavin reached out and gently turned my face toward his with a finger. "I know you were miserable. You retaliated by going out immediately with the man you met at the bookstore. I was so eaten up with jealousy I wanted to track him and place compulsion for him to leave you alone." Gavin's brows were drawn together in a severe frown. And compulsion? Who was Gavin kidding? He probably wanted to beat Tony into pulp. It was probably a good thing Gavin didn't know who Tony was, other than a potential rival.

"You have such faith in me," I retorted. "Even I knew that relationship was doomed from the start. It was just somebody who didn't know who or what I was that made me laugh. Is it wrong to want to forget that the werewolves are blackmailing you and the Council wants you dead?"

"I know you didn't go to bed with him," Gavin was the one to turn his head, now. "I would have smelled it if you had."

That was such a comforting thought. He'd checked. Great. "So, are you telling me that I can't ever date anyone else again? Is that what you're saying?"

"I have no hold over you now. You are free to do as you please. I am terrified that you will accept advances from this one or that; I have a feeling that offers are coming in already, both to Wlodek and your sire, and these are vampires who have yet to see you. All of them wish to meet with you."

"Oh, good grief," I muttered in alarm. Wlodek and Merrill were getting requests? What did that mean? And what did they want, these nameless, faceless vampires? The thought of it made me shiver. "I don't want to meet them, Gavin. Not that way. Good grief."

"This frightens you." He made it a statement.

"Of course it does." I wanted to pull my knees to my chest. I forced myself to leave them where they were.

"Will you sit with me?" He patted his knee. Sit with him? I wanted to crawl into his lap and huddle against him. Ask him to fend off this horde of vampires that had appeared from nowhere, asking to meet with me. Gavin ended up coming to me instead. "If I had known this information would frighten you, I wouldn't have told you," he whispered against my hair.

"Gavin, I don't have many pleasant memories of being around vampires," I mumbled, my head buried against his shoulder. "So far, they've either wanted to kill me or place compulsion. And they can all do it. I have no way of defending myself if they decide they want to toss the law aside and just tell me whatever they want me to do."

"You should not be this frightened," he said, rubbing the back of my neck with his fingers. "Not all vampires are that way. You were rogue so you were treated differently than you would normally be treated."

"Yeah. How about that?" I said.

"There wasn't any justice in it for you, my angel. None at all."

"So, vampires may come knocking who may be no different from Edward and Sergio. What do you suggest I do about that? If I tell them to take a hike, are they going to get all pissy about it and try to retaliate? Get me into trouble, somehow, so Wlodek will be sure and not hold you back next time? I don't know this race of yours, Gavin. I don't know how to react to this."

"This is your race, too, Lissa; you are just new to it. Most vampires will accept that they don't have any chance with you and leave it at that if you do not wish to see them."

"And the others?"

"Vampires are unpredictable at times. And the older they are, the more likely that may surface. The Council has been in place for six hundred years. Many of our race are much older than that and did not accept the new law graciously. Those may be the ones to watch for."

"You're not making me feel better about any of this," I burrowed against his chest.

"I don't wish to frighten you," he said, pulling his arms tighter around me. "I should not have said anything."

"What if I don't want anyone?" My words were spoken against his chest, causing Gavin to go still for a moment.

"Then that may be your choice, but the Council's decision may be otherwise. Lissa, I am begging you now to give me a chance. Give me some time, angel. Then tell me if you don't want to see me again." His fingers stroked my hair.

"I cannot tell you what I would give to go back to the night when I kissed and drank from you. I'd never had the opportunity to taste a female of our race. Your blood was so sweet, love. You gave yourself so willingly to my kiss; you trusted me at that moment. Now, that trust is destroyed. I must rebuild it, if I can."

"Gavin, if you hadn't chained me to the chair on that jet, or at least reassured me a little or told me where we were going, even, that might have gone a long way. But you didn't. I may never trust another vampire in my life. Not ever." I crawled out of his lap. We were done for the evening, he and I.

I saw him to the door; he turned to me as he was walking out. "Do we have some time, Lissa? Will you see me during that time so I may attempt to rebuild your trust?"

"Gavin, you have no idea how much I'd like to trust someone. To tell them what my worries and concerns are, ask them stupid questions and not have them look at me like I'm an idiot or something. I don't think that's possible." His face turned gray at my words. "That doesn't mean I won't give you some time," I sighed. "I'll give you some time. I'll give *us* some time. Goodnight, Gavin." I shut the door on him.

Franklin was coming downstairs for all his meals now and said he would be more than happy to take over his normal duties in another week. I handed him a bowl of beef stew and crackers. We talked while he and Lena sat there eating. "I never thought about putting pasta or rice in my beef stew," Franklin said. "This is really good."

"My mother put everything except the kitchen sink in her stew. I always liked the pasta and rice. The trick is, just don't go overboard with it. A little will do of each."

Merrill wandered in while they were eating and I was cleaning the kitchen. "Wlodek wishes to see you," he said when I straightened up after putting the stew pot in the dishwasher.

I wanted to mutter something long-suffering such as "not again," but didn't. I wouldn't be able to tell Wlodek no, no matter what it was that he wanted. "Let me go change," I said, wiping my hands on a kitchen towel.

I'd never seen Wlodek in anything except a suit and tie. If the man wore jeans, I probably wasn't destined to see it. Merrill also dressed most of the time but I did see him upon occasion in slacks and a nice pullover. Jeans, too, once in a while.

Therefore, I dressed nicely for this occasion, in a calf-length silk dress. I hoped I wouldn't be running across the English countryside as I slipped into low-heeled sandals. The dress was a deep green; one of my favorite colors next to blue. I even wore my gold hoop earrings, one of the two pairs I actually owned.

Merrill waited for me at the door when I was ready, and we went out to the garage together. He drove the Bentley, and it was a pleasure to ride in that luxury.

"You look beautiful, Lissa," Merrill said when he opened my door and helped me out of the car roughly half an hour later.

"Thanks," I said and followed him to the door of Wlodek's manor. Rolfe let us in as usual; Charles stood behind Rolfe, waiting to take us to Wlodek's office.

Wlodek was busy signing papers when we walked in and didn't glance up for several seconds. For a moment, I wondered if he were signing termination papers on anyone before shoving that thought aside. Eventually, Wlodek laid his pen aside and turned his attention to Merrill and me; we were sitting in the two chairs before his desk.

"Something came up missing recently," he said, in lieu of a greeting.

If I'd been talking to Don, I would have said automatically, "I'm innocent, as usual," and given him a smile. The Head of the Vampire Council, however, was as far removed from Don as I could possibly get. Instead of explaining what that something was, Wlodek lifted a paper from his desk and handed it to Merrill, who glanced at it briefly, raised his eyebrows slightly and then passed the paper to me. It was a photograph of the Cambridge Lover's Knot tiara and the Spencer family tiara. *Holy crap.*

"It has come to my attention that these items may be somewhere in France," Wlodek went on. "Lissa, I desire that you to fly to Paris with Russell and Radomir. While there, I wish for you to learn if these items are indeed where we think and retrieve them if you can. They will be returned to their rightful owners if you are successful."

There was only one reason I could see that Wlodek, Head of the Vampire Council, would involve two Enforcers and a mister in the theft of two tiaras. That, of course, would mean they were stolen by a vampire in the first place.

The fact that he wasn't intending to bring the vampire in for doing this meant that the vampire had to be important and the whole thing was probably going to be hushed up. Great. This involved vampire politics and intrigue, and I was being shoved into the middle of it.

Merrill asked the question before I could. "When?" he inquired.

"Tomorrow evening. Have her at the airport at nine."

"Very well," Merrill nodded.

"The annual meeting is also approaching," Wlodek said, flipping his gold pen in his fingers.

"I will be there," Merrill said, sounding as if that might be the last thing he wanted to do.

"I expect you to be there," Wlodek agreed. "I also expect you to bring Lissa. See that she is dressed appropriately for the ball. You look lovely tonight, my dear." He turned to me and almost smiled.

"Thank you, Honored One," I did what I'd seen some of the others do, dipping my head slightly. No sense pissing off the King of the Vampires.

Charles hugged me before I got out the door, telling me he intended to call sometime so we could see a movie when I got back. I grinned at him and told him I'd look forward to it. I hadn't gone to a movie since I'd seen one with Winkler, Gavin and the werewolf bodyguards in Corpus Christi. That seemed a lifetime ago, although it was only a bit over three months.

"If you were human, I'd take you for ice cream," Merrill said, once we were loaded into the car and driving through the huge iron gate that guarded Wlodek's drive.

"And if I were human, I'd eat it," I shrugged.

"Franklin, what are you doing still up?" I scolded him when we walked into the kitchen half an hour later.

"Waiting on you," he said.

"Did you drink your berry smoothie and take the flaxseed oil?"

"I did. I never thought I'd see a vampire so health conscious, before," he laughed.

"Those berries have antioxidants and the flaxseed oil does the same thing the fish oil does, it just doesn't have the taste to it," I said. "And even you can't stand there and say they aren't good for you."

"I'm convinced." He came over and hugged me. "I just want my goodnight kiss before I go to bed."

I kissed his cheek and watched him walk toward the stairs. "He's in great shape, I just want to keep him that way," I sighed as he walked out of earshot.

"I've offered to turn him many times," Merrill said. "He refuses every time and gets a bit testy over it, too. He tells me he likes to cook and to taste what he cooks."

"I'm right there with him on that," I said. "I only have the memory of what it tasted like. And that may go someday, too."

"Little girl, are you prepared for tomorrow evening? You should pack. Probably for four days, at least. I don't believe it will take that long, but one can never tell."

"All right," I nodded. "Goodnight, Merrill."

"Goodnight, child."

Merrill drove the Range Rover to the airport. It was a stormy night and rain was pelting us as we made our way to the Council's private strip outside London. My passport and other important ID was in my purse; Merrill had scrounged up a wad of euro and handed it to me before we left the house. I probably had twelve hundred euro in my purse when I left the house, in addition to my credit card.

Russell and Radomir stood beside the steps leading to the Council's jet, waiting for me when Merrill and I arrived. My bags were loaded in while I boarded, and I sat down before my two flight companions did. Radomir ended up sitting next to me, Russell right across the aisle.

"Will wanted to come but I told him he had to stay home," Russell grinned.

"Will is guarding Wlodek while we are away," Radomir added. I just sat there between both of them, trying not to let my breaths sound too shaky. I liked Radomir, but maybe not that close. I hadn't forgotten what Merrill told me about Radomir, either; whatever you said to Radomir you said to Wlodek, since Wlodek was Radomir's sire.

"Have you done anything fun, lately?" Russell asked, reaching across the aisle to pat my hand. I think he may have recognized my discomfort.

"No. I did learn to drive on the wrong side of the road, but Merrill still doesn't trust me with his cars," I offered Russell a smile.

"You should come out with Will and me, sometime," Russell offered.

"And what do you do that's fun?" I asked, quirking an eyebrow at him. I had no idea what vampires did for fun.

"Mostly they pick up women," Radomir said, a smile in his voice if not on his face.

"You pick up women? Do you put them down again?" It was out of my mouth before I thought.

"Oh, yeah," Russell grinned.

"The Monet you gave to the Honored One was a nice gift," I said, referring to the huge painting of water lilies that hung on a wall in Wlodek's study.

"He wanted it; I didn't particularly like it," Russell replied with a shrug. I knew it was a really nice gift; some of those paintings had sold for more than forty million pounds.

"So, did you hang up a print of dogs playing pool instead?" I asked. Radomir laughed.

"I did turn the space into a billiard room," Russell agreed with a stifled snicker.

"I knew it," I said, tossing up a hand. "And if you were human, your trash would be full of pizza boxes."

"I never got to taste a pizza," Russell observed.

"They're good," I said. "You strike me as a pepperoni kind of guy, leave the veggies off."

"Hear that, Rad?" Russell looked over my head at Radomir.

"Don't mess with him, he's the Italian sausage and extra cheese man," I said, pointing a thumb at Radomir.

"And what were you?" Russell patted my hand again.

"Canadian bacon and mushroom," I said. "Thin crust. Thick was just too much bread for me."

"Charles told me you can't even finish a whole unit of blood," Russell teased.

"Does everybody talk about my eating habits?" I asked petulantly.

"Well, we don't have a lot of other information about you, so we have to discuss what we have," Russell said.

"This is a fact finding mission, so you can pass around the dirt?" I was teasing him right back.

"Oh, yeah," he said. "And the darker the dirt, the better."

Okay, I was really starting to like this guy. And he had no qualms over cracking the stone-faced façade that most vampires wore. "Did Brock tell you that one of my sins while I was human was glazed donuts?"

"Nah, Merrill doesn't let him gossip about anything that goes on inside the house," Russell grumped.

"I won't be discussing Merrill, either," I said. "I'll talk about me as long as it's harmless. That's all you get."

"Damn," Russell pretended to be upset.

"You were married before?" Radomir asked.

"Yes. My husband has been dead eight months as of yesterday," I said. "As have I, I suppose. My ex sister-in-law can't wait to put the date of death on my headstone so she can get her hands on my house and the insurance money."

"You already have a headstone?" Russell asked.

"It was one of those double ones and my husband's information is on one side. They put my name and date of birth on the other. I'd left my side blank. My sister-in-law will have to wait the standard seven years unless she gets a sympathetic judge or something."

"Does it make you want to go back and slap your sister-in-law around?"

"No. That part of my life is over," I answered Russell's question as diplomatically as I could. "It's neither here nor there what she does with my stuff."

❦ ❧

The plane trip was short; we landed at Charles de Gaulle International Airport in no time. A car waited there for us, complete with driver. We stowed our bags in the boot—that's what Russell calls the trunk, (he has such a nice British accent) and we were on our way.

The safe house was on the outskirts of Paris, in Bobigny. Once again, our accommodations were underground while the tastefully furnished ground floor was for appearances only. The entire place was alarmed, of course; we let ourselves into the basement through a hidden door in the floor of a closet, using a keypad code.

There were three bedrooms; I would have been forced to sleep on the small sofa, otherwise. The sofa wasn't long enough for either Russell or Radomir to sleep on comfortably, so I was thankful for the third small bedroom. Radomir got the suite with the bath; Russell and I shared the second bathroom.

Neither of my companions offered information on where we were going the following evening, and I didn't ask. Russell did ask me after we were settled in if I wanted to go sightseeing in Paris. Humorous, I know—only vampires might plan sightseeing trips after midnight. I wanted to see as much of it as I could, so all three of us went out into a warm Paris evening.

I'd never been anywhere near France before; I'd lived in Oklahoma all my life and the closest I'd gotten to a foreign country was Mexico. My British driver's license listed an address in Kent; the U.S. license gave an address in New York—also somewhere I'd never really been.

A car was available at the safe house for our use, so Radomir drove us around for a while. At times, I caught a slight smile playing about his mouth but didn't say anything. I honestly believed that Radomir was enjoying himself, and Russell certainly was. I saw the Eiffel Tower, the Arc de Triomph and we passed close to Notre Dame de Paris; it was on an island, along with the Palais de Justice.

Radomir parked after a while and we walked along sidewalks where a few cafés and nightclubs were still open. There's a different smell to Paris. I was inundated with coffee, food, humans, perfume—all sorts of things.

"It used to be a nightmare to walk down some of the sidewalks; the smoke from cigarettes would be so thick," Radomir informed me.

"They passed a law recently banning smoking in all public places so the air has cleared up somewhat."

Since my nose is so sensitive now, it is difficult to stand near anyone smoking. The smokers at the courthouse where I used to work would congregate in an area outside and a cloud of smoke would rise over their heads whenever several of them got together. The smell didn't bother me as much back then. "So, vampires don't smoke, huh?" I asked quietly.

Russell laughed. "Not unless they're on fire," he replied.

"Hey now, don't even kid about that," I swatted at him.

※

My shower was rushed the following evening so Russell could get cleaned up. Loading into the car quickly, we drove away from Paris, heading into the Champagne Valley somewhere.

I watched the countryside roll past for an hour or so until Radomir pulled the car to a stop on a narrow lane. A charming (and rather large) chateau sat on a pretty hill off in the distance.

"We can't give any names," Radomir told me as he unrolled a roughly drawn map of the chateau onto the hood of the car (or *bonnet*, as Russell says). "There's a vent here," he indicated a spot on the lower level. "It leads into the kitchen. We believe the items in question are locked away somewhere in a basement or underground storage area. You'll have to find the vault and extract them." Radomir handed over a velvet bag. It was perhaps a fourteen-inch square of black fabric with a heavy cord drawstring. Slipping the drawstring over my head, I allowed the bag to hang around my neck while I wait for further instruction.

"Now, turn to mist and see if you can do this," Radomir said. Russell offered encouraging looks so I concentrated, slowly turning to mist. Russell timed it.

"Four minutes, twenty-three seconds," he said. I floated over their heads, making my way quickly toward the chateau.

The designated vent was harder to find than I thought and precious minutes were wasted while I searched for it. It was past midnight already and time might become a larger factor before all was said and done.

Once I located the vent and slipped inside, I swept through a kitchen that hadn't been updated in the past two centuries. The remainder of the chateau itself was richly decorated in Louis XIV furniture, with paintings appropriate to that period hanging on walls and luxurious fabrics covering windows. Somebody had a taste for obscene wealth, that much was certain.

What Radomir failed to tell me was that the vampire in residence was not only at home, he was entertaining guests. That worried me more than a little as I floated through the chateau quickly, searching for a means to get below ground level.

Locating a locked door that led downward, I misted through an old-fashioned keyhole and sped down narrow steps. The vault where the tiaras were was underground, all right, with a thick, locked metal door sealed tighter than a hatch on a submarine.

A tiny, oval window allowed me to see a part of what rested inside, and I could only imagine that some wealthy monarchs might be jealous of this vault's contents. The door would only open if I had the proper code to punch in on a lighted keypad to the right, and that stymied me.

Floated up and down the impenetrable door's length, exploring it carefully, searching for a crack or some other way in. The better part of half an hour passed during my examination of the door, but I was still unable to find even a hint of a crevice to slip through.

I considered that I might have to go back to Radomir and Russell, admitting to defeat by door, but the master of the house decided to show off his treasures to one of his guests. His voice filtered down to me as a key turned in the more conventional door above, so I hovered in a corner, waiting for him to walk downstairs.

He was handsome; no doubt about that, with dark-blond hair that curled slightly, a sensuous mouth and warm brown eyes. If I hadn't known him for a thief, I might not have minded talking with him sometime.

He spoke in rapid French; therefore, I didn't understand a single word he said as he punched a code on the keypad to allow his guest inside the vault. I might pick my way through written French but my college French classes were mostly useless in the real world.

What I did understand was the hatch opening with the same sound a very tight door on a freezer might make. Airtight, indeed. I floated inside, right above his head. His friend, not nearly as handsome with brown hair and eyes, dutifully admired the tiaras at length while I watched.

After roughly ten minutes had passed, the two vampires walked out again, locking me, the tiaras and a king's ransom in other treasures inside the vault.

If I could have gulped I might have, but one thing I noticed while I was there was that everything was alarmed. There was a small digital readout on the pad the tiaras rested upon, and right next to it was another pad with a necklace sitting on it that had enough rubies and diamonds to support me for a very long time.

Many other items were spread around the room, all out in the open so their owner could come in and peruse them at his leisure. Every single one of them alarmed, of course.

This vampire was taking no chances, but I was. I was taking a big chance. Taking a *huge* chance because if my plan didn't work, I was a very dead little vampire. Russell and Radomir would have to go back to England and explain to Wlodek and Merrill that I'd made a foolish mistake and died because of it.

First, I had to come back to corporeality and take the bag from around my neck, setting it aside gently on the black granite island that held the tiaras and ruby necklace. Then (and this is where the big risk came in), I concentrated on turning back to mist.

My hands and feet always turn to mist first, and they're the first things to reappear when I come back to corporeality. Once I was completely turned to mist, I concentrated once more on turning back but only until I could see my hands.

Hastily I snatched up the bag while my body was still mostly mist and raked both tiaras inside, drawing the string tight. I figured I had minutes at most, seconds at the least, and I was gambling with my life when I accomplished what I did next. I turned back to mist and like a miracle, almost, the bag turned to mist with me.

The alarm tripped the moment I'd swiped the tiaras into the bag, their weight removed from the electronic pad, which set off the warning bells. Consequently, the moment I was completely turned to mist I hovered as near the ceiling as I could, waiting for the master of the house to reappear.

He did, punching the code on the pad with fingers moving faster than lightning. He then rushed inside the vault, eyes red, fangs extended and claws out, ready to fight. If he'd seen me, no way would I have lived over that.

As it was, I zoomed invisibly through the open vault door, leaving a cursing vampire in my wake. If he'd had any sense at all, he might have closed the door behind him; there was another keypad on the inside of the door.

The vampire was now raising everyone inside the house seconds behind me. I was scooting up the stairs and through the house as fast as I could go, my mist rushing toward the kitchen vent.

Once through that and on the outside again, I sent desperate mindspeech to Radomir. He wasn't parked far from the chateau—not for a vampire, anyway. I was warning him as I fled in his direction.

Leave Now! I shouted mentally. *Open a window—I'll catch up to you!* I was halfway to the car but our pursuers weren't far behind; we were parked on the only road leading to the chateau.

Go, Radomir! I'll catch up. I'll let you know when I'm inside the car. My mental voice held frightened urgency and I was praying as I closed in on the now speeding automobile. I saw them moving away; thankfully, Radomir didn't need the lights to see as he hit the accelerator.

It took another minute or so to catch up, although I was moving as swiftly as I could. And I can't describe my feeling of relief as I was sucked inside the window Russell left open for me. I have no idea what, if anything, our pursuers saw when the car got away, but we didn't need to take any chances. I concentrated on turning back to myself.

"Well, look who's here," Russell said, peering over the back of his passenger-side seat. I heaved a grateful sigh and handed the velvet bag to him, glad to have it out of my possession. He looked inside briefly before flashing a beautiful smile. "Nice work," he said.

"It wasn't easy," I grumped, brushing my windblown hair away from my face. "Everything was alarmed."

"Save it for later, the plane's waiting. We already had someone pick up our bags and load them in," Radomir said. "We don't need to stay if we have what we came for. Father was worried it might take a while."

"I see," I said, even though I didn't. Once again, I was flying blind, completely out of the informational loop. I wondered briefly if I would ever be in it.

Another hour went by before we found our way to the airport. Russell tucked me under his arm and ran me up the steps to the jet like a football. Radomir took charge of the velvet bag, slipping it inside a locking case that he placed at his feet during the ride home.

We arrived in England barely two hours before dawn; a vampire waited for us there with a car. We were loaded up in no time flat and whisked away to Wlodek's mansion.

Radomir carefully placed the velvet bag on Wlodek's desk once we were inside his study. The Head of the Council opened the bag carefully, lifting each tiara out and examining it with solemn scrutiny.

"Very nice," he commented after several moments. "Very, very nice." He looked at me across his desk, his dark eyes enigmatic. "You must tell me how you did this, but not until after you rise for the evening. Merrill has already been informed that you're spending the night. Congratulations on a job well and swiftly done." Wlodek shocked me with a smile.

Charles led me to the same bedroom I'd occupied before after Wlodek dismissed me; the suite with the sky blue walls and white trim waited expectantly for my arrival. My bag was already there and I wanted a bath badly.

"I'll see you when you get up," Charles promised, closing the bedroom door behind him. My bath was quick—I didn't have much time before sunrise and I scarcely made it into my pajamas and under the covers before I was out.

"René, I warned you that she might succeed when we arranged this test," Wlodek spoke softly into his cell phone as he prepared for the rejuvenating sleep.

"Honored One, I did not expect such swift results," René muttered, working to hide the anger in his voice. He'd placed a wager with his two vampire children and now he owed them a great deal of money as a result. He'd insisted that no mister could get into his vault. Or, having accomplished that, might get out again, once they were locked inside.

This new one did both and in very little time. He was still puzzled over how a mister might turn so swiftly; less than thirty seconds had passed before he was opening the door of his vault once the alarm sounded, expecting to find a mostly corporeal female vampire inside. Instead, there was nothing and he'd lost the items he'd taken so much trouble to steal.

"René, when I asked you to steal something, I had no idea it would be such important and high-profile items. These will be returned to their rightful owners."

"Honored One, you left that option open to me. You know I enjoy a challenge."

"Then perhaps you will appreciate another. The girl will be brought out in this year's annual meeting. Take a look and tell me you might not desire that as well." Wlodek hung up abruptly. René muttered an obscenity in Latin and went to bed.

CHAPTER 3

"Lissa? Wake up, angel."

I was swimming through molasses—at least that's what it felt like. Somebody was talking to me while sitting on the side of my bed.

"Whuh?" I finally managed to vocalize something, whether it made sense or not. I lifted a hand to my head; it felt as if it were stuffed with cotton.

"You're sleeping late this evening," the voice came again. It sounded familiar, but my eyes wouldn't open and my ears weren't connected to my brain so I might determine who it was. Rolling over on my side with the hope that it would go away only brought hands to me—big hands that gripped my body near my hips and pulled me toward the edge of the bed.

"Henri says that he's this way too, whenever he mists several times in a short time span." Another voice I should recognize but didn't.

"What does Henri recommend, then?" the first voice offered dryly.

"Here," something changed hands.

"Come, Lissa, I'm taking you to the tub. I do not wish to spill this on the sheets." I was lifted and carried somewhere, and then settled against a cold surface. A hand gripped my jaw, forced my teeth apart and poured blood into my mouth. I choked and swallowed, fighting for air and struggling against whoever held me.

"Hush and drink this," he commanded. My eyelids finally unglued and I glared at an unsmiling and willfully determined Gavin, who was doing his best to get me to drink a unit of blood. Both my hands were held effortlessly in one of his while the other held a bag of blood at my lips.

"It would be easier if you'd let my hands go," I snapped as blood dripped off my chin. Yep—definitely not attractive, and I probably had bed-head on top of that.

"Are you going to drink?" A dark eyebrow quirked speculatively as blood continued to drip from the bag.

"Yes." My voice was sullen. I now had blood all over my face, my chest and my pajamas. Gavin was leaning over the side of the bathtub while I wriggled uncomfortably beneath his hands.

Charles stood at Gavin's shoulder, watching the whole thing with a bit of amusement in his eyes. Nope, not embarrassing in the least.

"Drink first, then we'll clean you up," Gavin said, letting my hands go. I snatched the bag of blood away from his hand and started sipping. Getting into a tussle with him while we had an audience seemed unwise.

Gavin sent Charles away when I was ready for my shower. I tried to shove him out the door too, but he wouldn't budge. It was like moving a mountain—a very grumpy and protesting mountain. Gavin wanted to assist me in the shower but I drew the line at that, so he was forced to wait inside the bedroom while I cleaned up. He did help me dress afterward, although I slapped his hands several times.

"What are you doing here, anyway? Aren't you supposed to be somewhere bashing heads in or something?" I snapped at him as he buttoned my blouse.

"I don't have to bash heads every day. I get time off now and then," he corrected me. "And Wlodek is waiting to hear from you, so I will be going along for that."

"Oh, joy," I muttered.

⚜

"I wouldn't have gotten in if he hadn't decided to show off the tiaras," I informed Wlodek later. "And I took a chance, allowing him to lock me inside. That vault was completely airtight; I couldn't find even a crevice to fit in," I added.

"So what did you do?" Wlodek watched me, his face expressionless as usual.

I explained that I'd turned back, took the bag off and set it aside before turning to mist again, then coming back to corporeality but timing it so only my hands and feet became solid.

After accomplishing that, I was grabbing the tiaras and stuffing them into the bag. And then turning completely to mist while the alarms went off. I described how the vampire had returned to open the door, allowing me to escape.

"No wonder you were exhausted," Russell said. He, Radomir and Gavin were all inside Wlodek's study with me, listening to my explanation.

"So, only your hands and feet were solid?" Wlodek asked.

"Yes."

"Fascinating."

I just shrugged at him, wondering where the tiaras were. It was none of my business now; I'd done what he sent me to do. Wlodek wouldn't be telling me anything else—I could see it in his eyes. I thought about going home and sleeping in my own bed. I was exhausted and my sleep during the day hadn't helped much.

Wlodek finished with us a few minutes later and Gavin took my elbow when we left the study. "Come with me," he said.

"Gavin, I'm tired," I complained. He didn't say anything; he just ushered me down the stairs, told Charles to have my bags sent to Merrill's and pulled me out the door with him.

A car waited outside; a silver Mercedes SLR McLaren that gleamed in the moonlight. Gavin placed me in the passenger seat, fastened the seatbelt around me and closed the door. He was on the driver's side in no time, starting the car and crunching over gravel as we drove away.

I had no idea where he was taking me and at the moment, I didn't really care. I just closed my eyes and catnapped. Vampires don't usually sleep during the night, I guess, unless they're really tired. I was exhausted, actually, and Wlodek's grilling had made the situation worse. I couldn't even keep my eyes open at times.

"Where are we?" I asked after a while when Gavin stopped the car, then came over to open my door and unbuckle my seat belt.

"My place," he said, lifting me in his arms.

※ ※

"She's asleep," Gavin explained to Merrill over the phone. "Nothing happened. Nothing will happen. She's exhausted, that's all." He listened while Merrill informed him that Lissa could have slept in her own bed just fine.

"I know that. It was a moment of weakness, nothing more. You'll have her back in one piece tomorrow night."

※ ※

"Lissa? Wake up, angel." There was a gentle kiss and a nipping on my lower lip. Part of that nipping was sharp. I was awake and huddled against the headboard of a huge bed in less than a blink.

Gavin stared at me as if I'd lost my mind. At least he was dressed—in jeans and a polo. Me? I was naked, thank you very much. I wanted to smack him across the room.

"Lissa, calm down, love. We can get you dressed in no time. I thought you might like to bathe first."

His eyes were a deep, liquid brown and the term *bathe* held such a note of hope in it. "I can bathe by myself," I pointed out acidly, trying to pull the sheet over my nudity. It wasn't working; Gavin was sitting on the edge of it. "And why is it you always see me naked," I gave another jerk on the sheet, realizing that I'd rip it if I jerked any harder, "and I haven't even seen you with your shirt off except when you were burned." I gave up on the sheet and buried my head in my hands.

"I can remedy that," he said, pulling the tail of his shirt from the waistband of his jeans.

"No! No, forget I said that," I held out a hand. "Just tell me where my clothes are, and where the shower is."

"You're so sensitive about this," he said, sliding off the bed. "You know it's almost impossible to embarrass an old vampire. That's an old saying, by the way."

"I'm not an old vampire," I snapped at him, sliding off the opposite side of the bed. His bedroom was dark and windowless; therefore, I had no idea where we were. We might have been on another planet for all I knew.

My clothes were on top of a tall chest on the other side of the bed. Gavin lifted them one-handed and shook them at me. I went over and snatched them away while thinking about stomping on his foot. He had shoes on and I was barefoot, so I'd more than likely come out the loser in that little battle. He might retaliate, too, and I didn't really want to know what he'd do.

I was turning on the taps in a huge walk-in shower when he came up behind me, his arms dropping around my shoulders. "Don't you want to know what it's like?" He nuzzled my neck and nipped it. I'd never seen Gavin this amorous before and it scared me.

"Maybe I will sometime, Gavin. But I need to stop being afraid of you first."

He backed away at my words, turning and leaving the bathroom after only a few seconds. We didn't talk much on the way home and I worried that I'd done something irreparable.

Gavin walked me to the door, where Merrill stood waiting. If he'd been human, Merrill might have been tapping his foot impatiently. As it was, the mask was in place so I had no idea if I was in trouble with him, too.

Gavin took my face in his hands before he left me, kissing me carefully before his deep brown eyes stared earnestly into mine. "I cannot take your fear away. If I could kill Sergio Velenci again, I would do it without hesitation." He kissed me once more, leaving me with Merrill.

"Did he harm you?" Merrill asked as we watched Gavin drive away.

"No," I replied. "He only kissed me."

"I could see that for myself," Merrill remarked dryly and led me into the house.

⁂

My lesson that evening was Vampire Law number six, when you were allowed to kill a human. "You may kill if the human is threatening your life or the life of another vampire or those of the vampire race as a whole," Merrill instructed.

"If a human has a flamethrower, as Niles Abernathy did, and it is a life-threatening situation for you or another vampire as in Gavin's case, you are justified in taking the life. However, if there are human witnesses, they must have compulsion placed to forget the incident. If there is a body, then you must make it appear to be an accident. You should hide it as well as you can, regardless, so it will never be found."

"Please tell me you're not going to take me out and have me kill someone," I muttered, refusing to look at Merrill.

"No. However, if there is a human taken down by an Enforcer or an Assassin and there is time, you will be conveyed to the scene and asked to cover it up. Occasionally humans learn of us and they hunt us. Many times over the centuries they have even banded together to seek us out and kill us. This seems to go in cycles, actually. We worry about the next wave because of the technology now available."

"Yeah. I can see that," I said, lifting my head.

"On another note," Merrill said, "Wlodek expects you to attend the annual meeting." I nodded; Wlodek mentioned it when he'd given me the last assignment. He hadn't explained what the annual meeting was, though, and I was afraid to ask.

"It is a gathering of our most influential members," Merrill explained it for me. "There can be as many as five or six hundred there, so a huge ballroom must be provided. Several of us own appropriate facilities and it is usually held in one of those. There is a grand ball scheduled first, to which many of the attending vampires will bring human dates and companions. Some may even be married to those companions. I will explain the laws concerning that at a later time. You are expected to attend the grand ball so that the ones who have been asking after you may see you, all at once, as it were."

"Gavin said something about that," I grumbled. "Merrill, what if I don't want to go? What if I don't have any desire to see any of these people? It scares me."

"Lissa, Wlodek recently informed me that you willingly went into a sealed vault, knowing you might not get out again. You risked your life, child, and yet meeting vampires frightens you?"

"Merrill, the next time you have compulsion laid so you can't even blink and are forced to follow along behind somebody that you trusted and thought was your friend, and that friend plans to kill you if so ordered, then we'll talk," I said.

"They can't get past my compulsion," he insisted, attempting to reassure me.

"Your compulsion. There's that word again. *Compulsion.*" I said it with as much distaste as I felt I could get away with. "Free will among vampires is mostly a joke, isn't it?" I got up and walked out of Merrill's study.

He came to find me a few minutes later. I was sitting on my bed, pillows propping me up against the headboard, my knees drawn up to my chest.

"My compulsion is only to protect you and the ones who live inside this house," he said gently, sitting down on the side of my bed.

"I know that." My forehead was now pressed against my knees. "But that doesn't keep me from wanting to go out and do something because I want to," I mumbled. "I want to buy my own computer. Maybe go find a pair of shoes or just wander around London because I still haven't seen much of it. And I haven't been to the bookstore in ages. You and Franklin have some good choices in the library, but those things aren't all I like to read."

"You feel confined." It was a statement.

"Yes."

"Lissa, one of the reasons I am reluctant to allow you out on your own is because of what you are and why all those male vampires wish to meet you. You are a rarity, something very desirable in our world. You shouldn't ever go out unattended, I don't think. London has a rather large vampire population. I would have failed in my duty if anything were to happen to you."

"Charles is so busy all the time or I'd ask him," I said. "We had a good time the night he took me shopping."

"I know. Perhaps I should look for a suitable companion so you may go out from time to time. And as far as a computer goes, borrow mine. Find what you want and order it online. I have a business address in London where it may be delivered; Lena can pick it up and bring it to you. She brings my deliveries from there when she comes to work most days."

"See, even Lena gets to come and go without supervision," I grumbled.

"Lena isn't sought after by a rather large number of males," Merrill observed.

"What makes me so special? They haven't even seen me."

"Thirteen of the sixteen female vampires are in a permanent relationship," Merrill sighed. "Most of those relationships are a result of the female having been a companion to the male vampire while they were still human. Theirs were successful turns. The two female Council members are unattached and then there you are, Lissa. Male vampires sometimes seek a relationship that could last centuries. With a human companion, this is not possible; they will age and die unless the turn is successful and the attempts far outweigh the successes."

"Merrill, this isn't making me feel any better," I said rubbing my forehead.

"I know. I am only trying to make you understand." He scooted up beside me and placed an arm around my shoulders, kissing my temple affectionately. "Feel better now?"

"Sure, Dad," I sighed. He laughed.

※

"We are going to Paris," Merrill announced a week later. "We must find a dress for you to wear."

"You're joking? There isn't anything here in London?" I stared at my surrogate sire in dismay. Merrill gave me the patient expression I'd come to recognize; the one that said he was dealing with my ignorance.

It was the middle of September and the only things that had changed for me was the fact that I had more knowledge of the vampire race because of my lessons and I was now the proud owner of a nice Mac laptop. I know—Gavin has one too. We had high speed, wireless internet at Merrill's manor.

Franklin bought a laptop for himself after seeing mine and became addicted to solitaire. I sometimes sent him e-mails, just for fun. The other thing that was different was Franklin's lover from New York had come to visit.

His name was Greg and he'd voluntarily submitted to Merrill's compulsion. He also didn't live with Franklin and hadn't ever. Franklin went to stay nights with him occasionally in New York on his days off and they'd been together for nearly twenty-five years.

"I almost had a heart attack when Merrill called and said Frank had surgery." Greg was usually more demonstrative than Franklin, but not overly so. I liked him; he was warm, witty and treated Franklin very well. Franklin introduced us when I'd come downstairs on the first night of Greg's visit.

"Be careful, she'll have you drinking berry smoothies and taking vitamins and flaxseed oil," Franklin put an arm around Greg.

"Well, it's good for you," I chastised Franklin.

"Honey, are you sure you're a vampire?" Greg asked.

"Honey, that's not the first time somebody asked me that," I put my hands on my hips.

"I like her," Greg declared and that was that.

Franklin and Greg went with us to Paris. Merrill has his own private jet (go figure). We stayed for nearly a week. Merrill took us out each evening while Greg and Frank offered advice on ball gowns.

I got a closer look at some of the landmarks, too. Merrill told me that he'd once climbed the Eiffel Tower, scaling up the sides when it was really dark one night. I almost laughed out loud, that was so unlike him.

I was also the only one in the party who didn't speak French like a native. I suppose I should learn. I suppose. The word I spoke the most, and even the designers and the sales assistants understood, was *no*.

"Merrill, this all looks like it was patterned after men's pajamas," I said, after viewing a very big name designer's current collection. I was doing my best not to gag. We weren't asking any prices but I had the notion that most of what I was looking at would cost more than I made in a year's time at the courthouse in Oklahoma. Some of it much more.

"Little one, we are running out of time," Merrill murmured against my ear. Franklin and Greg weren't saying anything, but I was beginning to feel pressured. Was I supposed to wear something I hated with a capital H, just because it had a name attached to it? "Come," Merrill said wearily and we walked out of the showroom. Greg and Franklin stopped to get coffee at a small café before we walked farther down the street.

"Now see, why can't I wear something like that," I pointed at a dress displayed in a window. The gown was a midnight blue silk with a sweetheart neckline. Thin straps crossed over the back, holding the dress up on the mannequin. The dress was simple, hugging the body around the breasts and waist, and then falling to a flared skirt that might float around the ankles.

"Let us look at this," Merrill was taking in the dress along with a few other things in the window.

Franklin interpreted what the sales assistant was telling Merrill when we stepped inside the shop. "She says this is an up and coming designer, who is only beginning to make a name for herself," he whispered.

"I want to try on that one," I said, pointing to the midnight blue ball gown. I got my wish.

"I think this is nice," Greg said. Turning this way and that in the mirror, I agreed with him. A pair of shoes were brought out—Jimmy Choos. This would be my first pair. They were silver, a heeled sandal in a watersnake pattern—at least that's what I was told, with crossover straps at the toes. I tried them on and the dress was like a dream, no longer dragging the floor. The assistant went into raptures over how I should do my hair, I think, according to her gestures.

"We'll take it," Merrill said, and also bought a couple of other things there in the shop, including a white dress that he liked very much when I tried it on and one in black as well that had a deep V-neck and a very low back. I almost felt naked in it. We bought three more pairs of shoes, too. Merrill spent a truckload of money that night. I hoped he was taking it out of what I now had.

The ball was scheduled for the first Saturday in October, beginning around nine with dancing and the whole bit. The meeting would occur on Sunday and I wouldn't be going to that, thank goodness.

Franklin and Greg taught me how to dance. Not up close dancing, I could do that well enough. They taught me ballroom dancing, but only the waltz and foxtrot. I was good on the waltz, a bit shaky on the other.

"No rumba or any of that other stuff." I explained my dancing lessons to Merrill, who took me a couple of turns afterward. My first dance at the ball was to be with him.

"You'll be fine," he insisted. I wasn't so sure.

"Do you think I'll be the only one who has ever attended the werewolf meeting and the vampire meeting?" I asked as he whisked me around the floor.

"Quite possibly," he nodded, turning me several times. Trying to trip me up, I'm sure.

"What does one talk about while one is dancing?" I was being sarcastic but Merrill either ignored it or it went right past him. He never batted an eyelash, either way.

"The female allows her partner to set the conversation," he said.

"Great. Lots of *nice weather we're having*, then," I said, not even pointing out that the *male* got to direct traffic, both in the dance and the dialogue.

"What would you prefer they talk about?" Merrill's eyebrow quirked upward.

"Well, they could tell me if their Springer Spaniel had puppies, or about their argument with Louis XIV or what they like to read." I put emphasis on the word *read*.

"And if they prefer Voltaire or Baudelaire?"

"Okay, you have me there," I conceded. "But they could try to convince me to read it if they're that passionate about it. Who knows, stranger things have more than likely happened."

"More than likely," the corner of Merrill's mouth tugged slightly.

"But if that's all they read, then they've missed out on a lot of contemporary fiction, which might be a shame," I said. "We're all a product of our times, are we not? Isn't it important to keep up with things and not just bury ourselves in the past, pretending that current events don't exist?"

"Some of those you may meet have most certainly buried themselves in the past," Merrill informed me dryly. He was trying not to smile; I just knew it.

"Then we won't have anything in common," I said. "Therefore and henceforth, they should get themselves gone." I made a shooing motion with my hand. It broke contact with my partner, which was a no-no in the dance. Merrill stopped right there, bent over and started laughing.

"Now," I went on, "while you may have been best buds with Voltaire and all that, I've seen his picture, that's some hairdo he had going, by the way, I've never met anybody important. Not while I was human, anyway, and I haven't read anything past Shakespeare I don't think, although I have seen quite a few movies. Does that make me insignificant? Maybe to you. But you have to look at it this way; in geologic time, we're all a blip on the radar." I walked away from him.

"That certainly does put things in perspective, doesn't it?" Merrill was back at my elbow and we went on with our dance.

"Are you aware of the controversy surrounding the last extinction—the one where all the large mammals disappeared?" I asked as we made another turn around Merrill's ballroom. Yes, he has a ballroom. Go figure.

"The one where some think it was caused by a comet or a series of comets while others think it was the Clovis people?"

"That's the one. I'm with the series of comets people, I think. Otherwise, those Clovis people had to be really hungry. There were some big, furry animals in that bunch. Made a lot of soup, no doubt."

"I agree," Merrill smiled.

※ ※

"Oh, you're kidding." I stared at Mr. Dalton, hair designer, who stood in front of me, looking my hair over. He had an assistant with him—a young woman who popped bubble gum while she did my nails and make-up. The night of the ball had crept up on me.

I was less than prepared to go and the gum cracking was so annoying at one point I nearly let a claw slide out to pop a rather large bubble. Holding back that urge, I ground my teeth instead and hoped she'd finish soon. Merrill was already dressed and waiting impatiently while Mr. Dalton and Co. worked me over, gum chewing notwithstanding.

Mr. Dalton worked on my hair while the girl did my nails, toenails, and then my face, handing me a mirror afterward so I could see the results. Mr. Dalton had piled my hair atop my head. It looked decent, even if it did feel somewhat weird at first. My fingernails and toenails had never looked so good. Lena stayed late and helped me into my dress afterward.

"That looks incredible," Franklin said when I and my dress floated downstairs. Greg had gone back home only two days before and Frank and I both missed him.

"This will finish it off," Merrill slipped a diamond necklace around my neck, handing the matching earrings to me.

"I don't even want to know how much these cost," I said, slipping the earrings into my ears.

Brock was waiting to drive us, and I learned that he'd acted in that capacity for Merrill for a long time before becoming an Enforcer. He also piloted Merrill's jet and often flew for the Council when needed. We rode to the ball in the Rolls Royce Phantom.

Brock explained during the drive that it was a Diamond Black and not just black in color, in addition to giving me information about the engine and other car parts I didn't recognize.

As he talked, I nodded like one of those dogs that some people stick to their dash. He gave me a nice grin. "What kind of pizza am I?" he asked. Russell and Radomir must have been talking.

"You're the ham and pineapple guy," I said without thinking.

"Well, I was a ham and pineapple guy," he agreed. "Good guess."

"If it wasn't that, it was the shrimp and lobster."

"My second favorite. How do you know these things?"

"I'm a good guesser," I said, smiling at him. Actually, I had no idea what kind of guesser I was.

Merrill settled my wrap a little better around me when Brock dropped us off outside a very large building on the outskirts of London. I hadn't paid much attention to where we were going; Brock had talked most of the way. Merrill let me ride up front with Brock while he sat in the back, watching and listening to his two youngest vampire children.

Vampires were waiting outside to assist guests when they arrived, some of them working as valets, others as escorts and doormen. The scents came the moment Merrill handed me out of the car. I could have told you which ones were the oldest and which the youngest.

Two vampires opened the double doors leading into the building, allowing Merrill and me inside. I didn't miss the look of shock on the face of the one closest to me; he inhaled sharply and almost banged himself in the nose with the heavy wood door.

I also learned that any Enforcers or Assassins that weren't out on assignment were there to watch the crowd. I spotted Russell against a wall, watching everything carefully while Will stood on the opposite side, doing exactly the same. I hadn't seen Will since I'd ridden in the Council's jet with him and I'd been chained to my seat at the time. I still appreciated his attempts to argue with Gavin over my treatment, however.

What I wasn't expecting to see inside the huge ballroom was the rather large number of human women there as dates and escorts. Merrill warned me they might be there, but I wasn't expecting so many. I guess vampires hated going to a do without a date as much as humans did.

I smelled the human women intermixed with a heady, spicy scent of very old vampire. Once inside, Merrill led me to a cubicle where a vampire took my wrap and laid it on a shelf, handing Merrill a small slip of paper, which he pocketed.

Merrill was decked out in a tux, just like all the other males. If the people who made the *James Bond* films could have seen him dressed like that, they would have swooned and tried to sign him on the spot.

"There's our little female." I remembered this Vampire Council member; Charles said his name was Flavio, who was also his sire. More than likely the most beautiful man in the room, although his eyes were very dark as opposed to Merrill's piercing blue. Flavio took my hand and kissed me, European style, on both cheeks. I returned the favor as well as I could. "You are well?" he asked me.

"Of course," I nodded. "It's nice to see you." At least he'd voted not guilty when the Council was deciding whether to let me live or not. Wlodek wasn't far away and I already knew that Wlodek had sired Flavio, just by the scent. Of course, I was keeping that information to myself—apparently, it was something other vampires couldn't tell for themselves.

"Come," Merrill said, leading me farther into the ballroom, where several vampires waited to greet us. Some of those vampires had very old names and the scent of extremely old vampire to accompany them. If I hadn't been too afraid to ask, and if they'd been gracious enough to answer, I could have received a lesson in ancient world history from those who'd experienced it firsthand.

I was given Greek names. Or Roman. I also heard French, Italian, Spanish, Russian—everything. Most, however, spoke excellent English and employed it. Many of them were also eyeing me speculatively, which made me uncomfortable. How could it not? I felt as if I was the meal of the month and they were all staring hungrily.

Merrill steered me toward the wall near Russell's post, asking the tall Enforcer to keep an eye on me while he went to run some errand of his own. That's when I was approached by three human women, who sidled cautiously up beside me.

"That hunk you're with is gorgeous," one of them ventured.

"You're welcome to tell him so," I said. She had blonde hair, but it hadn't always been that color. The other two were darker-haired and showing off as much of their charms as they could. All three were dressed in low-cut gowns, clouded in expensive perfume and wore jewelry that must have cost a mint.

"I may just do that," she said, her voice thick with a Georgia accent. Georgia in the U.S., not the Russian one. I didn't think it would impress

Merrill all that much if she expressed her interest. I'd seen the photograph on his bedside table following my fainting fit. The woman in that photograph was stunning, with pale blonde hair and blue eyes. No way could Miss Georgia compete with that. No way.

"You know Rudolf will object if you show interest in another man," one of the blonde's companions cautioned.

"Honey, you may as well call them what they are," the blonde laughed. "We know they're vampires. Are you with him?" The blonde nodded toward Merrill, who was making his way through the crowd.

"It depends on what you mean by with," I said. "He's my sire."

"Holy Christ, she's one of them," the third woman spoke for the first time.

"Unintentionally, I assure you," I said.

"Did it hurt?" the blonde asked.

"I don't remember it," I shrugged.

The blonde took her chance, moving next to Merrill and touching his arm when he arrived. His voice and his compulsion were icy when he told her to run along. She and the two women with her trotted away.

Briefly, I thought about Winkler and how he wouldn't have passed up the opportunity. Nope, not him. He probably thought I was dead, now. The certificate that Weldon sent pretty well said as much.

A full orchestra was now warming up at the front, striking up a waltz quickly.

"That's our cue," Merrill bowed politely and took my hand. "Now," he told me, as we went twirling around the room, "a good, standard answer is always *thank you; I will consider your offer.* You should know by now not to be rude."

Actually, I was afraid to be rude, but I didn't say that to Merrill. And offer? What offer? What did Merrill mean by that? While we danced, I saw how the others nodded to my surrogate sire and gave him space. Merrill was powerful in the vampire community and, with the exception of Wlodek, older than all of them.

The vampire who approached for my second dance was someone named Wellington. He appeared to be English, was quite old and of the nobility. And stuffy, on top of that. He blustered about the House of Lords and the House of Commons, regaling me with current events as they concerned the monarchy. As he blustered, I was afraid my eyes might glaze over.

Next came someone of Russian heritage who offered to teach me his native language. Merrill's standard answer came in handy on that one. One of the many vampires I danced with after that was Italian and introduced himself as Paolo Moretti.

"I can make love to you so easily," he said. If my shoes hadn't been strapped on, I would have come out of them, I think. Merrill's answer didn't work for him.

"I think I would have to know you better, first," I said, which caused him to laugh. Mostly I listened, nodded, and concentrated on my dancing, except when my partner asked a question.

Another one offered to take over my teaching, insisted that he knew Wlodek personally and could accomplish this immediately. I told him I would discuss it with Merrill and that caused him to back off.

The worst one of the evening was also the best one in most respects. He was charming, handsome and funny—and also the one from whom I'd stolen the tiaras. No. No future in that one.

I smiled, answered when he asked a question, laughed more than once and thanked him for the dance when it was over. If vampires actually sweated, I'd be hoping my deodorant wouldn't fail me right about then.

"This last dance is mine," Gavin smoothly cut in front of another vampire. I think it was all right—Gavin was older than the other vampire, who backed away immediately with a polite nod.

Where had Gavin come from? I hadn't seen him the entire evening, yet here he was, claiming the final dance. I'd only gotten to dance with Gavin once before and I'd enjoyed it, plus, it was a relief not to make polite (and forced) conversation with him.

"So, what have you been up to?" I asked as another waltz began. I hadn't heard from Gavin for several weeks.

"Hoping you would call," he said softly against my ear.

"I was supposed to call? Who's making these rules? I want to have a talk with them. I don't call you, mostly because I don't want to interrupt if you're doing something important. Breaking bones and smashing heads require a lot of concentration, I hear."

"If I don't answer, then I am busy or dead," he informed me stiffly. I'd offended him.

"Now there's a comforting thought; imagining that you're dead if you don't answer your phone," I rolled my eyes at his cavalier attitude.

"You'd truly worry over me?" That sounded a bit warmer.

"Of course I'd worry over your sorry ass," I said tartly. "I can't help it. And you smell good," I couldn't help adding.

"I smell good?" Gavin sounded confused.

"To me, you do. You did from the start and I couldn't figure it out. I can't believe I was such an idiot, thinking you were anything but vampire."

"What did you think I was?" He offered a small smile.

"I don't know," I said, puzzled over the whole thing. I didn't even know why I was telling him that and hadn't realized I'd said it aloud until he chuckled.

"If we weren't surrounded by this crowd, most of whom want to sleep with you, or take you home and then sleep with you, I'd kiss you," he said. "Wlodek may want to punish me for dancing with you anyway, but I have an invitation, just as many holdings as most of the others and am older than seventy-five percent of them. He—and they—can stew about it." He turned me smartly and we took off again.

The dance was ending when I heard someone having an orgasm off to the side. It was a female and she was having a good time, from the sound of things. Gavin growled. "They are not supposed to be doing that here," he said angrily. "Come."

Wondering if all vampires had that "come" thing down pat, I followed along behind, almost trotting to keep up with him. His legs were much longer than mine and he was moving swiftly.

Russell and another vampire were already there and ushering the female (who was human) and her vampire lover toward the door. Wlodek stood nearby, looking thunderous. Merrill came up beside Gavin and me.

"What happened?" I asked Merrill.

"This is considered a public place, little one, and therefore the no biting rule applies. I know we haven't discussed this, but I will explain it later. Suffice to say, they did wrong." I nodded, still feeling confused. I did see two other vampires, their fangs out and eyes red.

"They get the smell of blood and it cannot be helped at times," Gavin whispered, leaning down and pulling me against him protectively. "It is warm blood as opposed to chilled, and it has a greater attraction, especially to the ones who were born in an era where only warm blood was available." That included him, but I didn't say anything; I chose to move out of his embrace instead.

"Gavin," the vampire from whom I'd taken the tiaras walked over and greeted Gavin as if he knew him, and knew him well.

"René, how are you?" Gavin nodded politely.

"I saw you dancing with our little rose, here," René de la Roque said, offering me a lovely smile.

Stepping closer to Gavin, I looked up at René. If he ever discovered that I'd taken the tiaras—I'd seen his face and his fangs—I'd be dead, no doubt about that. Gavin placed his arm around me, his eyes locking on mine. Then he said something that chilled my soul. "René and I are cousins, turned by the same sire at nearly the same time."

I shivered under Gavin's arm, so he pulled me tighter against him. Vampire politics and intrigue, indeed. Did Gavin know exactly where I'd been? Whom I'd taken those tiaras from? It hadn't come up in my conversation with Wlodek while Gavin had been there. I did my best not to let it show in my face.

"René, Gavin," Wlodek walked over to us and nodded at both vampires. "We have the problem sorted out now," Wlodek went on. He knew. I know he knew, but that vampire habit of showing absolutely no emotion was coming into play for him. Perhaps this was why they all cultivated it. No guilt or recrimination on either party's face.

"Always a pleasure," René nodded respectfully at Wlodek.

"Gavin, please bring Lissa and follow me," Wlodek commanded. Gavin had a hand at my elbow and steered me into Wlodek's wake. We picked Merrill up on the way out the door; he came along behind us, my wrap slung over an arm.

"We are expected at Flavio's town home; it is nearby," Wlodek said, ushering Gavin and me into his limo. Merrill rode with Brock in the Rolls—we were all away in minutes.

Flavio's town home was very nice; a three story in an affluent part of London. "He only uses this when he must," Gavin told me quietly as we pulled up to the house.

Flavio arrived before we did and was waiting on us as another vampire opened the door to allow us inside. He showed us through a long hall and then into a very nicely appointed drawing room.

There were paintings on the walls that could have been done by Gainesborough, but I wasn't about to ask. They were beautiful landscapes and certainly looked like his work. There was also a large fireplace in the center of the back wall. Faberge eggs and other little knickknacks were sitting on the mantle—all probably worth a fortune.

"I received two very strong offers for our Lissa tonight," Wlodek said when we sat down, causing me to draw in a shocked breath. Flavio had not opted for period furniture, settling instead for modern sofas and chairs that were ultimately more comfortable.

Gavin made sure I was seated next to him, and I wanted to huddle against him after hearing what Wlodek had to say. Offers? Someone had made offers? What did that mean? Was I being auctioned off? Was this what Merrill had meant earlier? I forcibly held back a shudder.

"From whom?" Merrill was still standing, his face showing no emotion.

"From Ivan Baikov," Wlodek began.

"The Russian?" Flavio asked. He didn't sound pleased. I couldn't help myself—I did huddle against Gavin. Gavin's gaze was trained on Wlodek, listening intently even as his fingers stroked my elbow.

"And the other?"

"René de la Roque," Wlodek said. I must have whimpered because Gavin placed both arms around me.

"There is a third offer," Gavin said, sounding angry.

"Which one is that?" Merrill asked, lifting an eyebrow.

"Mine," Gavin growled.

Wlodek studied Gavin for a moment. "Then we have three viable offers," he conceded. "Lissa, you will not be bound by marriage to any one of them until your five years of instruction are finished," Wlodek said. "And perhaps not then if things do not work out, but accepting one of these offers now will prohibit the others from coming forward later and bombarding Merrill with requests. Each of these candidates is strong enough and old enough to make the others back away."

"And what if I don't want any of them?" I asked. I was terrified and being backed into a corner. "Is Merrill going to make this decision for me, even if I hate the one he picks?"

"Lissa, I will only make that decision for you if you will not choose for yourself," Merrill informed me. Why had they not told me this before? Why?

"I don't want to pick one and I don't want Merrill to pick one either," my voice was shaky as I stared at my hands. My fingers were laced together as tightly as I could make them, to keep the others from seeing how upset I was.

"Then they will struggle against one another, attempting to win your favor and attention. None of those who danced with you tonight were disappointed," Wlodek's eyes bored into mine as I looked up at him.

"Wellington found you quite charming and interested in English politics and the Royal Family, with which he is obsessed." Wlodek almost smiled. "He only backed away when he learned that Ivan and René were making offers."

"Oh God, I may be sick," I said, hanging my head and trying to steady my breathing. "Please tell me the Italian guy didn't say the same thing."

"Oh, he was quite taken with you, but René gave him a look and he backed away for the time being."

I didn't realize it, but I'd somehow tangled my hands in Gavin's tuxedo jacket while Wlodek was speaking and was now hanging on for dear life. Where was my freedom? Where was my right to live my own life, away from sniffing hounds? The truth was that I had none of those things.

The stark reality of being female and vampire was only now hitting me. Unless I was very, very old, like the two females on the Council, I was something in demand by the males of the race. "You're saying I need the protection of someone's claim? Is that it?" I tried desperately to keep the panic out of my voice.

"Mine will only go so far," Merrill agreed. "They know I do not have an interest in that part of your life. I am only teaching you. Therefore, they feel free to make offers of this nature."

"These vampires may be willing to fight one another for you and we do not need such conflict within their ranks," Wlodek's voice was stiff and unrelenting.

I didn't know the evening was going to end this way. I realized that Wlodek and Merrill had most likely known all along and once again, nobody was telling me anything. I wanted to shout at them. Weep angry tears and throw priceless art objects at Flavio's tastefully painted walls.

They'd trapped me like a wild animal. The inescapable power of the Vampire Council was herding me down a path I had no desire to tread. I couldn't run away, Merrill's compulsion saw to that. His was a velvet glove covering the steel of the trap, but it was a trap nonetheless. I'd had more freedom while Winkler was blackmailing me.

"You may put a stop to further offers if you accept one of them tonight," Merrill said. "You will be consenting to a lengthy engagement, with a courtship during the five-year period. The Council will not allow a vampire to marry until he or she has successfully passed their probationary period." Yeah, Wlodek already said that. Apparently, Merrill didn't think it registered the first time.

"And I have to get married after the five years is up?" I had to know. I wanted to curl up in a ball and whimper. Hanging onto Gavin would have been frowned upon under any other circumstances. I was supposed to develop the mask they all had; none of them showed any emotion.

"Yes, unless you petition the Council to dissolve the engagement. And unless both parties wish to have the engagement dissolved, it will be put to a vote, I warn you," Wlodek informed me coldly. "Therefore, if they decide against you, your marriage will take place. Marriages between vampires last a period of one hundred years and may be renewed for additional periods of one hundred year intervals, from thereon."

"You're not going to let this go, are you?" I searched Wlodek's face for any empathy or emotion. There was none.

"An unmated female vampire is too much of a temptation, Lissa," Wlodek said. "Males will challenge and fight over you as long as you are unclaimed."

Gavin had been watching and listening the entire time, his face in that expressionless mask that I was coming to recognize. All of them had it—it was the face they showed each other most of the time. No way could I go to René. He'd kill me if he ever found out what I'd done. Ivan? I think I'd rather die at René's hand. "Gavin, you're not going to become insufferable, are you?" I turned to him, begging with my eyes as well as my voice.

"Only if you refuse me," he replied softly. "And especially if you turn me down in favor of my cousin. He likes to acquire things. It would give him great pleasure to snatch you from beneath my nose."

I wondered where my time was—the period Gavin had requested to earn my trust. Had he known about this? I had no idea. Everything was turned upside down and I had no way to sort it all out now.

"He's not about to snatch me anywhere," I said, struggling to keep my voice even. "Ivan scares the crap out of me. Wellington almost put me to sleep. Moretti? He wanted to have sex, right there on the floor, I think." I shuddered, just thinking about it. "Gavin, I'm not turning you down, but you have an uphill climb." I let his arm go and sat up straight, leaning my body away from his.

"You are accepting Gavin's offer?" Wlodek quirked an eyebrow again.

"Yes. I suppose so," I sighed. I really didn't have much choice.

"Gavin, you will bring a ring and make the formal offer within the week," Merrill said. "The acceptance will be listed in the Council's records immediately."

"There's a ring?" I must have sounded lost. I thought it was just some sort of promise, I suppose, with all of that coming later. I hadn't even been widowed a year, yet.

"There will be," Gavin growled. I think he knew not to push things right then; I was still feeling stunned.

"Gavin, if I lend you my car, I trust you can get Lissa home before dawn and in one piece?" Wlodek asked. "Merrill will drop me off. We have business to discuss."

"I can do that," Gavin nodded.

"You may spend the night at the manor, if you wish," Merrill said. "In a separate bedroom, of course."

"Of course," Gavin nodded. "Come, Lissa," he said, helping me off the sofa. Gavin laid his jacket across my shoulders once we were outside in the cool air, opened the car door and put me up front on the passenger side. The driver gave the keys over and Gavin pulled out of the driveway, heading away from London.

"We're engaged?" I tried to keep the trembling from my voice.

"Love, it will be all right," Gavin reached over and patted my hand.

※ ※

"She will be protected; I cannot imagine many who would willingly challenge an Assassin, especially this one," Wlodek sighed. "Had I the penchant, I would have wagered against her acceptance of Gavin under any circumstances, and I was quite surprised he arrived tonight before the ball was over. He was on assignment in Madrid. No matter, she has made a choice so I will make the announcement at the meeting tomorrow and see if anyone has a complaint."

"She still doesn't trust him, but the others were unknown to her and they frightened her more," Merrill said.

"Especially de la Roque. Did you see the look on her face? She has no idea that this is a game to him. She is terrified that he will kill her if he discovers that she took those tiaras. I imagine she witnessed his anger when he discovered that he'd lost this round," Wlodek said. "Too bad she didn't come away with some of the other things, but we didn't send her after those. I had no idea she'd come out of this as successfully as she did. This bodes well for us in the future. And, now that she's with Gavin, it may be easier to persuade her to work for us once her probationary period is up. In the meantime, we will send her out on other supervised assignments so she may gain the experience she needs. This one will definitely be an asset for us."

"Wlodek, I wouldn't count too heavily on your being able to strong-arm that one," Merrill observed. "She is new, now, and somewhat afraid. If her confidence improves, she may not only surprise you with her abilities but with her defiance as well. Do not play with her, Wlodek."

"Lissa, I am feeling hungry," Gavin informed me when we reached the house. Merrill had showed me where the key was kept outside, so I pulled it out of its hidden brick and opened the door.

"I have some blood in my fridge," I said, returning the key and locking the door behind us. Gavin followed me upstairs and looked around my bedroom while I handed the unit of blood to him. It was after four and he drank almost the entire pint of blood.

"Want what's left?" he asked. I took it and drained the rest. Some days, I couldn't believe how easily this came to me now. Once, in my human life, I'd not been able to watch while they drew blood from my husband's arm. Now I didn't even bat an eyelash.

The empty blood bags were destroyed once we were finished with them. Merrill or Franklin dropped them off somewhere; we kept separate covered wastebins just for that. Probably one of the things I was destined to learn.

"Now, how about cuddling with me so I can watch the news?" Gavin reached for my hand and kissed it. I led him to my sitting area, which held a sofa, a chair and a chaise.

Gavin opted for the sofa; it was directly in front of the flat screen that hung on the wall. Grabbing the remote, he turned the television on, pulling me down onto the sofa with him. Gavin stroked my neck and cheek absently while listening to an early news program; I was tuning all of it out until a journalist announced breaking news.

"The Cambridge Lover's Knot tiara and the Spencer family tiara have both been returned anonymously," the journalist said. I stiffened in Gavin's arms. "There were no fingerprints on the tiaras or the packaging and they were mailed from a facility in Wales," the correspondent went on. "The employees at the shipping business have no recollection of the mailing and no recording of the incident was made."

"Cripes," I muttered.

"Nice work, ma petite ange," Gavin bent down to kiss me.
"You're not going to teach me Russian, are you?"
"No immediate plans."
"Good."

CHAPTER 4

Merrill was back before dawn and chased Gavin out of my bedroom. He'd been content to watch television there until he fell asleep, I think. I managed to get out of my pricy gown and diamonds before I went to bed, wondering briefly if Merrill wanted the diamonds back. *I'll have to ask*, I thought, as I set them on my dresser.

A quick shower followed; I shampooed all the hairspray and mousse out of my hair before going to bed. I was engaged. How the hell had that happened? And to Gavin, on top of that. It was probably better than the alternatives I'd been offered. There wasn't much time to worry over the whole, confusing mess; I dropped off the moment dawn arrived.

"Gavin said to tell you he'd be back—he went to trade cars and run another errand or two," Franklin advised when I made my way downstairs.

I'd dressed in black fleece pants and a pink top, with a black fleece jacket. I'd been thinking about going to the roof. The night before still hadn't settled well, leaving me adrift on uncharted waters. "Merrill has already left for the meeting," Franklin went on.

"Are you doing all right?" I asked, giving Franklin a hug. "If you didn't belong to Greg, I might take you for myself."

"You're welcome to whatever Greg doesn't want," he hugged me back. "I understand that Mr. Gavin has a prior claim, now."

"Oh, yeah. *That*," I grumped. "Nothing like getting strong-armed into an engagement so the dogs won't come sniffing around. Is it too late to get a sex change operation?"

"More than likely," Franklin laughed. "And I wouldn't want to be the one to break the news to Gavin."

"He'd be pissed all right," I agreed.

"Merrill gave him a key," Franklin said soberly.

"He did what? I don't even have a key." I was upset, now.

"And the bedroom down the hall from yours, where he slept last night," Franklin added.

"He's going to be staying here?" My voice squeaked.

"At times, it appears," Franklin said.

"Well, this just gets better as it goes along," I grumbled. "I'm going to the roof. Tell Mr. *I can just waltz in and get whatever I want* that he can float up if he wants, I can't stop him."

"I wouldn't imagine that you could. I can take the broom to him," Franklin offered with a grin.

"Franklin, that is a vampire and an Assassin on top of that. Get Merrill to take a broom to him if he needs it," I said.

"Fair enough," Franklin nodded.

Gavin did float up after a while but I was expecting him. I'd heard his Mercedes in the driveway minutes before. "I brought a swimsuit and some clothing," he said as he settled his tall frame beside me. "I was thinking about soaking in the hot tub. Might you consider joining me?"

"Maybe." I hadn't been in the hot tub in days. "How did you get out of providing security for the meeting?"

"Wlodek gave me two weeks off to celebrate my engagement," Gavin leaned over and nuzzled my neck. "And sent someone else to finish my assignment in Madrid."

"Lucky you," I said.

"Yes. I am lucky. Quite lucky. I think you may be able to hear my cousin's angry shout when he learns I made away with you," Gavin was now kissing my neck. "Do you know how fine your skin is?"

"How did both of you get turned at nearly the same time?" I asked, trying to distract him. He was nipping while kissing.

"We were both fighting in the Roman army and were defeated by the Goths," he mumbled against my skin before pulling back for a moment. "I was turned first; René was turned three days later by the same sire. Of course, our names were different then, but we adopted France as our country after a time. René still lives there, as you know," he hugged me. "Both of us are nearly seventeen hundred years old."

"That's not scary or anything," I muttered, hunching into my fleece jacket with a shiver. Gavin was more than sixteen centuries older than I.

"Lissa, your lifespan is no more than a blink to us," Gavin confirmed my thoughts as he pulled me into his lap. "But a very important blink. To me, anyway." It was so nice to know that even at my age, I was considered a vampire infant.

The night around us was crisp and cold. It was October in Kent and Gavin was hugging me tightly as if that might warm me or something. Vampire bodies are cool; blood doesn't pump through our veins as it does in humans.

Considering that I might ask Merrill what our normal body temperature was, I lifted my head to ask Gavin about it first when I received mindspeech from Robert, one of two other known vampires with the talent.

Lissa, there is trouble, he sent. *Bring Gavin and come quickly.*

"Gavin, I sure hope you know where the meeting is," I said instead. "Robert just said there was trouble and to bring you quickly."

Gavin had me off the roof so fast I was nearly dizzy, and we were in the Mercedes and speeding away in less time than that. "Did he say what the problem was?" Gavin asked while I kept an eye on the speedometer. Kilometers per hour still evaded my sense of time and distance.

No time to do research now. He'd bought the car in Germany, that was apparent, as the steering wheel was on the left. It might have seemed somewhat normal if he weren't racing along on the left side of the road. Pushing my thoughts away from how fast we were going, I concentrated on Gavin's question instead.

"No," I answered. "Let me contact him to find out." *Robert*, I sent, *Gavin wants to know what the problem is.*

The Council met after the formal meeting. We were attacked and are being held captive by six humans and three vampires. One of the humans has explosives strapped to his body and a detonation device in his hand, Robert returned.

"Robert says the Council is being held by six humans and three vampires, and one of the humans is strapped with a bomb." I shivered as I passed the message to Gavin.

"A bomb will kill a vampire, just as it will a human if the bomb is strong enough and the detonation takes place near enough," Gavin informed me. "If a vampire is blown to bits, he cannot survive."

We'd pulled up to an intersection, but there were no waiting cars so Gavin blew right through, ignoring the red light. "Both our misters are out on assignment; They would be most useful here, but they are called for elsewhere, more often than not," Gavin went on.

"Then if you need one, I'll go," I offered.

"Lissa, I do not like risking you in this way, that is a *bomb*," Gavin said, as if I didn't realize it to begin with.

"I know," I said. My shivering hadn't stopped. "Why are vampires working with humans?" I asked, attempting to control my quivering.

"At times they form an alliance, each attempting to take advantage of the other race in order to achieve their goals. The humans can move about in daylight. The vampires are strong. Some vampires desire a return to the old ways and look to change or destroy that which keeps the laws. The humans may think of us as evil and wish to exterminate us. It is an unholy alliance between the two factions."

"The enemy of my enemy is my friend theory?" I asked.

"Temporarily," Gavin agreed. "Both sides realize that their alliance is never meant to last; it is just that each intends to come out the ultimate victor, and that is seldom the case." Gavin shifted angrily as we turned a corner at a high rate of speed.

His statement informed me that he'd seen all this before. With sixteen centuries behind him, it wasn't that much of a surprise. It took us less than fifteen minutes, with Gavin driving more than one hundred eighty kilometers per hour at times, to get to Gravesend where the meeting was being held. I smelled the Thames nearby when we leapt from the car; it was mixed with other scents of the city around us—petrol and automobiles.

"What are they waiting on?" I asked Gavin as we ran swiftly toward a single-story brick building. "If they were going to blow the Council up, why not go ahead and do it?"

"Because the vampires are in charge and realize that something of this nature may not be accomplished by merely killing the Council. They are attempting to change the laws."

"Great," I mumbled. "I suppose the Enforcers are all inside with the Council members?"

"Yes. They would be."

"We need to get the bomber. The others can be dealt with after that," I said. I concentrated on turning to mist.

"Lissa, what will you do?" Gavin's voice held worry and that wasn't like him.

Where's that stiff upper lip? I sent to him, watching my hands and feet disappear.

"That is British, which is not my nationality," he grumbled. "Lissa, do not do anything foolish."

That's easy for you to say, I sent. My record for turning may have been broken that night, but there wasn't anyone there to time me when the change was complete. Floating as invisible mist, I made my way toward the building.

Coming in now, I sent mindspeech to Robert.

We are in the basement, he returned. Gavin positioned himself at the building's entrance. I didn't think any of the bad guys would get past him alive.

The door to the stairwell was locked with a keypad, but there was space at the bottom and I misted underneath, making my way down the stairs. The Council was in a wide chamber below, all of them seated at tables against the far wall.

The three rogue vampires threatening them stood behind the human strapped with a bomb. It looked like a vest to me; something that a road repair crew might wear. It was orange in color and well-padded with explosives. The detonator was in his hand and he stood a bare fifteen feet away from Wlodek, who sat at the center of a long table.

I was terrified. Not just for myself but for some of the vampires at the table. Charles was there, along with Flavio and the others, and behind them were the Enforcers, including Robert, Russell, Will and Radomir.

What frightened me the most, however, was who was standing off to the side, at the very end of the Enforcers. *Merrill*. This was going to take some strategy and a very big chance on my part. If I failed, then it was likely the entire building would go up and me with it.

"You are just a figurehead," one of the three rogue vampires shouted at Wlodek. "Change the laws and we will let you live."

"Do not lie to me," Wlodek said sharply. "Step forward and we will discuss your demands."

"Old man, I know what the range of your compulsion is," the vampire laughed. So, that's why they were all standing as far away as they were. Otherwise, Wlodek would just command them all to give up and they wouldn't have a choice.

Slowly and cautiously, I misted between the bomber and the rogue vampire standing a few feet behind him. Hoping he'd keep his eyes straight ahead instead of looking down, I stood behind the bomber so my hands would appear only in front of him while using his body to conceal their appearance from the vampire. My feet would be revealed at the same time my hands were and things could go downhill fast if the rogue saw them while I was attempting to do the only thing I could.

In their usual way, Wlodek and the rest of the Council never blinked when my hands coalesced against the human's torso. It was my plan to take away the detonator and drag the human toward Wlodek so he'd have control of the would-be bomber, but even I wasn't expecting what happened.

My misted body came in contact with the bomber's, and just as the tiaras had disappeared in my grip, so too did the human. He, the detonator and the bomb instantly turned to mist the moment I touched him.

The vampire behind us shouted and slashed out at me the moment the human disappeared, but I was invisible mist and he only managed to disturb the air around me, forcing me forward for a moment.

I had no idea what status the bomb was in and took no chances, turning and flying toward the stairs and then beneath the locked door. I thought I heard fighting behind me as I fled but I didn't have time to worry about it; I had to get the bomber out of there and then decide what to do with him.

Flying straight up into the night air once we cleared the building, I felt the human's emotions as I carried him with me. He'd suddenly found himself in a state he never expected to be and was sending out his fear in waves and vibrations.

Turning quickly, I saw the river barely a quarter mile away, the dark water sparkling under a few nearby street lamps. Hoping there weren't any boats traveling the waters nearby, I rushed toward the Thames.

Feel free to explode, I sent to the man as I dropped him over the center of the river. The moment we separated, he became whole again, screaming and flailing as he fell toward the water.

He detonated only a few feet above the river itself; his hand had probably released his grip on the detonator as he dropped. The explosion sent my misty particles blasting upward at a tremendous rate of speed, and I was frightened out of my wits when I finally stopped tumbling through the air.

Emergency sirens were sounding and vehicles with flashing lights were converging on the river when I came back to my senses. I wasn't sure what they'd find, if anything, but they were far enough away that I wasn't immediately worried for the vampires I'd left behind.

Robert was sending desperate mindspeech by that time. *Lissa? Lissa, are you all right? Lissa?* They were all vampires; they'd heard the explosion.

Keep your shirt on, the blast sent me into another country, I think, I returned, my mental voice sounding shaky. I felt dizzy (if that were possible in my current state), after turning several time in an attempt to get my bearings. I couldn't determine immediately from which direction I'd come. Finally, floating off in what I hoped was the right path, I slowly made my way back.

The rogue vampires must have been killed already when I arrived; I didn't see any evidence of them, but two humans were still alive when I floated inside the building. The ground-level floor was the place for questioning, it appeared; I could tell that compulsion had been laid already as I came back to solid form.

Merrill came to my side, wrapping me in a tight embrace, which surprised me. He kept me in the crook of his arm while we both listened to the interrogation. Wlodek asked questions while Gavin and Russell held the two humans.

"We wanted to expose both the vampires and werewolves and get rid of all of you," one of them hissed in anger. "You're an abomination. Filthy blood drinkers."

"And just how did you learn of our existence?" Wlodek asked in a conversational fashion, ignoring the insult.

"Tate, here, told us all about you," the young man said, indicating his companion. "You're devil spawn, straight from hell. I hope you all die." Wlodek never turned a hair or blinked, even. Likely, he'd heard all this before.

Tate stood by, frowning at his companion, angry that they'd been forced to spill everything they knew. Dark-haired with a thin build, Tate couldn't be more than twenty, I figured. His companion looked a bit older, but his eyes were wild and filled with hate.

"Are you all right, Lissa?" Merrill whispered against my ear.

"Yeah, I just got disoriented when the guy blew himself up over the water," I whispered back. "I dropped him into the river and he exploded just above the surface." Merrill hugged me against him and we turned back to the conversation.

"So, Tate," Wlodek turned to the other young man, "How did you learn of us?"

"My father was a werewolf. He was killed when he made a challenge," the kid's voice was sullen. "I want all of you to die. Vampires and werewolves."

"Get Weldon Harper on the phone," Wlodek snapped at Flavio, who whipped out a cell phone and began punching numbers.

"Don't turn me over to them," Tate whined.

"We do not interfere with werewolf justice," Wlodek said indifferently, turning back to the first human. "Do you have connections to the werewolves? Are you related to any of them by blood?"

"No."

Wlodek nodded to Russell, who held him tightly with only one hand. The death was swift. I'm not sure I ever saw Russell move, but a broken neck is an effective way for a human to die. Russell allowed the body to fall while the one who'd been identified as Tate looked on in horror.

"Weldon is on the line, Honored One," Flavio held out the cell. Wlodek took it. "Weldon, we have a young man in custody who claims his father was a werewolf. He and some of his human friends attempted to destroy a few vampires tonight." Wlodek listened for a moment. He hadn't informed the Grand Master that he'd been one of the vampires threatened. "What's your full name, boy?" he asked instead, holding a hand over the phone.

"Tate Briggs," the kid said.

"Oh, lord," I put a hand over my mouth. Wlodek heard, whether I wanted him to or not. He lifted an eyebrow at me.

"I believe there's someone here who may have information for you," Wlodek said, motioning me forward.

The phone was held out to me. My fingers shook when I took it. Weldon thought I was dead. He was about to find out differently. "Grand Master?" I spoke into the phone.

Weldon, to his credit, barely hesitated, and I'm sure he knew Wlodek was listening in on both sides of the conversation. "Lissa, I'm glad to hear your voice," Weldon said smoothly. Gavin watched me closely while he held Tate Briggs.

"Grand Master, this young man says his name is Tate Briggs. Is this Lester's son?" I knew the answer before Weldon gave it to me; the kid drew in a shaky breath.

"Yes, it's Lester's son," Weldon growled. "Is the little bastard causing trouble?"

"You might say that," I confirmed. "He and a few friends took up a career in terrorism tonight."

"Are any of them still alive?"

"Just Tate. He's the only blood relative to a werewolf."

"Lissa, do something for me, all right?"

"I'll do my best, Grand Master."

"Look that punk in the eye; tell him you are *Pack* and that the Grand Master will come to deliver his justice in person."

"All right, Grand Master." Lowering the phone, I studied Tate Briggs. He bore a resemblance to Lester—I could see it, now. Plus, once I'd had a chance to get close enough to scent him, I knew. "The Grand Master says to tell you I am Pack," I said. "He also says to tell you that he is coming to deliver justice himself in your case. I want you to know, and this is from me only, that I helped fight off your father and his followers. There was no honor in your father and there is none in you. Your father would have condemned you if the peace had failed. I pity you and your short-sightedness." I held the phone back to my ear. "The message has been delivered, Grand Master."

"And then some," Weldon chuckled in my ear. "Let me talk to Wlodek again, so we can hammer out an execution date."

Dutifully I handed the phone back to Wlodek, who nodded at me and spoke again to Weldon. Merrill put his arm around me again when I returned to his side.

Russell and Radomir ended up taking custody of Tate Briggs. They placed cuffs and chains on him and hauled him off toward a waiting car. I wondered if he was going to be locked inside one of the cells I'd been kept in, but put it out of my mind.

"Now, what shall we do with this?" Wlodek toed the body with the broken neck. "We have four others just like it in the basement."

"Too bad I got rid of the bomb," I said. "That would be an ideal situation."

"We may be able to come up with something," Wlodek said, glancing at me. "What did you have in mind?"

Merrill and Gavin helped me while Charles typed the note on his computer (using gloves, of course). The note was then placed inside one of the cars the young men had driven to the site. Someone else would be getting rid of the second vehicle.

Actually, Wellington, the stuffy old British vampire, had given me the idea. He'd blustered about a faction gaining popularity in Great Britain, which wanted to eliminate the monarchy altogether. Even followers from other countries were joining the movement. When the charges were delivered by vampires driving up in an unmarked van, Robert and Will, both wearing gloves, set them up.

The note we'd left in the car spelled out their dissatisfaction with the monarchy and that the five young men were planning group suicide as a form of protest. At least one member of the Council snickered softly over the whole thing.

"Who owns the building?" I asked Merrill quietly while the charges were being laid. Since this was my idea, I was going to be responsible for destroying somebody's property.

"Wlodek, I believe," Merrill smiled slightly.

"Ah."

"Come along, Lissa," Gavin lifted me one-handed and hauled me toward his Mercedes.

"Hey." I tried to slap his hand but it wasn't working very well. Gavin buckled me into the passenger seat in no time and then came around to the driver's side. "We need to be far away when this blows," he said, putting the car in gear.

"Can we go home slower than we got here in the first place?" I grumbled, pulling the mirror down to look at my face. "Crap, why didn't you tell me I look like I've been in a hurricane?" My hair was quite windblown and I may have had a black smudge or two on my face.

"Lissa, I was afraid you were dead when we heard the explosion," Gavin said, zooming around a corner.

"He didn't explode until just before he hit to the water," I said. "I didn't know he was going to turn to mist when I touched him—I just wanted to take away the detonator." Gavin wasn't doing much in the slowing down department, so I held onto the edge of my seat as he rounded another corner at a blinding rate of speed.

"Lissa, stop talking. If I had a heart, I'd be having an attack right now." I stopped talking and drew my knees up to my chest in the seat.

※ ※

"Franklin, why are you waiting up?" I gave him a hug when Gavin and I walked into the kitchen.

"I was worried," he said, brushing strands of tangled hair away from my face.

"I'm fine, Gavin's fine and Merrill's fine, too. In fact, Merrill should be here any minute," I patted Frank's shoulder and let him go.

"Merrill's here, now," Merrill walked in behind us. "Franklin, go to bed. You look worn out."

"All right," Franklin said. "At least I know you won't want breakfast in the morning so I can sleep late." He took off toward the stairs.

"I'm worried that he's the one who'll have the heart attack," I said softly as Franklin walked away.

"Lissa, I would very much like to take you over my knee," Gavin said, changing the subject.

"And I will fight you every step of the way and most likely never speak to you again," I said.

"That's why I only said I'd like to," Gavin frowned at me. "You have no idea what I was thinking when you went off like that, and when the others came upstairs afterward and said you'd disappeared with the bomber…" he didn't finish.

"I didn't know what else to do, Gavin. Honest. Can we leave it for tonight?"

Merrill stood nearby, listening. "We'll leave it for tonight," he sighed. "I think I'll go sit in the hot tub and forget this for a moment."

"That is an excellent idea." Gavin grabbed me up again and took off at full speed toward the spa room. That's how he and I both ended up in the hot tub, completely naked. Gavin just ripped through my clothing while I attempted to stop him. His claws were out and there wasn't any way I wanted to argue with those things.

He dumped me in the water first, before removing his own clothing. I got to see every inch of him that night, and some of those inches were rather large and rigid. I had to look the other way.

Merrill, dressed in a swimsuit, dropped in on the other side, lifted an eyebrow slightly and never said a word. Merrill was nicely built but Gavin's shoulders were wider and there wasn't any part of him that wasn't tight or a pleasure to see.

The hot, frothing water was pure bliss as I sat there, even though Gavin held me firmly against his side. At least he wasn't pulling me onto his lap; that might have been a bit much.

Instead, I leaned my forehead against Gavin's shoulder. Merrill climbed out after a while and left us. Gavin began speaking in French, murmuring words against my hair. I didn't understand any of it, with the exception of one short phrase, *je t'aime*.

※ ※

Wlodek spoke by phone with Merrill the following evening during my lesson, informing him that Weldon would arrive in a week for the execution. Wlodek expected Merrill, Gavin and me to be there when Weldon carried out the sentence against Tate Briggs, since the Grand Master requested my presence. I didn't want to go.

"You must," Merrill said after hanging up with Wlodek. "It is considered an honor to receive an invitation such as this."

"Merrill, this is an execution. Remember, I've seen werewolves fight before. This is going to be bloody."

"Lissa," he held my chin in his fingers, "look away if you want. Wlodek wants you to be there and I'm sure Weldon desires your presence because you are a member of his Pack."

I blinked up at Merrill and sighed. "What should I wear," I asked, turning away from him.

"Wear something dark but tasteful."

"Because the fur and the blood are going to fly, no doubt."

"More than likely."

"I have to get used to this, don't I?"

"Yes. It is difficult to understand, Lissa, how you can fight someone so successfully, or drop the boy's companion into the water so he may blow himself up, and yet hold back from something like this." His bright blue eyes examined my face carefully.

"I can't explain it either," I shrugged. "Maybe because this is a spectator sport and not in defense of my life."

"I see," Merrill said and left it at that.

Gavin brought a ring, just as Merrill had instructed and presented it to me in Merrill's study (in Merrill's presence), before the designated week was up. The center diamond was two full carats with smaller, round diamonds twisting and swirling around the band. It was huge and beautiful and it felt like a great weight around my finger when Gavin slipped it on. Gavin took me out afterward, to a restaurant.

"What is this?" I asked, as he led me down a sidewalk on a narrow street in London.

"You'll see," he said, guiding me down brick steps that led below street level. After reaching the bottom of the steps, we walked forward for perhaps twenty feet before coming to a thick, steel door. Gavin pulled a card from his pocket and swiped it through a reader at the side.

The door opened automatically, closing behind us once we were through. We walked another ten feet in darkness before coming to a small pool of dim light, where two vampires stood guard before another door. I was beginning to worry at that point.

"Gavin," one of the vampires acknowledged while the other opened the door for us. I was ushered into the only vampire restaurant in the London area.

Muted sounds of silver and glasses clinking mingled with voices talking and soft music. The interior was dimly lit, but it may as well have been daylight to the vampires present. Perhaps twenty private booths lined the square perimeter of a spacious room, with a bar at one end, complete with a vampire bartender.

The scents of human women mixed with that of vampire males, varying in ages from younger to very, very old. And the décor? Human five star restaurants might compare to this one. Maybe.

"This is *El Diablo*," Gavin said, removing my wrap. He'd insisted I wear a dress, so I'd worn a cocktail length black dress he found adequate. Gavin was dressed in a suit; I seldom saw him in anything else.

A Maitre d' came, passed my wrap off to another vampire and led us to a booth. I think he might have bowed to Gavin if he thought it might get him somewhere and not look pretentious.

Glasses of blood were offered right away, in champagne flutes, no less. "This is the place for vampires to bring their dates, mostly human," Gavin explained quietly. "They have a fully functioning kitchen in the back, with a human chef. The waiters and bartenders are vampire. Flavio owns this and it has been in operation for nearly twenty years."

A woman moaned in the throes of orgasm across the room, making me lift an eyebrow at Gavin. "This falls outside the rule," he said, reading the question in my eyes. "It is considered a private club and not a public place, plus it is common knowledge that you should have a date if you come here. This way, if you get excited from the smell of blood, you have your own ready supply available."

"Okaaay," I breathed, glancing surreptitiously about the barely lit room.

"It is my hope that you will allow me to take from you, love," Gavin nuzzled my neck. "You may replenish yourself with blood from the bar or drink from me in return. And, as this is somewhat public, you will not be obligated to have full sex. Also, be aware that anything said here may be overheard and repeated."

"Oh, tell me that now," I hissed quietly.

"My love, they serve blood mixed with the alcohol of your choice. You may drink safely here; I will make sure you come to no harm." He pushed my glass of blood toward me. "This is the house specialty, blood with champagne."

"And what if I make a lot of racket and pass out if you bite me?" I whispered. Honestly, why hadn't he warned me before bringing me here? I figured it would be reported if I smacked his shoulder, so I kept my hands in my lap.

"Then I will carry you out and be the envy of everyone here," he smiled.

"You are a piece of work, you know that?" I grumbled.

"Come, try this," Gavin nudged the glass of blood in my direction again.

"On your head be it," I said, lifting the glass. "I should warn you, I can't hold my liquor; it goes right to my head. Four glasses and poof, I was vampire," I said, waving an arm. Gavin placed an arm around me and lifted my free hand for a kiss.

The alcohol-laced blood was good. Really good, I suppose I should say. Gavin handed his off to me when mine was empty and called for two more. I was drunk after the third one.

"Now, little Lissa," Gavin nuzzled my neck, pulled back to kiss me and then nuzzled my neck again, nipping it lightly. "You will remember this time, my love," he gripped the back of my neck in his hand, pulled my body against his and sank his fangs into me.

My breaths were coming in a series of whimpers as he brought me to climax just with his bite. Sure enough, just like the other times, I blacked out for a while. When I woke, I was in Gavin's arms. He was murmuring my name and kissing me again.

"You taste so sweet, my love," he murmured. "Take from me, Lissa. I want to feel the nip of your teeth."

"Gavin," I slurred his name.

"Come, love. Just a little. Let me know what the true pleasure is."

I blinked at him before putting my arms around his neck. "I'm supposed to kiss you, first," I put my mouth on his throat, over the point where his pulse should be. His scent was drugging me, so instead of kissing him, I licked his neck and nipped his skin. Then I placed the kiss, holding the back of his neck as firmly as I could. Wondering how my small fangs would feel to him—would they be enough to satisfy? I pierced his throat and drank.

Gavin groaned and gripped my body fiercely against his. "Yes, Lissa," he moaned, and then moaned again when I disengaged. I licked his neck to eliminate any stray drops of blood. Now it was his turn to close his eyes. I don't think he passed out or anything close, but he was definitely happy.

"I have only read accounts in the past concerning the pleasure one may receive from the bite of one's mate or lover," Gavin whispered against my ear. "Those accounts did not do justice to the reality." He smiled down at me. "You may take from me any time. Rest assured I will most certainly enjoy it."

Gavin didn't have to carry me out of the restaurant, but he certainly had a tight grip on me when I wobbled out. I heard the whispers behind us as we left—vampires telling their dates or companions about the first female turned in seven hundred years.

CHAPTER 5

Gavin watched me dress for Tate Briggs' execution, his eyes betraying a bit of appreciation as I paraded around in underwear and bra. I chose black slacks and a black sweater, braided my hair and pulled on a pair of black, low-heeled boots while his eyes followed me silently.

Gavin kept his arms folded and displayed a slight quirk at a corner of his mouth. He helped me into a short, black leather blazer, my last item. "You need jewelry," he breathed against my ear. "More earrings and necklaces and such. When I return from assignment, we will remedy that."

I put my platinum hoop earrings on, causing him to step back with a sigh. I knew he wanted to have sex and had been hinting at it for days, but I didn't know what to do about it. I was feeling a bit queasy over the execution thing, really didn't want to go in the first place and had been told that it was an honor to be invited. Well, Gavin was Roman. I wondered if he'd had season tickets to the Coliseum.

Merrill arrived in a separate car and was already at the site when Gavin and I reached the designated execution area. It was set up on the grounds near Wlodek's manor and the entire Council was attending. No lights were provided; they weren't needed since vampires and werewolves could all see perfectly fine on the darkest of nights.

The site was already roped off; it consisted of a twenty-foot square of dead grass on a chill October night, far away from everything human. Vampire Council members lined the rope on one side, some talking quietly to those beside them.

I didn't listen in or give them more than a cursory glance, choosing instead to keep my revulsion over the whole thing from being noticed. Merrill made sure I was standing between him and Gavin behind an adjacent rope. Wlodek arrived after a bit, accompanied by Weldon and (to my surprise) *Winkler.*

"Lissa!" Weldon boomed before walking over and wrapping me in a bear hug, which aggravated Gavin. Gavin didn't get a greeting, but I wasn't surprised about that. He'd fooled everybody while watching Winkler and me.

I hoped Winkler had somehow figured out that Gavin was keeping an eye on him over the recognition software he was developing. The fact that Winkler sold it exclusively to the NSA was our little secret.

"Good to see you, Grand Master," I nodded to Weldon after he let me go. Winkler grinned at me and frowned at Gavin, who displayed his usual unreadable expression.

"Honored one," Weldon turned to Wlodek, "it is my intention to allow my temporary Second to perform the execution." Weldon indicated Winkler.

"That is acceptable," Wlodek nodded to Weldon.

"It is also customary to my race for the one performing the execution to share the blood of the kill with a chosen member of the Pack if they so desire. Winkler wishes to bestow that honor upon Lissa."

Merrill stiffened beside me while I drew in a gasping breath. I didn't want any part of that, and I wasn't even sure what it was. No way did I want to share the blood of an executed half-human. No way.

"Lissa will accept this as the honor it is," Wlodek gave me a pointed look. *Fuck.* I was pulled inside the roped-off area and shown where to stand, which was in a corner with Weldon. My skin was shivering and I only wanted to curl up in a ball. That wasn't an option, so I stood as straight as I could next to Weldon, who placed an arm around my shoulders and hugged me.

The first thing to happen after all the Council members quieted expectantly was Winkler's preparation to turn to wolf. He removed his clothing. Winkler should definitely pass his genes off to someone; he could have posed for a few nude statues. He stretched his lithe, well-muscled body before nodding to Weldon and turning to wolf. His wolf was huge and solid black; only his eyes gleamed golden in the sliver of moonlight shining down.

"We are ready for the prisoner," Weldon informed Wlodek. Wlodek nodded to an attendant vampire and Tate Briggs was brought forward, struggling between two Enforcers that I hadn't seen before. I almost buried my face against Weldon's side at that point.

Tate was naked, just as Winkler was before he changed. I imagined that if Tate were werewolf, he'd be making the change as well. Unfortunately, he was the half-human son of a werewolf-human mating, and they were unable to turn. He was also crying, which made things worse. The vampires and the werewolves all looked on, their masks in place, no emotion evident.

"Tate Briggs, you are sentenced to death, according to the Law of the Pack," Weldon spoke beside me, his voice measured and even. "You have threatened the Pack by exposing the Pack, attempting to destroy it for your own petty revenge. These acts are in violation of the Pack oaths you swore, not only to your father, but to me as well. Make your peace and prepare to die."

"Shut up, you fucker!" Tate shouted, struggling against the two vampires who held him. He was placed inside the roped off area. Winkler was already growling at him.

"Let him go," Weldon said and the vampires released their prisoner. Tate screamed and ran, but Winkler was already on him, savaging his body. He nearly ripped a leg off first, causing Tate to scream louder. An arm was completely severed next and blood was indeed flying. I think I was whimpering by that time.

Winkler then ripped out Tate's belly, spilling intestines and bloody viscera across the dead grass. Lastly, Winkler snapped the head from the neck, allowing it to roll away. He changed to his human form quickly and before I knew what was happening, Weldon shoved me forward. I found myself staring at Winkler, whose mouth and face were drenched in blood. He also had an erection as he came toward me.

Stunned as I was, I couldn't move when Winkler lifted me in his arms and kissed me, his mouth transferring warm blood from Tate's death into mine and humping his erection against me until he achieved release.

Winkler set me down when he was done and lifted his head to howl. Shocked beyond comprehension, I almost dropped to the ground. Weldon was behind me, holding me up. "Stand up, Lissa," Weldon whispered in my ear. I did my best to stand as steadily as I could.

The scent of Winkler's semen was all over me now, along with Tate's blood. Winkler was done howling after a minute or two and warm, wet towels were brought to him. He made a huge production over cleaning himself off.

Someone should have warned me about this, I thought, only then beginning to feel exceptionally angry over the whole thing. Tate's body parts were gathered into a body bag by Enforcers. Who knew where they would be taken? I certainly didn't. Winkler dressed, once he'd cleaned himself up.

"You are welcome to stay at the manor," Wlodek extended an invitation to the werewolves. I gaped at Wlodek and Weldon, who were exchanging pleasantries while I, horrified and covered in blood and semen, looked on in obvious disbelief.

"We have a place to stay; one of the local Packs has offered," Weldon nodded to Wlodek. "We appreciate your invitation just the same, Honored One." Wlodek hadn't expected them to accept; I could see it in his face, but he was obligated to offer anyway. I wanted to smack both of them, as furious and humiliated as I felt at that moment.

"Lissa, I would very much like to hear from my Pack member, now and then," Weldon turned me to face him. "You are an official member of the Dallas Pack, by permission of the Packmaster. You should check in with him from time to time as well." He smiled at me. He was giving Wlodek instruction by talking to me within Wlodek's hearing. Wlodek's face was unreadable as he listened.

"She is a member of the Dallas Pack, by the *demand* of the Packmaster," Winkler added. All right, I not only had his come all over me *and* the blood from his kill, but now he was ordering me to keep in touch. *The colossal schmuck.*

"Haven't changed much, have we, Winkler?" I asked, doing my best to hide my fury and horror over what had just happened.

"Not one damn bit," he grinned. "You have my e-mail address. You could call, too, once in a while."

"Good to see you, Lissa," Weldon bent down and kissed my cheek. Winkler leaned in, gave me another tonsil-licker, grinned again, let me go and strode off after Weldon, leaving me dazed and speechless.

As soon as they were out of sight, Gavin jerked me out of the enclosure, ripped my blazer, sweater and slacks off, tossed them on the ground and left them lying amid Tate's blood, threw me over his shoulder before I even had time to squeak out a protest and took off. I was now wearing only a bra, lacy panties and my boots.

I was beating on Gavin's back by the time we made it to the car, but he was ignoring me completely. The door was slammed shut once he'd tossed me inside and Gavin was in the driver's seat before I knew it. He wasn't jealous. Uh-uh. I just hoped I was going to survive the next few minutes—Gavin was scaring me. His face was set and he hadn't said a word since the whole debacle started.

On top of everything else, I couldn't get Tate's screams out of my head. Winkler hadn't tried to make the kill quick and merciful. He made sure the kid suffered. Maybe this was a deterrent to others who might consider breaking the law, but it didn't sit well with me or my stomach. Briefly, I considered telling Gavin that I'd like to walk home, even dressed as I was, but thought better of it.

"I think I'm needed at home," Merrill informed Wlodek quietly when Wlodek invited him to stay for a few minutes. "Perhaps to keep Lissa alive."

"If he harms her, I'll void his claim myself," Wlodek said, frowning. "René's offer still stands."

"I'll let you know," Merrill said, rushing toward the door.

※ ※

Gavin was cursing. At least that's what I thought he was doing; it was all in French or Spanish or Italian; he appeared to be switching around. How was I to know? I didn't understand any of it. He was also pacing inside my bedroom.

He'd tossed me in the shower, boots and all, when we arrived and I'd struggled to pull the boots off while Gavin ripped off my underwear. He proceeded to scrub my skin and hair twice under practically cold water, then watched while I brushed my teeth and rinsed my mouth with mouthwash.

He didn't like Winkler's scent on me one tiny bit. Honestly, I didn't appreciate the scents Winkler left on me either, but there wasn't anything I could do about it. Now, I was wrapped in a bath towel and sitting against the headboard of my bed, listening to the rant.

"Slow down, honey," I ventured after a while. Gavin growled at me and started up again. Well, this was going nowhere fast. I pulled my knees up and hugged one of the many pillows there. That's how Merrill found us; I was huddled on the bed and Gavin was still having his fit.

"Gavin, enough," Merrill said, his voice a soft command. Gavin slowed down and then stopped. "Lissa, did he harm you?" Merrill turned to me.

"No. Unless you consider getting your skin scrubbed harm."

"Gavin, she didn't want to go and she didn't want what they did to her. Let it go." Merrill frowned at Gavin.

"You didn't want him to touch you?" Gavin looked at me.

"Not like that," I shuddered. "I was so shocked, I couldn't even move. Somebody is going to have to explain all the rules to me someday before dumping me in the middle of a situation like that."

"Lissa is yours, Gavin," Merrill said. "She is here with you. She came home with you. She accepted your claim. This jealousy accomplishes nothing." Merrill stalked out of the room.

"Well, I guess he told me," Gavin drawled.

"At least you're speaking English, now," I said, refusing to look at him.

"Lissa, anyone has the power to arouse my ire where you are concerned," Gavin rubbed a hand over his head. His hair was growing back slowly; he now had about a quarter inch of dark hair over his scalp. He looked to be growing it faster than the half-inch a year Charles had estimated.

"That was some ire," I said. My arms were still gripping my pillow tightly and I was still huddled against the headboard. I'd had a traumatic evening and Gavin hadn't helped matters any, flying off the handle like he did. "You're some kind of over-achiever, aren't you?" I added, looking up at him.

"It was not my intention to make the situation worse." His dark eyes betrayed no emotion.

"I don't know whether it's a good thing or a bad thing that I didn't understand anything you said."

"More than likely a good thing." He came to sit on the bed beside me. "I will not harm you," he reached out a hand and trailed fingers across my bare shoulders. I almost shrank from his touch.

"Your skin quivers when you are upset or frightened," he leaned in and placed a kiss against my shoulder. I still wore his ring; it was the only thing he hadn't removed when I'd been shoved into the shower earlier. Wanting to curl into a smaller ball, I lay there while Gavin stroked my skin, wondering what my life would be like when I had to marry him.

"How close are you and René," I asked instead. "He'll want to kill me if he finds out I took those tiaras."

"René and I, well," Gavin sat up straighter but still kept a hand on me, his thumb making circles on my shoulder. "René sometimes performs special services for the Council," he said. "We are not very close, but we don't ignore one another, either. We are family, he and I, where most other vampires no longer have family. Robert and Albert are close as brothers, as are Henri and Gervais, the misters. René and I are the only other two who are truly related in the vampire community."

"There are two sets of brothers who are Enforcers?" I hadn't thought about that before.

"Yes. As you can probably tell, the gifts sometimes run in families. Three years ago, we lost our Chief of Enforcers, Adam Chessman. His uncle was a mister and when Adam was turned, it was fortuitous for the Council that he also had the gift. Russell now holds the Chief position, but he doesn't have mindspeech or misting ability. We have difficulties as you might guess, finding the rare talents to begin with. Therefore, we often search out siblings who might carry the same abilities."

"So, you and René exchange Christmas gifts and birthday cards?" I asked, focusing on Gavin's only relative in the vampire realm.

"Nothing such as that, although René might find it humorous if I sent either," Gavin replied. "I was hoping to love you tonight but you are not in the proper mood." He sighed and stood up. "I must leave tomorrow and fly away from you, little angel. Remember to call me from time to time." Gavin left my room swiftly.

⚜

Gavin was kissing me when I woke. "I do not know when I shall return," he said and kissed me again before walking out my bedroom door. I blinked back tears as I watched him leave.

I sent an e-mail to Winkler that evening, telling him that as an honored tradition among werewolves, what he'd done sucked. Of course, I skirted around the term werewolf and didn't describe the incident just in case, but he'd know what I meant. He sent an e-mail back after a few hours, due to the time differences, I'm sure, and told me that usually if a female was involved, they got full sex and not a dry hump.

"Thanks for that, O furry one," I replied.

"Howling with laughter," he sent back. The man was a lunatic in every sense of the word and that's what I e-mailed back to him.

※

Merrill and I finally discussed biting in public during my lessons. "It is considered a public bite if there are other vampires around that may become frenzied if they smell blood," Merrill explained. "If they cannot control themselves, humans may be killed as a result. This is not the same as when you bit that young man in the alley. There were no vampires close enough, you took the blood properly and not as a deliberate act of sex, which is what happened the night of the ball. The vampire was not hungry; he merely wanted his escort to experience a climax. He should have taken her outside and away from the others if that is what he wished to do."

"Gavin took me to *El Diablo*," I mumbled, staring at my hands.

"And I'm sure he explained the differences to you."

"He did. I e-mailed Winkler and told him his traditions sucked," I lifted my eyes to Merrill.

"And he more than likely informed you that normally, the actual sex act is included instead of what he did."

"He may have mentioned it. I called him a lunatic."

Merrill smiled. "Tomorrow," he said, I will take you and Franklin to London, where we will inspect the building that Sergio Velenci owned which now belongs to you. You may decide whether to keep it or sell it. There is also the matter of the villa in Spain. I have photographs of it." He handed a large envelope over that he'd pulled from a desk drawer.

"I don't need this," I said, going through the pictures. It was a grand estate, no doubt about it, and more than likely still contained Sergio's scent. I had no desire ever to smell *that* again.

"I can have someone pack up things such as jewelry and the like and have them shipped to you, so you may go through them and decide if there's anything you'd like to keep. Otherwise, a prestigious auction house will be more than happy to offer those things for sale," Merrill said. I nodded. "Do you wish to keep any of the furniture?"

"No."

"There are buyers who would like the villa furnished as it is," Merrill said. "Here is a listing of the artwork, along with photographs." We looked at those for a while. There was some Baroque art, even a few Rococo pieces, along with a Neoclassical piece or two. What really drew my attention was the Vermeer; I drew in a breath at that one.

"Merrill, I want this one," I passed the photograph back to him.

"You have excellent taste," Merrill smiled. "That one is priceless. It probably hasn't seen the light of day since Sergio acquired it—shortly after the artist painted it, no doubt. I'll have it packed up and shipped directly to my business address. Is there anything else you might like?"

"The Rubens. Do you think the Honored One would like the David?" It was a Neoclassical piece, depicting Napoleon.

"I think he would like that very much," Merrill said, smiling slightly.

"Do you want the Rembrandt?" I passed the photograph over to him.

"Are you sure you want to give this away? It is worth millions."

"I know. I'm asking if you want it. If you do, I'd like to give it to you. As an early Christmas gift."

"I would be honored to accept," he smiled. "I have a spot for it in my drawing room."

"Let me ask Gavin if there's anything here he wants; I guess I'll have to call or e-mail," I said, leafing through the photographs again. "Franklin, too."

"You know quite a bit about art," Merrill said.

"I have an MFA in fine art, you know. They don't hand those out unless you take a truckload of hours in art history."

"I see." Merrill's smile deepened.

"So, you can keep Baudelaire and Voltaire," I said. "I can talk art with anybody, including those vampires who painted on cave walls, I think."

Franklin had a hard time choosing between the Fragonard and the Boucher, so I asked Merrill to have both of them packed up and sent to him. Franklin tried to stop me, so I hugged him into submission. Who knew Franklin would want a painting of Louis XV's mistress?

"The prospective buyers for the villa are vampires and have offered a fair amount for the property," Merrill informed me later. "They understand that the art work will not be included and didn't expect it."

"They're not like Nyles Abernathy, with an ax to grind, are they?" I asked. I just wanted to make sure.

"No. I know these personally, and that will not be the case," Merrill hugged me briefly. "Actually, Henri and Gervais, the misters, wish to buy. The countryside is beautiful there."

"Then more power to them," I said.

※ ※

"Honey, I just need to know if you want any of the paintings," I spoke with Gavin on the phone later. I'd left a voice-mail earlier and he'd called me back.

"You don't miss me?"

"Of course I miss you. I don't miss your temper; you can leave that behind when you come home."

"Amusing," Gavin grumbled.

"I'm teasing you. I don't think a surgeon could separate you and your temper."

"Then I am pleased you realize that."

"Charles wants to see a movie and asked me to go along." I winced, expecting the jealous rage. It didn't come.

"Charles would be a good companion," Gavin acknowledged. "I trust you have only a platonic interest in him?"

"I think of Charles as a friend, nothing more," I said.

"He's not your type," Gavin said, right at the moment I said almost the same thing.

"We say jinx when people do that," I laughed.

※ ※

Charles and I did go out in early November. We saw a romantic comedy (I guess some vampires actually enjoy those, he and I did). He had a place in London, although he stayed at Wlodek's most of the time.

The best part about the outing was the fact that we had fun and it was nice. He knew not to get too friendly, I don't think many vampires would want to tangle with Gavin, after all. The trouble with having Charles as a friend was his job—Charles didn't have a lot of spare time.

"Have fun?" Merrill was reading a newspaper at the kitchen island when I got home. He likes to keep up with the stock reports and his subscriptions to business magazines alone were staggering.

"I did and we liked the movie," I said.

"I thought you might be interested in the fact that René de la Roque is moving to his London home," Merrill said, turning the page of his newspaper.

"No way," I said. "Please tell me he isn't coming because he found out I—you know."

"I think he's past that," Merrill said. "René has issued an invitation to visit with him after he arrives."

"And what will Gavin say?" I was trying to wiggle out of the whole thing.

"Why don't you call and ask?"

"I don't want to see René." I was whining and I knew it.

"Vampires tend to live a very long time," Merrill reminded me, lowering his newspaper. "It is never wise to offend any of them, as enmity can last as long as the vampire can."

"Now you tell me," I grumbled. "So, I'm supposed to go and make nice, even if he scares me?"

"Especially if he frightens you," Merrill said. "You should learn not to show any weakness."

"Yeah. I've seen the lack of expression," I muttered. Pulling out my cell phone, I dialed Gavin's number. He actually answered.

"First off, I miss you," I said. I didn't want to start the inquisition. "Second, Merrill tells me René is moving to his London home and expects us to visit. I don't want to see René but Merrill says we should go. He says it's about living a long time and not making enemies or something like that."

"Lissa, you must learn to slow down," Gavin sounded almost happy. "René will not harm you and he is quite charming as a host. Merrill is correct—you should go."

"Gavin, you are not helping," I said.

"Lissa, are we going to waste precious time arguing over this?"

"Gavin, I'd really like to make up my own mind once in a while," I was back to whining.

"I know, love. We will talk about this some other time. I must go." He hung up.

"Well, that was useless as phone calls go," I ended the call and stuffed the phone back in my purse.

"Lissa, be patient with us, please," Merrill pleaded. "I know you feel trapped and smothered, most of the time."

"I miss walking in daylight and not worrying that vampires are going to jump out of every closet and dark alley," I said, walking toward the stairs.

"Lissa, you are vampire, and generally we do not jump from closets," Merrill said softly at my back. I just hunched my shoulders and kept walking.

René de la Roque's home was not in London proper—it was outside London with stables, a gardener's cottage and various outbuildings. In other words, it was huge. There were even horses in the stables.

"I enjoy riding," René said as the human servant ushered us into a den of sorts.

René didn't do anything in a small way, I discovered. We were introduced to other guests, one of whom I recognized from my thieving trip to France. Merrill suggested I wear something nice and mentioned the black dress he'd purchased for me in Paris. I wore it with a heavy wrap since it was low-cut, front and back. The servant took the wrap and my small purse and carried them away.

"You are stunning," René appraised my appearance with a smile. I had to smile back and thank him; that was the proper thing to do. He looked very nice himself; I could see a bit of family resemblance to Gavin in his eyes and the shape of his face. I could also tell by scent that they'd been sired by the same vampire. At least Rene' still had his hair; it was a thick, dark blond, whereas Gavin's was a very dark brown. Gavin's hair was still growing out at the moment.

René invited us to sit in a beautiful, museum-quality receiving room, decorated in René's favorite Louis XIV period. This home was furnished much like his chateau in France and none of the furniture was something I'd want to flop down on to read a book. It all smelled old and horsey to me. Probably stuffed with horsehair, no doubt, although the chairs, sofas and settees were covered in silks and damasks.

Instead of commenting on the scent of his furniture, I complimented René on his excellent taste. He flashed me a dazzling smile. Oh, he was handsome, all right, and he knew it, right down to his little pinky toes.

His three other guests consisted of a vampire named Aubrey, along with two other vampires named Devlin and Jacques. Aubrey was the vampire I recognized from France—he was the one who'd gone inside the vault with René. I intended to do my best to stay away from him as well; René trusted Aubrey enough to show him what he'd stolen. Aubrey had been quite impressed with the tiaras.

I didn't know Devlin and Jacques. They both kissed my hand when I was introduced, and I wasn't sure I was comfortable with that. Merrill was as smooth as could be, talking about this or that with all of them while we were served glasses of wine by the human servants.

René entertained us with stories about getting caught inside Louis XIV's court. He'd crashed a ball to dance with someone and ended up befriending the French king. René was funny, it was true, and doing his best to make sure I enjoyed myself. He had other things on the agenda, however.

While I'd already discovered that René was fond of adventure and liked to steal the impossible at times, (the contents of his vault in France attested to that) he also liked to gamble and not in the traditional sense. He was a master strategist, carefully crafting a plot—just to take what he wanted or to steal something from someone else. I learned that night just how devious he could be to achieve his goals.

He invited Merrill to his bedroom to view a painting that, in his words, was not fit for delicate sensibilities (mine), but was attributed to one of the masters. I was left with Aubrey, Jacques and Devlin.

Merrill had only been gone a short while when the trap was sprung. Aubrey moved from his seat across from mine and came to sit beside me. Quite close, in fact. He set his wineglass on the table in front of the small sofa where I sat and breathed a cool breath against my cheek.

"You will look fine on René's arm," he said. "And you must accept his offer over Gavin's, you know. René and the rest of us here know what you did."

He'd made me uncomfortable the moment he sat down and the way he leaned over me was frightening. My cell phone had been taken away inside my purse; I had no idea where it was at the moment. I couldn't send a hasty message to Merrill that way so I attempted mind-speech, begging Merrill to come.

He didn't hear and Aubrey kept right on pushing against me, telling me I would regret it if I didn't accept René over Gavin and that Wlodek would be happy to make the exchange, one fiancé over another. "Come, now, you stole from René and you owe him. He is willing to forgive if you accept his offer."

"I'm sorry, I have no idea what you're talking about," I lied, doing my best not to make a face at his closeness. I did try to scoot away from him, but there wasn't much room between me and the delicately carved arm of the sofa.

"Yes you do. You took the tiaras; René knows of this. If you know what is good for you, you will do as I say." He was smiling at me but I'm sure my face must have registered my shock. My body began its inevitable shivering. Aubrey's fangs slipped out. "Perhaps I will taste you, just to make sure René is getting the best for his efforts."

That had me off the sofa in a flash and racing toward the door. Devlin and Jacques were prepared for such an attempt; both of them had their hands on me before I reached the exit. I fought with both of them, earning a slash across my cheek before pulling out my own claws.

They turned me loose amid a bout of howling, so I flew down the hallway, heading for the front door and freedom. Another two vampires had the front entrance blocked; I veered away from their grasp, running to the left.

I wasn't familiar at all with René's home—I'd only seen the entrance and the hall leading to the sitting room. Blindly, I ran through the manor until I came to a formal dining room where a very long, heavily carved table took up a great deal of space. Ornate chairs lined both sides of the dark, wooden behemoth.

Situated in front of the table was a window, constructed of floor to ceiling glass panes. With five vampires almost on my heels, I did the only thing I knew to do, running headlong through the window and shattering it in my flight, tearing my skin with shards of glass as I leapt onto the lawn in front of René's home.

The vampires were now shouting and running after me, which frightened me more. I gasped and sobbed as I ran, trying to concentrate on becoming mist while I raced over René's manicured lawns. I had no idea if misting would work; I was moving as swiftly as I could, frightened out of my wits as I ran.

I don't know how far I ran or how fast I changed, but I did change. What I didn't count on, once I'd gone to mist and lifted off the ground, was the fact that it was my intention to escape. Merrill's compulsion kicked in while I was mist and my misty particles were suddenly on fire. Not merely the burning from flames but as if I'd been dipped in acid.

I had no mouth to scream but I was screaming mentally as I plummeted to earth. I'd been flying high overhead to escape my pursuers before the agony overcame me. Still in the form of mist, I lay next to the ground, convulsing somehow; even I was aware of that. Somewhere, in some small part of my brain that seemed detached from the pain and horror, I knew that I was suffering. Blackness came after only a few minutes.

CHAPTER 6

"I will kill you, René, if we do not find her." Wlodek had come, along with Radomir and Ian, another of the Council's Enforcers, after Merrill reported Lissa missing.

"It was meant to be a harmless prank," René growled, glaring at Aubrey. Wlodek stood inside René's entry while several others were outside, searching the grounds. "We had no idea she would try to run."

"Through a glass window, René? How badly did you frighten her?" Wlodek didn't expect an answer and received none.

※ ※

"She is here," Griffin knelt by the small patch of dead flowers on the edge of René's property. Lissa had gone as far as she could go before Merrill's compulsion activated, and she'd even traveled a bit beyond that. Merrill knelt beside his friend. As mist, Lissa was still invisible to Merrill, but not to Griffin's powerfully sharp sight.

"Can you bring her out of this?" Merrill pleaded. Griffin had very strict rules to follow, the strictest of which was that of non-interference.

"I will bring her out, but you will have to take care of the situation past that point," Griffin said, holding his hand over Lissa's mist. A bit of light formed and Lissa's body slowly became solid.

"She's cut to ribbons," Merrill sighed, lifting her carefully. "Thank you," he nodded at Griffin, who disappeared.

"*Mon Dieu*," René swore when Merrill carried Lissa's unconscious body inside the house. Merrill didn't speak to René; he was so angry he could have taken on every vampire inside the manor.

"As your punishment, René," Wlodek surveyed Lissa's body, which was bloody and sliced in many places from breaking through the window, "You are going to call your cousin immediately and explain what you did."

"No, Honored One, I beg you," René said, his voice barely a whisper. "He will kill me."

"I can't say that I'd stop him," Wlodek grumbled. "Very well, let us table this for now. Merrill, what must we do to take care of her?" He nodded toward Lissa.

"We should clean the wounds and assess the damage," Merrill said. "The rejuvenating sleep may take care of most of this, but if she wakes before dawn, she will be in terrible pain."

"I never meant for this to happen," René walked over to Merrill, reaching out a hand to touch Lissa's forehead. "I only meant to frighten her a little."

"Lissa is terrified of you," Merrill's fangs slipped out, which happened only when he was as angry as he could possibly get. "I was hoping that by bringing her here, she would find her fear of you unfounded. And what do you do? She will never want to come within sight of you again."

※

I woke before dawn and my multitude of cuts and scratches were all an agony. "It will be fine, Lissa, once dawn comes," Merrill was leaning over me with Radomir standing at his shoulder. Under normal circumstances, I might have told Radomir it was nice to see him. These weren't normal circumstances. Tears must have fallen; Merrill wiped one away with his thumb. "René will not threaten you again," Merrill assured me.

"Dead?" I asked, unsure how I felt about that.

"No. Not yet anyway. If Gavin decides to kill him when he learns of this, I certainly won't try to stop him." My eyes closed and I didn't know another thing until nightfall.

≼ ≽

René asked to see me before Merrill ushered me out of his home after nightfall, but I refused. I also told Merrill that Aubrey and the others were now on my shit list, only I didn't quite put it in those terms. He nodded and we walked out of the place.

They'd have to drug me or place compulsion to get me to come within a mile of René's estate again. There were still a few scratches left over from my trip through the window and I had no desire to discuss what the compulsion not to escape had cost me. Neither Merrill nor I wanted to mention *that*.

Franklin was nearly beside himself when we got home and Lena looked as if she'd been crying. "I'm all right," I said to both of them, giving them a hug. Merrill told me to soak in the hot tub and we didn't have lessons for three days.

Wlodek decided not to tell Gavin what happened until he returned from assignment, which occurred a week after my injuries. Wlodek told the story, I suppose, after calling Gavin into his study. Gavin, as a result, was so angry when he arrived at the house that Merrill sent Franklin to his suite while he and I faced Gavin as he walked through the door.

My ribs may never be the same after being crushed against Gavin's body, which was trembling with rage. He glared over the top of my head at Merrill, who stood steady, the usual expression on his face.

"This happens and no one tells me?" Gavin almost shouted.

"Wlodek's instructions. I'm sure he's already informed you of that," Merrill said. I was glad Wlodek had given the order; I didn't want to be on the other end of the phone when Gavin exploded.

"Wlodek tells me I may not kill René," Gavin paced while still holding me in his arms. I wanted to ask him to put me down; my face was held against his chest and my body tight against his. "I tell her he is safe, charming, even, and he does this? He has much to answer for."

"Gavin please put me down." I couldn't stand it anymore—my cheek would more than likely have an imprint from the fabric of his suit.

"Lissa," he shifted me in his arms so he could look at my face, "tell me you are well. That he did no lasting harm."

"I'm still afraid of him, Gavin, but I was afraid of him before." I looked into Gavin's eyes. They were normally such a beautiful brown, but now they were clouded with anger. Gavin carried me to the island, setting me down there. He then moved his body between my knees before pulling me against him.

Merrill left us at that point; I heard his footsteps as he walked away. Gavin started kissing me. He didn't stop kissing me, even while he lifted my top over my head and clipped through my bra with partially formed claws. His teeth and eventually the tips of his fangs against my nipples were doing something to me.

Yes, I was afraid. But that wasn't the only thing I was feeling at the moment. Gavin was giving me a different kind of fire; one that made me want to press myself against him. I was completely naked in his arms and he, still fully clothed, floated me through the manor, up the stairs and into my bedroom.

How strange and sensual it is, having someone with centuries of experience love you. Gavin held nothing back. There was no part of me that he failed to explore, kiss or nip. When we joined, his body worshipped mine in sinuous, erotic thrusts, urging my body to twine with his, while matching and mirroring his movements.

Too bad most human women who've had a lover of the fanged variety don't recall the sex—women everywhere would be hunting vampires just for the multiple orgasms.

One of the most intense moments came when Gavin sank his teeth into my femoral artery to drink. The climax was incredible. Like a gentleman, he waited for me to regain consciousness before continuing. He was gentle when we joined the second time, punctuating thrusts with kisses until I was nearly mindless as the climax came.

Gavin convince me to drink as much of a pint of blood as I could afterward; he finished off what was left of it and then insisted I bite him. I couldn't take much, but his body convulsed against mine. I learned that vampires do indeed ejaculate, only it is nearly clear, much like my tears.

⁂

"Are we holding back from taking the world apart tonight?" Franklin ventured to ask Gavin when he and I made it downstairs the following evening.

"For now." Gavin pulled me close and gently nipped my neck.

"I see." Franklin went back to his cooking.

⁂

Gavin was home for three days before he was sent out again, and he wasn't pleased that Wlodek had another assignment for him so quickly. During the three days he was with me, I learned a new term: *Vampire lust*. Gavin's had been held in check for a while and during his three days off, he had me in bed as often as possible (or as often as he could get me to say yes, that is).

Merrill explained, (without my asking because it was embarrassing) that it was tied to the need for blood. "Wlodek has always held the theory that it is payment for the blood we take—giving the donor sex of one kind or another, along with intense orgasms." He'd smiled slightly while he said it.

I wondered about the blonde in the picture by his bed and was curious if she'd ever gotten the benefit of Merrill's lust. No way was I going to ask, though. No way. Merrill never spoke about her so it was a private matter.

Two days after Gavin was called out, Wlodek asked to see me. Merrill drove me over, as usual. Maybe someday, he'd trust me enough to drive myself. That someday wasn't yet.

"First, there's this." Wlodek handed a thick, cream-colored envelope across his desk. I rose from my chair to take it. He gestured for me to read it so I pulled the note from the envelope.

"*Little rose,*" the letter began, "*it was never my intention to frighten you as I did. Aubrey is my child; he was only following my instructions when he said those things to you. I assure you that they were only meant in jest, mostly aimed at my cousin, who sometimes needs a bit of a jolt to keep him from complete stuffiness. When I saw your body brought back into my home in such dire condition, I nearly melted on the floor. You have my apologies and I will continue to send them to you until you pardon my abysmal behavior. Gavin is my cousin and only true family remaining; therefore, you are family as well. I should have realized this before playing my little joke. Please forgive me.*

Yours ever, René."

I knew two things when I handed the note to Merrill to read—René most likely was sincere in his apology, but he was also lying. Aubrey wasn't his. I did know who made Aubrey, and it wasn't René. Of course, I couldn't say that and tip my hand. That was a talent I was going to keep to myself if at all possible.

Of the three who'd been in the room that night, only Devlin was René's and Aubrey was Devlin's. The thing was; Aubrey was nearly as old as Devlin, which might mean that Devlin had turned Aubrey before the five-year training period was up. Vampire intrigue, indeed. If René knew I held that piece of information, he truly would try to kill me, I think.

"What do you intend to do about this?" Merrill held up the note as he asked the question.

"Do you know how many panes of glass were in that window and how big they were?" I asked sweetly.

"Why do you wish to know that, child?" Wlodek was curious too, I could tell.

"Because I want to send René a gift, along with an acceptance of his apology," I said. "Enough panes of glass to re-do his window, all taped with an X for the next person to break through."

"I'll handle it," Merrill nodded, pulling out his cell, which was vibrating. "I'll take this outside," he said and walked out the door.

Wlodek handed over some very nice stationery he pulled from a desk drawer, I wrote out a quick note to René, telling him there was nothing to forgive and noted that I was sending a gift.

Wlodek read the note with interest before sealing the envelope and promising to get both items to René after Merrill purchased the glass. Wlodek placed the note in a drawer, picked up his gold pen and gave me a smile. "Thank you for the painting," he indicated the David portrait of Napoleon that now held a place of honor on one of his walls. It replaced a Meissonier, which I didn't like as much.

"I thought of you the minute I saw the photograph of the painting," I smiled back at Wlodek. "I never liked Meissonier as much as I did David."

"You seem to know a little about it."

"I have some hours in art history."

"Merrill has told me as much." I wondered what else Merrill had told him but didn't ask. Who knew what information Wlodek kept inside his head? He was still the oldest vampire I'd met and likely held a great deal of information.

Merrill came back, apologized for the interruption and sat down again. "Now, back to business," Wlodek said. "Weldon Harper has requested that Lissa provide security for him while he performs some of his yearly duties across the United States. He managed to accomplish the European portion while he was here, but now he is scheduled to travel across the U.S. And, since his Second's wife is pregnant, the alternate who was here with him will be going. The Grand Master has asked for Lissa as extra security. I have given permission, since she is officially a member of the Pack, as it were."

"Lissa?" Merrill blinked curiously at me. I hadn't said a word.

"I'll go," I shrugged. "I just hope there's no more of," I hesitated, searching for the words to describe what Winkler had done to me, "whatever it was that happened last time," I floundered.

What was I supposed to call it? Dry humping? *In front of Wlodek?* It had only been dry on my part. I wondered what happened to the clothes Gavin ripped off me, not to mention the total embarrassment of being dragged away from the execution site in my underwear.

Gavin had stripped me in front of the entire Council and the Enforcers. If the observers hadn't been vampire, I imagine that my image would be all over YouTube by now.

"We'll send you tomorrow evening; you'll spend the night in a safe house in New York before making the second leg to Grand Forks," Wlodek said. "Russell and Will are going with you since you don't have the information and codes for the safe house and such."

"How long is this going to take?" I asked.

"Three months," Wlodek said. "With a short break for Thanksgiving and Christmas. If Merrill wishes, you may join him for the holidays."

"I already have other plans," Merrill said. I turned sharply in his direction but didn't say anything. Merrill's face was unreadable, as usual. Franklin had plans to be with Greg, I knew that already. Well, I'd have to make my own plans, looked like.

"Well, then, if Gavin isn't busy," Wlodek smoothed it over. "He is your intended, after all." I didn't want to be the one to tell Wlodek how firmly Gavin had staked his claim, but then Merrill may have already supplied that information.

"Franklin, I'll e-mail you and do my best to get your Christmas card to you," I said as I folded clothing to tuck into one of four bags I was packing.

"You have my phone number and Greg's," Frank said as he watched me pack from a chair beside my bed. I'd gotten Greg's number while he visited earlier, just in case I needed to call him about any other emergency that might crop up with Franklin.

Franklin declared that there weren't going to be any other emergencies, but I'd taken the number anyway. "You can come and stay with us during Christmas if you want," he offered.

"I hate to interrupt the time with your honey," I said. "But I'll call if everything else falls through. Who knows, I may see how the wolves do the holidays."

"You know if Gavin's available, he won't leave you alone."

"I sort of do know that."

"You still don't trust him."

Franklin must have known by my expression just what I was going to say before I said it. "I don't trust any vampire," I said. "They're all full of secrets and they squeak when they turn one of them loose. And, when one of those secrets gets me in trouble or nearly killed, they don't really give a shit. Do they?" I tossed underwear into my suitcase a little harder than was warranted.

"Lissa, they're a secretive race. It's difficult for them to invite trust. They anger quickly too, for the most part."

"Well, same here," I said. "If it took going to bed with Gavin so he wouldn't kill his cousin, then so be it."

"Is that why you did it?"

"Not the whole reason, no," I grumbled. "I'm still pissed about all this. Why didn't they tell me up front they wanted to sell me off to somebody instead of parading me in front of a bunch of old vampires, just to see who put up a winning bid?"

"Do you have any feelings for Gavin?"

"Yes. Of course I do. It's just, I don't know." I sat down on the bed and put my head in my hands. "How did my life get so fucked up, Franklin? How?"

"Terrible things happen all the time, little girl," Franklin came over to sit beside me. "Come on, you're better than this. I know you're stronger than this. I don't know too many vampires, werewolves or humans who would willingly rush in, grab somebody strapped with a bomb and haul them out of the building, just to save a bunch of people who almost killed you to start with."

I lifted my head and looked at Franklin. "It was bad enough, seeing all of them there and about to get blown up, but what scared the bejeezus out of me was that Merrill was there, too. Now, I still haven't forgiven him for getting me sick when he ordered me to drink from a kid who'd taken a whole medicine cabinet one night, but I sort of like him."

"I know," Franklin patted my back. "And in a perfect world, well," he didn't finish.

"Frank, I've seen the picture on his nightstand. There's only one reason for a man to have a woman's picture on his nightstand. I can't compete with that. Not now and not ever. *Love looks not with the eyes, but with the mind, and therefore is winged Cupid painted blind*," I quoted Shakespeare. "It's as simple as that."

"Is that your favorite quote?"

"No. But it's the one that fits," I sighed. I sat on the edge of my bed, contemplating the twists and turns my life had taken in a short span of time. "I get the idea that the woman in that photograph is so special, nobody can come close," I added.

Franklin smiled at me. "Shouldn't you be packing?" he asked, tapping the edge of my suitcase.

"Yeah. Don't remind me. I have to go guard the king of the werewolves and his court jester, who came all over my clothes the last time I saw him. Can you explain that to me? What kind of custom is that?" Franklin laughed and we were back to normal.

Merrill drove me to the airport the following evening, after making sure I had plenty of money, my credit card, passport, driver's license and anything else I might need for the next three months.

I wasn't sure how I felt about spending three months with the wolves. Gavin already knew when I phoned him; Wlodek asked Charles to give him a call. He wasn't happy, but then I knew he wouldn't be.

Being merely unhappy would have been an improvement over what Gavin was. He was angry when he called, and he lectured me quite extensively over the whole thing.

Lots of *don'ts* came out of his mouth. "*Don't* let that werewolf put his hands on you. *Don't* trust any of them. *Don't* let them put your life in danger like the last time."

The list went on, but those were the big ones. It's a good thing vampires don't have heart attacks, strokes or aneurysms. Gavin would be well on his way to vampire limbo if that were true. He also ordered me to check in regularly. In his eyes, he owned me, and I was tired of being owned already.

Russell waited for me when I got to the Council's private hangar. It was misty outside—London at its November finest. Merrill talked while he'd driven me to the airport.

I was the experiment, he'd said. The first officially cooperative effort between vampires and werewolves (like I hadn't been there already). Merrill said he was hopeful that the trend could continue; future alliances could be beneficial to both sides.

I realized that as well as he did. Werewolves could move about freely during the day, something the vampires would never be able to do. A single vampire was generally much stronger than a single werewolf. If they combined their efforts, rogues could be captured swiftly. On both sides.

I hadn't heard any more about the Briggs family—did Lester have others out there, waiting to cause trouble for the werewolf community?

Briefly, I wondered about Tony, whom I'd met in Corpus Christi. He was the Director of the joint NSA and Homeland Security Department, and sole purchaser of the software Winkler had developed. He'd been such a nice person to talk to and to know.

"And there's our little mister now," Russell grinned at me while another vampire loaded my luggage onto the plane. Will arrived shortly after I did, and I surprised him greatly by giving him an unsolicited hug.

"Thank you," I said.

"For what?" He was completely confused by my gratitude.

"For standing up to Gavin as much as you did when he brought me back from Corpus Christi," I replied.

"Now, is this the same Gavin you're engaged to?" Russell looked puzzled.

"Yeah. The schmuck."

"It's the same Gavin, all right," Will snickered.

"Lissa, I am not even going to mention to Gavin that you hugged someone else," Merrill muttered.

"Good," I said. "Russell, do you want a hug, too?"

"I'll take whatever I can get," Russell said, embracing me.

"Now, there's another one you can hide from Gavin," I handed Merrill a level glance.

"You must be quite angry with him," Merrill observed.

"I am. Have a nice Christmas." I waved at him and trotted up the steps to board the jet.

※ ※

"Gavin's a little controlling," Merrill almost coughed into his hand.

"No. Gavin? No way!" Will's voice dripped with sarcasm. "That girl was crying the whole way from New York to London and he sat there and did nothing. Fucker." Will never minced his words.

"Come on, Will, let's get going. You can talk to Lissa and trade horror stories about Gavin on the way," Russell slapped Will on the back.

※ ※

"Merrill," Franklin looked up from the grocery list he was writing at the kitchen island.

"Franklin?"

"Father."

"Child?"

Franklin sighed and looked at the only father he'd ever known. Merrill would always look as he did; Franklin was growing older with the years. "Lissa feels trapped, Father."

"Tell me something I don't know," Merrill grumbled.

"If Gavin doesn't loosen his grip, he's going to lose her."

"I know that too."

"I don't really know how to say this next part." Franklin felt uncomfortable for the first time in a long time. He'd considered telling Merrill that Lissa cared for her surrogate sire in more than a fatherly way, but eventually decided against it. Merrill's affections lay elsewhere and nothing Franklin might do could change that.

"Then just say it. That's the best way." Merrill wasn't in the mood for subtlety.

"Lissa knows things, father. Somehow, I get the feeling that there will come a day when none of you will be able to control her. And she won't forget how she was treated or what was done to her."

"Griffin says the same thing."

"Well, Griffin would know if anyone would." Franklin went back to his list.

※ ※

Russell and Will made me laugh on the trip, which was a welcome change. They called each other names, too. I heard a lot of "prick" and "asshole," among other things, all while teasing each other unmercifully, along with several dirty jokes, which also made me laugh.

The day we spent in New York was uneventful; we got back on the jet the following evening and flew into Grand Forks. Unsurprisingly, Winkler was there waiting for me, along with a werewolf I hadn't met before—someone named Kelvin Morgan.

"Kelvin's new in the Dallas Pack. Davis is there keeping things in hand while I'm away," Winkler grinned at me while Will and Russell handed my bags off to him and Kelvin, who stowed them in the back of the Escalade Winkler was driving. The man had more money than was decent. Or werewolf, I should say.

I got a friendly hug from both Will and Russell before they ran back up the steps to the Council's jet. They were heading to Chicago and then on to assignments from there. I didn't ask and they didn't tell me.

"Come on, time's a wastin' and we have to get you into bed before sunrise," Winkler teased. Honestly, I just wanted to tell him to shut the hell up. He'd ruined some really good clothes the last time I'd seen him, never mind the fact that Gavin had been so pissed he could have spit and then scrubbed me in a shower afterward, all while cursing in multiple languages.

"I sure hope you're not offended by vampires," I told Kelvin when he leaned over the passenger seat to look at me while Winkler drove like a maniac over the dirt and gravel roads leading to Weldon's place.

"Nope. Not a problem," he grinned.

Weldon was still up when we arrived, although it was nearly five in the morning. "Kathy Jo and Daryl are asleep," Weldon whispered as he led us through the house.

Weldon had added onto his log home since I'd seen it last. It was now nearly twice as large. I complimented him on the changes. The inside had been redecorated; more than likely from Kathy Jo's influence and the fact that she was going to give birth to Weldon's first grandchild before long.

I was given the same bedroom I'd had the last time. The deer head had been removed from the wall and I was grateful for that.

Honestly, that glassy-eyed stare right above my head would have given me nightmares if I'd been capable of having them.

Maybe I should have asked Weldon to put Lester Briggs' wolf head on the wall instead; I might not mind seeing that, to be honest. Lester and his seditionist werewolves nearly killed me months earlier with their bites and the werewolf saliva that was subsequently trapped in my body.

"We leave tomorrow afternoon for Des Moines," Weldon informed me as we both stood before his massive fireplace. He also gave other information that might have made my blood run cold if it weren't already. "We have a body bag for you and we'll be packing you inside it, so wear something to sleep in that you won't mind us packing you up in," he said.

"Weldon, if I had any way to do it, I would march right out of this house and leave you and Winkler to your own affairs," I said, my hands on my hips. "It's bad enough being dead to the world between dawn and dusk, but to be manhandled by somebody in the meantime? Does the Council know about this?" I figured if Gavin knew about it, he'd be having a fit and on his way to North Dakota if he didn't have an assignment to take care of.

"Um, Wlodek is the one who suggested it, in case we needed to move about during the day," Weldon offered sheepishly.

"You know, I've never called the Head of the Vampire Council a rat bastard before, but I'm thinking about it now. Rest assured he wouldn't let somebody treat his most holy self this way." I was mad and thinking that all of Weldon's newly decorated log home might be turned to kindling in a matter of minutes.

"Lissa, we'll take good care of you, I promise," Weldon said.

"Weldon, if you knew how close your house was to becoming toothpicks, you'd save those empty words for later," I snapped.

"Lissa, you should know we won't let anything happen to you during the day," Winkler was now making an attempt at reassurance.

"William Wayne Winkler, do not even try." I swatted his hand away as I blazed past him. The bedroom door was nearly torn from its hinges when I slammed it behind me.

"I didn't think she was going to take that well," Weldon muttered, but of course I heard.

No way was I going to wear pajamas. No way. I went ahead and took a quick shower, dressing in navy fleece pants and a t-shirt. I also kept a bra on and I hate going to sleep in a bra. My hair was braided, too, so I wouldn't have bed-head. At least I hoped I wouldn't.

Who the hell would be picking me up and stuffing me inside a zippered bag? Would they be taking liberties? The whole thing pissed me off and I would have tossed and turned if that was possible. The last thing I put on before conking out at sunrise was socks.

"If I didn't know from the smell, I'd say she wasn't vampire," Kelvin said as he lifted Lissa and laid her inside the body bag Winkler held open. "She doesn't weigh much. Seems like she should be more, oh, substantial, I suppose."

"I wouldn't say that to her face," Winkler said. "She's substantial enough to put you through a wall, along with a dozen of your closest friends."

"Are all vampire women that pretty?" Kelvin watched as Winkler carefully zipped Lissa inside the bag. He'd laid an extra black cloth over her face and the front of her body; he didn't want any burns from leaking daylight.

"There are precious few vampire women," Winkler said. "The vampires would never have agreed to this if it weren't important, and since she's considered Pack, she was the logical choice. Weldon had to pull as many strings as he could, still, to convince them. She's a rarity, or so I've heard."

"Is she going to be able to breathe in there if she wakes up?"

"I have the alarm set on my watch for half an hour before sunset," Winkler said. "We should have her someplace safe enough to open the bag by then, in case she's claustrophobic or anything. I didn't get a chance to ask her last night and we've got extra bags in case she punches right through this one."

"I guess there's that," Kelvin nodded. He was getting his education in vampire 101 on this assignment. According to his paperwork, he'd just finished his residency at a New Mexico hospital, moved to Dallas to join the Pack and Winkler had agreed to set him up in his own practice when he got back after this assignment. Kelvin just didn't have experience with what he termed the *undead*.

Winkler's private jet waited at the airport in Grand Forks. All the luggage was loaded in, along with Lissa's body bag, which Winkler tossed over his shoulder in a fireman's carry. Weldon was the one to suggest making it look like a garment bag, so they'd placed loops on the ends to give that effect.

They made it to Des Moines just as the sun was setting on a mid-November evening. Winkler's watch went off so he walked to the back of the jet where Lissa's bag had been stretched out in the floor.

"We'll wait until she wakes to take her off," Weldon came up behind Winkler, who was kneeling on the floor, waiting for the first signs of life. Winkler glanced at the windows; dusk was settling around Des Moines International Airport.

He unzipped the top of the bag and pulled the black cloth away from Lissa's face. He'd watched her wake before and it always sent tingles through him, watching her take the first breath of the evening.

This time, however, she must have remembered what they were doing because she came awake with a start, gasping in a breath and attempting to claw her way out of the bag. Winkler knew then that she was a tiny bit claustrophobic.

"Stay away from the claws!" Weldon jerked Winkler back; he'd been trying to get to Lissa.

"Lissa, listen to me," Weldon soothed after he'd shoved Winkler onto a seat off to the side. Winkler was awkwardly trying to climb out of it again. "Lissa, you're all right. We're in Des Moines, sweetheart." Lissa's eyes were wild as she ripped the carpet on the jet's floor with deadly claws, all of which were extended to their full, one-foot length.

"Jesus, I didn't know they were that long," Kelvin came to stand behind Weldon.

"Shut up," Winkler hissed. "Lissa, wake up, baby. It's just us. Nobody's here to hurt you."

※ ※

I blinked, seeing nothing at first. My breaths were ragged and I was shivering as I tried to come to terms with unfamiliar surroundings. Winkler's voice was in my ears but I didn't understand what he was saying at the moment. Disorientation was clouding my brain and I blinked again.

"Lissa, nobody's here to hurt you." Winkler repeated off to my right. Slowly I focused on him while sight and colors returned. I was on the floor of his jet, my claws extended and my breaths trembling in my lungs.

"Lissa, you can stop shredding the carpet, now." Weldon's voice, this time. Looking down at my hands, I noticed that I had indeed shredded Winkler's carpet. Like he couldn't get it replaced—probably in the next five minutes if he wanted.

No way was I going to apologize for that. I was still sitting inside a half-zipped body bag on the floor of his jet. My claws retracted and Weldon breathed a sigh of relief.

"Want some help out of there?" he asked.

"No, thank you," I said as stiffly as I could. It wasn't the most graceful thing I've ever done, but I crawled out of the bag on my own.

Winkler offered to carry me off the plane. I offered to remove his liver. He allowed me to walk down the steps on my own. The Des

Moines Packmaster (I'd never gotten his name when he'd introduced himself to Weldon at the werewolf meeting earlier in the year), was there waiting for us.

All I remembered from our previous meeting was his smell and that he'd taken down someone named Corwin, whom Weldon had obviously liked. The man was around five-ten, stocky and looked to be pure muscle. No way could he take Winkler or Weldon, though. No way. This guy had probably gone as far as he could go.

He introduced himself to Winkler, who nodded and took his hand. "Avery Phillips," he said, nodding and smiling when Winkler gave his name. Avery already knew who Winkler was, I could tell.

He fawned all over Weldon, asking about Daryl and his new wife. Weldon was tactful, I'll give him that. Avery remembered me, too; I could see it in his eyes, although he didn't speak to me.

I figured most of the Packmasters remembered me quite well. I'd killed at least twenty of them, more than likely right under their noses while I'd protected Weldon from Lester Briggs and his henchwolves. Only two wolves eventually came to help, along with Daryl, Weldon's son.

"We're here to do the inspection. Weldon does it for all new Packmasters after six months or more," Winkler dropped back to speak quietly with me. I still felt rumpled from being tossed around in a body bag. Winkler and Kelvin had flung my purse and everything else inside my suitcase, so I didn't even have a mirror to check my hair.

"He's doing it tonight?" I squeaked, staring at Winkler in alarm.

"Oh, no, we're going to dinner. Avery will drop us off at our hotel first and wait while we change clothes before taking us to a restaurant. He'll do his best to impress, but the meeting with the werewolves of the Pack will come tomorrow night. If there are any grievances or problems, The Grand Master will hear them. Weldon has experience sorting out truth from fiction."

"If not, there's always compulsion," I shrugged.

"Exactly," Winkler grinned at me. "Actually, you're a big part of the reason we're making such a lengthy trip—you accounted for many Packmaster replacements across the country."

"Don't blame this on me," I elbowed him in the ribs. "Mr. *I was in Corpus Christi at the time* werewolf."

"Too bad I wasn't there; I might have saved you a few bites," Winkler chuckled.

"You got eyes on your ass?" I snipped. "That sounds like hindsight to me."

⁂

We had three suites in a hotel near a bridge on the river. Each of the wolves was getting his own suite. Winkler and Weldon had connecting doors and I was set up in the living area of Weldon's suite so I could provide night security for the Grand Master.

Winkler already offered his bed for me to sleep in during the day; it was his and Kelvin's job to see that I wasn't disturbed and the curtains remained tightly closed. Fortunately, my body bag had been left inside the jet. The werewolf pair that had flown us got rooms at a hotel near the airport so they could see to the plane, getting it refueled and ready to go in two days.

A quick bath and a change of clothes made me feel much better. I dressed in a nice pair of slacks, boots and a sweater with a jacket to go to dinner with the wolves. It was just below freezing outside so I wore appropriate clothing.

Avery had two cars waiting for us outside the hotel as we trooped through the sliding glass doors at the entrance. Winkler and Weldon went with Avery and another werewolf while Avery's Second, Norwood, drove Kelvin and me.

Norwood and Kelvin sat up front talking; I sat in the back seat and listened. I learned that Norwood worked as an EMT with the local fire department. Kelvin explained that he'd just finished his residency in oncology, so they found quite a bit to talk about. Fine with me. I pretty much hate small talk and listening to a conversation about intubating a patient almost made me glaze over.

Of course, we ended up at some ritzy steak house; werewolves are notorious for eating half a cow at one sitting. I listened while they ordered a ton of food and then watched as they tore into it. Wisely, I kept my comments about their eating habits to myself.

Avery didn't speak to me and neither did Norwood, since I was the vampire security detail and beneath their notice. Maybe I should have reminded them I was Pack, but Weldon probably wouldn't appreciate that. Not one tiny bit.

Avery turned out to be a namedropper, and enjoyed tooting his own horn a little too much for my taste. I'm sure he might have regaled Weldon with his exploits on taking his predecessor Corwin down, but even Avery realized that bragging over that feat would be a major faux pas. See, I do know some French—not that it would impress Gavin in the least. An old friend of mine used to call that term fox paws. I smiled at the memory.

"What are you smiling about?" Avery's Second looked at me and asked.

"I was just thinking about an old friend," I said and let it go at that.

CHAPTER 7

The books that I'd ordered online before leaving home got me through the night. I read two. One was political humor, the other a mystery. Kelvin, who was up early the next morning and drinking a cup of coffee, asked if he could borrow the mystery. I handed it to him and told him it was good.

Winkler was still in bed, propped against half a dozen pillows while he sipped coffee and watched the news on a flat screen television when I walked in. He grinned and patted the bed beside him. I just patted my butt, my signal for him to kiss my ass.

His grin widened so I gave him the standard rude gesture. He was laughing when I stalked into his bathroom to change into pajamas. Winkler politely vacated the bed when I crawled into it and as usual, I was out like a light the moment daybreak occurred.

※ ※

"That's just uncanny." Kelvin stuck his head around the connecting door. Weldon was showering so Kelvin caught the moment between Lissa's consciousness and unconsciousness. Winkler bent down and placed a careful kiss on Lissa's forehead before covering her completely with the sheet, blanket and comforter.

"You know how many germs are on that comforter?" Kelvin asked, watching Winkler perform this duty.

"And she's not susceptible to a single one of them," Winkler said. "Just like us, pretty much."

"Werewolves still get diseases when they're old," Kelvin pointed out. "Arthritis. Cancer, sometimes."

"I've never heard of that happening unless we're over two hundred," Winkler said, handing Kelvin a cursory glance.

"Well, me either. I see you've done your research."

"Yep. And we generally don't live long after we reach two hundred anyway."

"But the vamps, they don't get anything, ever. Do they?" Kelvin came over, reached under the covers until he found one of Lissa's arms and checked her pulse. "Nothing," he said.

"It's like that when she's awake, too," Winkler frowned at Kelvin, who placed Lissa's arm beneath the blanket. "No heartbeat—nothing. My father always said they had some sort of metabolism, but it's nothing like humans or werewolves."

"But they breathe when they're awake. This just fascinates me." Kelvin heard Weldon coming out of the shower next door. "Time to keep the Grand Master happy," Kelvin said and walked through the connecting door.

※ ※

Yawning, my eyes still closed, I stretched on Winkler's bed and discovered I was buried beneath a mountain of covers.

"Time to wake up, sleepyhead," Winkler tugged the blankets off my face. He was sitting on the side of my bed. Again.

"What is wrong with you?" I asked, flipping the covers off and sliding my legs over the side of his king-size bed. It would take a king-size for him; he was six-three or thereabouts in his socks.

"I just enjoy watching a pretty woman get out of bed in the morning. Er, well, evening."

"Jerk." I smacked the top of his head when I stood and headed for the bathroom.

"Did I say your ass looks good in those PJs?" he called after me. I'd already shut the door so it was too late to give him another rude gesture. Maybe I was going to have to learn to curse in multiple languages, like Gavin did.

"Now what are you doing?" Winkler hovered while I pulled out my laptop and set it up next to his on the hotel room desk.

"I need to e-mail somebody," I said. "He worries, so I was going to tell him I'm fine."

"What's his name?"

"Franklin, and he's gay. Schmuck."

"Him or me?"

"The gay part or the schmuck part?"

"The schmuck part. You know I'm not gay." Winkler snorted.

"Yeah. How about that?" I said, tapping out a quick message to Franklin and hitting send. I shut my laptop and turned to Winkler. "Where's the cooler?" I asked. I had no idea where they'd put it.

"In Weldon's room. Locked, of course."

"Of course," I mumbled.

"I have the key." Winkler pulled it out of a pocket and shook it at me.

"Are you going to tease me with it all night or do I have to go hunt my dinner?"

"You take the fun out of everything," Winkler grumbled.

"Oh, like I'd stand between you and a half-raw piece of bovine when *you're* hungry," I retorted.

"I may eat sheep now and then. The occasional lobster, with plenty of butter."

"Maybe two lobsters," I said. "I've seen you eat, remember?"

"Maybe." Winkler grinned. "We can't help it if our metabolism is so much faster than a human's."

"At least you were born that way; you have a legitimate excuse," I grumbled.

"But I love full moons," Winkler was waxing poetic, now. "I love venison after a kill."

"You get two next month," I said. I'd checked the calendar; December actually had a second full moon.

"Yeah." Winkler's eyes closed in pleasure. "It's like a Christmas present for the werewolves." He opened his eyes and looked down at me. "I don't suppose you know how to do Thanksgiving dinner?"

"Who do you think you're talking to, here?" I asked, tapping my chest. "I make very good turkey and dressing. I just wish I could still eat it."

"You can eat it, you just can't taste it," Winkler reminded me.

"Yeah. And then I have to cough it all up later. Why are you asking about this, anyway?"

"Because we're all going to be in Dallas for Thanksgiving—Weldon's consented to come, Daryl will bring Kathy Jo down, and Whitney and Sam are coming. Unfortunately, most of my staff will be off. I thought I was going to have to get the thing catered."

"Oh, yeah. Those are never the same as home-cooked," I said. "I'll do turkey for you, Winkler. But only because it's you." I waggled a finger at him.

"Can I get an inflated ego now?" he smirked.

"You already have one the size of Canada," I said. "If it gets any larger, it may damage the ozone layer."

"If you'll make a list, I'll send it to the staff at the Dallas house; they can buy what you need and have it waiting when we get there." Winkler was still on the subject of dinner and not the self-aggrandizing.

"Good enough," I said. "But if they shop for the turkey only a day or two ahead, have them buy a fresh one. I hate thawing turkeys at the last minute."

"I'll be sure and tell them that." He wanted to laugh at me, I could tell. I wanted to kick his ass.

We were having dinner with one of the more affluent members of the Des Moines Pack. He'd made his money in alternative energy production (mostly ethanol, this was Iowa). He had a nice, large house, had hired the meal catered and the Pack had come, adults only.

Of course, the werewolves were on their best behavior while the human caterers were there, but the food service employees were instructed to lay out the meal buffet style and then leave. They'd arranged to pick up pans and utensils the following day.

Avery also made plans for four of his wolves to guard the perimeter of the property. The owner lived outside Des Moines on an acreage surrounded by (no surprise) corn fields. It was my job as well as Winkler's and Kelvin's to watch over the Grand Master in closer quarters.

The staff left, the meal was eaten and then the ceremony began. I didn't eat with the others; I stood outside the large dining room while the werewolves laughed and talked. If anything came in that wasn't scheduled, it was my duty to take care of it.

Weldon was giving his blessing, werewolf style, to Avery when one of the wolf guards from outside strode through the front door. That normally wouldn't worry me, except he was dragging a young human woman along with him and she was crying. I followed along behind the wolf and the girl as she was hauled into the dining room and tossed to the floor at Avery and Weldon's feet.

"She sneaked back onto the property," the guard declared. "She saw Ruben and Jasper as wolves."

"I didn't sneak, I swear," the girl sobbed. "I left my rings in the kitchen. I took them off to rinse out a few pans before we packed them up. I drove up, two men were at the gate and they told me to park and come inside. That's when I saw the wolves. I just came back for my jewelry. Please let me go." She was terrified. I had no doubt she'd seen werewolves, all right.

"Well, girlie, that's too bad, isn't it?" Avery growled. He wore a nasty grin as he studied the human at his feet. "Looks like we may have a hunt tonight, folks."

Even Weldon looked shocked, I could tell, but he wasn't interrupting. I was about to. Stalking over to Avery and the wolf who'd brought the girl in, I let them know exactly how I felt.

"You will do no such thing, you poor excuse for a flea-bitten mutt," I shouted, shaking a finger in Avery's face. "If I have to take on every one of you, I will. But all it takes is just the barest of compulsion," I lowered my voice. "Honey," I lifted the girl to her feet and took her face in my hands; "we'll get your rings. You just drove up and came in, asking us to get your rings for you, didn't you? You didn't see anything except people having their dessert, isn't that right?" The girl nodded, her eyes going blank. The sobbing stopped.

"Here, now, let's go find your rings," I led her toward the kitchen. We found them in no time. Avery wasn't done, however. "How the hell do we know she won't," Weldon lifted a hand, stopping Avery in mid-bluster, before coming to the girl.

"Ask her to tell us what she saw," he ordered.

"What did you see when you drove back here, hon? Tell the truth." Compulsion dripped from my tongue.

"I drove through the gate and walked up to the house. Everybody was eating dessert and I asked you for my rings. We went to the kitchen to get them. See?" She held the rings up.

"Take her to her car," Weldon growled. I figured I was about to get a fast trip right back to Wlodek and the rest of the Council with a big F on my report card. There wasn't anything else I could have done, however. No way was I going to let Avery and his wolves tear this girl apart because she'd seen two of them who were fool enough to change out on the grounds.

We walked to the girl's car; it was a small import and she chatted on the way, thanked me for my help and then drove off. The wolf who'd dragged her in came out and warned away the other wolves guarding the property.

The four werewolves followed me inside the house where Weldon looked as if he were about to have a stroke. Winkler was up and leaning against one wall of the large dining room, Kelvin was doing the same on the opposite wall.

"Now," Weldon said to the wolf who'd dragged the girl inside the house, "tell me what happened, and in the proper order. I warn you, I can smell a lie a mile away and if you want confirmation, then I'll have Lissa here place compulsion on you to tell the truth. What the hell happened with that girl? Start at the beginning. Don't stop until you reach the end. I'm waiting." Weldon crossed his arms angrily over his chest.

"She drove right through the gate and pulled up in front of the house," the wolf who'd brought her in said. "We told her she couldn't come in so she got belligerent with us. Ruben and Jasper had to change when she started fighting with us."

"Lie," Weldon said. "Try again and make it the truth, this time."

I wanted to snicker. That girl couldn't have weighed more than a hundred and twenty pounds, looked to be around five-four and definitely hadn't worked out. If four grown werewolves in their humanoid shape couldn't subdue somebody her size, then they needed to find another form to shift to. Skunk came to mind. I figured they'd seen this as an opportunity to tear someone apart just for the sport of it.

"She wanted to argue with us so Ruben and Jasper changed," the werewolf whined.

"A little closer to the truth, but still not the truth." Weldon's eyes were hard. "Lissa, come here." I went.

"Now, wait just a minute," Avery said but Weldon growled low, forcing Avery to back up. He didn't argue past that.

"Place compulsion on this one to tell the truth," Weldon ordered. I walked up to the werewolf and studied him for a moment. Not willing to take any chances, I allowed my claws to slide out the entire way. A few gasps sounded around the room.

"You will speak only the truth from this point forward," I said, looking the wolf straight in the eye and pointing a claw at him. He nodded. I stepped aside.

"Now," Weldon said. "Tell me exactly what happened."

"She drove up to the gate and Ruben was there, waiting," the werewolf began. "Jasper was on the other side. She asked Ruben if she could come in to get her rings. Ruben told her to park halfway up the drive and wait for him and Jasper to come and escort her to the house. They changed before they got there and started growling. I had to come along and bring her in."

"And why did they change?" Weldon asked almost casually.

"Because we thought it might be fun to hunt with the Grand Master," the wolf muttered.

"You thought I'd find sport in hunting that poor girl down and tearing her to pieces?"

"Yeah." When he said that, I wanted to kill him myself. I'd moved aside so Weldon could question him, pulling my claws back in. Too bad. I might have used the excuse that my hand just slipped. *In the vicinity of his neck.* Winkler, I noticed, was no longer leaning against the wall. Neither was Kelvin. Both stepped forward. Winkler was prepared for anything, I could tell.

"You, sit." Weldon barked at the wolf, who sat down at the table. "Avery, Lissa, come with me." Weldon stalked into the kitchen with Avery and me close behind. Winkler and Kelvin stayed outside to watch the others.

"Lissa, place compulsion to tell the truth on Avery, here," Weldon ordered. Avery started to protest but I just used compulsion to make him shut up and stand still. Then I placed the one to force him to tell the truth.

"Do you condone this kind of behavior?" Weldon asked. "Has this sort of thing happened before?"

"Simms does seem to have a knack for being around when this happens," Avery whined. "We've had to take care of things several times since I took over."

"And how many times when Corwin was in charge?"

"None that I remember." Avery was now sweating.

"And you weren't suspicious?"

"Simms is one of my best guards."

"Really?" Weldon wasn't happy. It looked like I wasn't going to be sent back to the Council, after all. "Well," Weldon went on, "I'll be interviewing the Pack one at a time, then. Lissa, send Avery back out and tell him not to go anywhere. Have Winkler send in the others, beginning with the owner of the property."

I nodded at Weldon, then laid compulsion for Avery to go back out, sit down and not cause any trouble. He went.

Winkler sent the Pack in one at a time after that. Most of them told the same story; that Simms or one of the other three assigned to guard duty would bring a human in on the pretext that they'd seen them change and then instigate a hunt.

The rest of the Pack would hang back and allow Simms or one of the others to make the kill, which generally ended up quite bloody. The worst of the stories involved a sixteen-year-old boy whose car had broken down on the side of a road. It was all I could do not to march right out and do all four of them in over that one. Now, there were grieving parents in the area who had no idea what happened to their son.

The stories continued, one on top of another, until Weldon and I learned that Avery and his four pet guards had accounted for at least fourteen disappearances in the Des Moines area.

The Pack as a whole found the whole thing reprehensible, but none were willing to challenge their new Packmaster. I got the idea that Simms and his cronies might have interfered with the challenge anyway. None of the Pack came out and said it, but they didn't like Avery's leadership at all. They all talked about Corwin and how good it had been before.

"Those four guards have acquired the taste for human blood," Weldon growled after the last werewolf left the kitchen. I figured I knew what was coming, only this time I wasn't about to argue over it.

Innocents had died. They weren't threatening a room full of old vampires who most likely had killed many times. These were humans, who hadn't known werewolves existed until they'd been chosen by a handful and hunted down to die.

And the sixteen-year-old? One of the werewolf women wept as she described his death, and went on to say that according to local media, he'd gotten a night job to help his parents pay bills during some difficult times. His car had broken down on the way home one evening. That information made me so angry my eyes were likely blood red.

Weldon walked back into the dining room after the last Pack member was questioned. "Avery, I had no idea I'd be doing anything other than officially confirming your status as Packmaster when I arrived," Weldon sighed. "As of this moment, I am revoking that status. You and those four over there will be executed. Tonight." He turned to the owner of the house. "I don't wish to do this in your home," Weldon said. "We'll go out back for this. Who wants to help hold them?"

Several male werewolves stood, including the property owner. There were only two female werewolves in the bunch to begin with, both of them mated. Weldon nodded at the Pack members who stood, Avery and the four were taken, and the rest of us trooped out to the fence behind the house.

Avery looked like a deer in the headlights by that time. I had no idea how he'd thought his four guards weren't up to something, and he'd hunted those humans right alongside them. Now, he was going to pay for that with his life.

Weldon turned to wolf and took Avery down himself. Winkler got three of the others. Simms was now the only one left; he'd been the one to haul in the boy. Weldon deliberately held him back until last.

"Lissa, do you want this one?" Weldon asked me softly. I walked up to Simms, who'd watched all the others die in front of him. He swallowed hard when I approached.

"I don't know, Weldon," I said, turning around and forcing the claws out on my hand. My back was to Simms so he didn't see. Whirling so fast I was merely a blur, I sliced through his neck. The two who held him looked on in amazement as Simms toppled, his head never leaving his body until it was flat on the grass. His face frozen in an expression of surprise, Simms' head rolled away after that.

"Yeah, I guess I did want that one," I said, retracting my claws.

I washed my hands inside the house while Weldon talked to the rest of the Pack, who decided in a democratic fashion which wolf they wanted as interim Packmaster. It ended up being the property owner, who appeared to have leadership qualities. I didn't think anybody was willing to challenge him, either. He chose his Second right away; Norwood had argued several times with Avery over what Simms and the others were doing.

Weldon gave his blessing to the interim Packmaster, told him he'd be back in six months to see how things were going, thanked the man for the meal and we left. The Pack had some accidents to arrange to explain dead bodies.

"Some days, I hate my job," Weldon shrugged out of his shirt first thing when we got back to the room. Avery may have gotten a bite or two in, but he wasn't much of a challenge for the Grand Master.

Winkler, having done away with three of the others, also had a few bites but nothing that wouldn't heal quickly. At least they didn't seem to have the vampire's allergy to werewolf saliva like I did. I sat outside in Weldon's little sitting area, doing my duty as a bodyguard while he took a shower and cleaned up.

"Lissa, I hate to put you back in that bag, but I want to leave first thing in the morning," Weldon said when he walked out of the bathroom dressed in a towel. He called the pilot and co-pilot, had them bring the body bag over and take the cooler and most of the other luggage back with them. We only kept what we'd need for the following day.

I pulled out more fleece to dress in, since I was going to be unconscious when they hauled me out of there in the morning.

⁂

"It's a good thing she's small and limber," Weldon mumbled to Winkler, who'd folded up the body bag that held Lissa's sleeping body. He had her not only folded up, but hanging from a hook on the cart the bellboy wheeled toward the cab. Winkler tossed the bag into the trunk on top of the other bags. Weldon gave him a hard look, Winkler shrugged and they climbed into the cab after tipping the bellboy.

The jet ran into turbulence over Lake Michigan on the way to Grand Rapids. "I think Lissa's lucky she's missing this," Weldon observed while bouncing around in his seat. Winkler ignored the turbulence and continued to tap away on his computer; Kelvin hummed *The Wreck of the Edmund Fitzgerald* while staring out a window.

"Wrong lake," Winkler muttered in Kelvin's direction.

Once they left the lake behind, the turbulence cleared up and the jet landed in Grand Rapids without further incident. It was still early but nearing noon, so the three werewolves rented an SUV, loaded it up and drove toward a hotel.

The local Packmaster wasn't expecting them until later that evening. Weldon wanted to leave the dust of Des Moines behind him as quickly as he could; the Pack there had mourning to do and needed time to regroup without his interference. Three rooms were reserved at the Marriott downtown, which was also near the Grand River; Winkler preferred a water view whenever he could get it.

After checking in, Weldon made the call to the local Packmaster, letting him know they'd arrived early and where they'd booked rooms, assuring him that they just wanted to relax before going to dinner with the Packmaster, his wife and Second later on.

※ ※

Sunset was after five that Thursday and we were one week away from Thanksgiving when my eyes popped open. Winkler had already pulled me from the bag and settled me on his bed, propped up with extra pillows. He had a bag of blood out for me, too, handing it over the moment I realized he was sitting next to me.

Kelvin, who walked in from the Grand Master's room through the connecting door, watched in fascination as I drank my meal. Winkler took the third of a bag that I couldn't finish and locked it inside the cooler.

He still had the key with him for some reason and hadn't given it to me. He and I both knew that I could pop the lock off the cooler if it was necessary, but I still couldn't figure the whole thing out. Winkler wasn't taking any chances with my blood supply, and that puzzled me.

I cleaned up and changed after my meal; Weldon called the Packmaster for the name of the restaurant where we were eating and said he'd meet him there. I think Weldon wanted as little small talk and chitchat as possible without appearing rude. The night before hadn't settled well with him, I could tell.

This Packmaster had a werewolf wife, and while she'd been informed that Weldon was bringing a female vampire as a bodyguard, I think she was expecting somebody dressed in a revealing black leather bustier and stiletto heels while showing fang to everybody.

When I showed up in a nice, charcoal gray suit with a black turtleneck under the jacket, I almost heard her sigh of relief. My short boots didn't have more than a two-inch heel.

"Are you really, oh, you know," she said across the table. I smiled and nodded at her, hoping to put her at ease.

She sat between her husband and Weldon; I was wedged between Winkler and Kelvin on the opposite side of the booth. The Second, a quiet werewolf, had an extra chair on the outside edge and seemed content to listen while everyone else talked. Once again we were at a steak place, only this one also served ribs, seafood and chicken. Winkler went out on a limb and ordered two lobsters.

Kelvin ordered chicken and ribs; I ordered a salad and the soup du jour. My phone rang while we waited for food to be served. I checked caller ID—it was Gavin. I'd sent him an e-mail when I woke earlier, telling him everything was fine. That wasn't sufficient, I guess.

"I'll take this elsewhere," I said, attempting to scoot Winkler over so I could get out. He had the seat on the outside.

"It's all right, you can take it here," Winkler refused to budge. My phone rang again so I rolled my eyes at Weldon, whose expression was unreadable. I'd have to talk to Gavin with everybody listening in.

"Hi, honey," I said as brightly as I could when I answered. No need to transmit to the Packmaster and his missus that the vampire on the other end was more than likely frowning deeply and waiting to lecture me about staying away from Winkler and every other male on the face of the planet.

"Lissa, are you well?" I'd just told him I was in the e-mail. Maybe I should have translated it into French or something so he'd understand it better. I didn't say that, though.

"I'm very well," I said. "We're having dinner, right now." I was hoping he'd make this short and sweet as a result. Ever since René's little fiasco and the thing with the bomb, well, he'd gotten worse.

"Lissa, I just wanted to hear your voice," he said. He almost sounded lonely. *Fuck.*

"Honey, I miss you," I said. I tried to get Winkler to let me out again, but he wasn't moving, choosing to grin as he crunched into a breadstick. More than likely, werewolf hearing is just as good as vampire hearing so everybody at the table was getting to hear my conversation with Gavin. "Honey, are you going to be available for Christmas?" I asked, trying to point the conversation in a better direction. Plus, Weldon was supposed to give me a break and I'd only told Winkler I'd do Thanksgiving dinner.

"I don't know, Cherie. Right now, there are no assignments but that could change as it usually does."

"All right." I sighed. "Let me know, okay?"

"Of course I will. If I find I have the time, I will either come to you or bring you to me as quickly as possible."

"Okay, honey, that sounds good," I said.

"Cara mia, ti amo troppo," Gavin said, and hung up. I must have blinked a couple of times because Winkler was watching me closely.

"You don't know what he said, do you?" he asked ungraciously. I was glad at that moment that I couldn't blush.

"No. I wish he'd translate sometimes, unless he's cursing. *That* he can keep to himself."

"When did he curse the last time?" Winkler lifted an eyebrow.

"When somebody messed up my outfit," I said, hanging my head so Winkler wouldn't see my grimace. "He threw me in the shower and scrubbed me twice, while cursing in at least three languages." Weldon snickered at my explanation. I wasn't about to mention the René fiasco. That would involve even more explanation, and I'm sure Wlodek wouldn't approve.

"Someone messed up your outfit?" The Packmaster's wife, Jewel, said across the table.

"Oh, yeah," I elbowed Winkler. Not as hard as I'd like, but hard enough.

"You got scrubbed twice?" Winkler was grinning hugely. Obviously, I needed to be harsher with my elbow.

"And shampooed twice. And then wrapped in a towel while more cursing was going on. He's not jealous or anything."

"How did you get engaged to him anyway? Honestly, Lissa, that's the last thing I expected from you." Winkler emptied the scotch the waiter brought out.

"Well, that makes two of us," I muttered. "Winkler, do you know how many females of my kind there are? Do you?"

"No. Do you?" He was grinning again.

"Sixteen," I said. Winkler almost choked.

"Do you need the Heimlich Maneuver?" I asked sweetly. Kelvin perked right up at that. It might have been a chance to show off his medical skills, but then again, maybe not. Winkler straightened up.

"Are you telling me that they were going to auction you off to the highest bidder?" Weldon buttered a roll from the basket the waiter set in front of him.

"In a way," I said. "Gavin was one of the top three and out of those three, well, the Russian guy scared the bejeezus out of me, same with the Frenchman, for different reasons. Gavin's was the third offer."

"You don't love him?" Jewel sounded sympathetic.

"No, that's the trouble. I do, but all it takes is a couple of near-deaths and one insane bout of jealousy and he wants to hover."

"Is he handsome?" she asked curiously.

"He is," Weldon supplied for me. "He was here, earlier in the year. When he was called back to Europe, he took Lissa with him."

"We don't want to discuss that," I said. I got all riled up every time I thought about *that*. "He's growing his hair back," I added.

"How did he lose it?" Winkler's eyes were dancing.

"Um, a rogue with a flame thrower," I said. "We were worried he wouldn't make it for a while."

"And there I thought you might have been responsible. I did notice he looked almost shaved," Weldon said, smiling slightly. He and Winkler hadn't spoken to Gavin when they'd come to handle Tate Briggs. I couldn't blame them; Gavin held them under compulsion while he was in the U.S.

"Enough about me," I said. "Jewel, how do you like being the wife of the man in charge?"

"I don't see him as often as I'd like," she put an arm through his. Theirs was obviously a love match, one way or the other. "But I'm proud of him, too," she looked up at him; he smiled down at her.

Weldon got into the conversation then and I was thankful for that. He asked how the finances of the Pack were. The Packmaster who'd gotten killed with Lester Briggs back in the spring had been siphoning off funds that the Pack paid in for emergencies and such.

"We're rebuilding, Grand Master," James Naylor replied. "I have the books and the bank statements ready for your inspection."

"I'll take a look tomorrow evening," Weldon nodded. I was beginning to be hopeful that tomorrow night wouldn't turn out like the last one.

It didn't. Everything went smoothly. The guards did their job and were well behaved, several of the wives got together to supply the meal and I could tell they were all pitching in to replace the money the previous Packmaster had stolen. Weldon and Winkler both enjoyed the home-cooked food. Kelvin ate with them; clearly, he could eat just as much as any other werewolf I'd ever met.

Kelvin. It was hard to tell about him, at times. He never talked much—at least not with me. I also wondered why Winkler had taken all three executions in Des Moines rather than allowing Kelvin to take at least one of them. Oh, well. Not my business.

※

We made it to Jamestown, Pennsylvania, and Houlton, Maine, before we had to fly back to Dallas for Thanksgiving. We had three towns in West Virginia to visit after that and the first full moon in December fell on the third one, Sugar Grove, which bordered the Shenandoah Mountains. That's where the local Pack was scheduled to run and Weldon, Winkler and Kelvin would be running with them.

We started the trip to Dallas in the afternoon while it was still daylight, so I was packed into the plane inside my favorite bag. The sun set after a while and Winkler pulled me out so I wouldn't wake zipped inside the thing. That just terrified me for some reason, although I could punch or rip my way out easily enough. Merrill also called; I found his voice-mail after we landed in Dallas. I called him back; he was in New York, so the time difference wasn't bad.

"Franklin and I decided to pack up and come here through the New Year," he said. I asked him if Franklin was well. Franklin always said he was in his e-mails, but then he was one of those people who'd say that if he was on his deathbed, I think.

"Franklin is very well and will be making dinner for himself and Greg on Thanksgiving," Merrill informed me. "I have checked your credit card charges, Lissa."

"Really? Has someone been using my card? What did you find?" I knew I hadn't used it for anything; there'd been no opportunity.

"That's just it, there isn't anything," he said.

"And you're complaining?"

"I expect you to buy something for yourself, now and then," he told me gently.

"All right, I'll go out and buy a bus," I said.

"See that you do," he chuckled.

We talked for a bit longer before hanging up. "Who was that?" Winkler asked. We'd been picked up at the airport by a werewolf I didn't know and were on our way to Winkler's mansion, which sat on a tract of land between Denton and Dallas.

"My surrogate sire," I said, stuffing the phone inside my small purse.

"The black-haired one?" Weldon asked. He'd seen Merrill during Tate's execution.

"Yes. That's Merrill."

"Why didn't you take him?" Winkler asked out of curiosity.

"Because he's not interested," I replied. "He already has a woman on the hook. I don't rate next to that."

"Lissa, you'd rate next to anybody," Winkler tried to nuzzle my neck. I had to push him away.

Weldon commandeered the front passenger seat so Winkler, Kelvin and I got the back seat of the van while our luggage was piled in the cargo area. My bag was filled with dirty clothes, so I was hoping to get my laundry washed while I was at Winkler's place.

Driving through the gate to Winkler's mansion almost felt like coming home and Winkler offered a grin and a hug as we pulled in.

"I'll get the turkey in the oven when I get up tomorrow," I told Winkler as we unloaded luggage from the van. "Eat a late lunch; I'll have dinner ready around nine or ten. I'll see if I can do pies tonight."

Pies were what I did, along with my laundry. Winkler wouldn't let me stay in the guesthouse this time, so I got a huge bedroom inside the house. Whitney and Sam were there as well, but they'd already gone to bed.

I baked all night and did other little prep things like chopping onion and celery and putting it in baggies, ready to add to recipes. I was thankful that there was a double oven in the kitchen; it saved a lot of time.

The turkey went into the oven shortly after I woke the evening of Thanksgiving Day. Whitney and Sam came in to hug me and Davis gave me a huge kiss, shocking me. Kelvin was most likely shocked too—he'd witnessed it.

He and the others lounged around the kitchen when things started smelling good. Whitney helped set the table; there was a beautiful linen tablecloth laid down with napkins, silver and china that was extremely expensive. It was all getting hand-washed afterward.

Weldon carved up the turkey for everyone and the werewolves stuffed themselves on turkey and dressing, mashed potatoes and giblet gravy, green bean casserole, a broccoli rice casserole in case you didn't do green beans, corn on the cob, yams, fresh rolls, pumpkin, pecan, apple and chocolate pies. This was the way you did Thanksgiving where I came from. Daryl and Kathy Jo had arrived shortly before the meal was served, and Kathy Jo was happy as could be, even if she was five months pregnant.

"I can't believe a vampire still cooks," Kelvin said. He'd been drinking and was now slurring his words. Davis kept pouring wine for everybody except Kathy Jo, who was having soda. I had a glass of wine with all of them, although I couldn't taste it.

"I still have fond memories of what it tasted like," I shrugged and sipped my wine. "So, nowadays it gives me pleasure to know someone else is enjoying it."

Whitney, Kathy Joe and Davis helped clean the kitchen. I gave Davis an extra hug for being the only guy who made the effort. He grinned at me. Believe me; I was ready for sunrise to come when it did.

CHAPTER 8

"Here he goes," Winkler said. He, Weldon and Davis watched the monitor hooked up to the hidden security camera inside Lissa's bedroom. Kelvin had stolen inside after telling everyone he was going to the convenience store two blocks away for a few personal items.

"What the fuck is he—oh no," Weldon didn't want to see this. Kelvin was undressing Lissa, who was completely unconscious and had no way of knowing what was being done to her.

Kelvin removed the speculum from his bag first, did a quick pelvic exam, took specimens, screwed lids on tightly after dropping samples inside sterile tubes and jars, then set about getting blood, hair and tissue samples. Lissa was dressed again; Kelvin gathered his things and stole quietly from the room.

"I want to kill him now," Davis growled.

"We can't. We have to wait and see who else is involved in this," Winkler said. "If I hadn't had that trace on the messages he sends, I wouldn't have caught this. How did that Tate kid get so many people involved?"

"I'm sure we'll find out and I hope it's sooner rather than later. I don't like watching my back where he's concerned," Weldon grumbled. "I know I'm safe if Lissa's up, but it's a different story if she isn't. I worry when Winkler has to go take a piss."

"I'll try to keep my pissing to a minimum," Winkler muttered.

"Piss on Kelvin," Davis suggested with a grin.

"Who do you have following him?" Winkler asked Davis.

"Glen and Hastings," Davis said. Winkler nodded. He could trust those two. "They'll give us a call, but I figure he's hauling that to a lab somewhere to drop it off. Once we find which one, we can keep tabs on who comes in and goes out."

"We need to substitute something else for those samples," Weldon pointed out.

"We'll get right on that," Winkler pulled his cell out and made a few calls.

Winkler received a message from Glen roughly an hour later; Kelvin had gone straight to Healdton Labs with the small bag of samples, dropping them off and leaving shortly after. He then drove to the convenience store as originally planned before returning to Denton. Glen, who was very experienced in tailing someone, never made Kelvin suspicious.

Winkler's hospital employee slipped into the lab two hours later, sniffed out the vampire samples, traded for some he'd taken just recently from a patient at the hospital and then called Winkler. Winkler arranged to meet with the technician, who handed everything over. Winkler passed a significant amount of cash to the man and carried Lissa's samples to Davis.

"Bury these," he said. "Destroy them as much as you can, then bury them where they won't be found." Davis nodded, grabbed the bag and took off.

※ ※

"Get what you wanted?" Winkler came into the kitchen, finding Kelvin seated at the kitchen island, helping himself to a piece of leftover pie. Winkler forced himself to be calm, polite and interested in Kelvin's answer.

"Yes. But the convenience store didn't have the shampoo I liked, so I had to go somewhere else."

"Leave any pie?" Winkler looked inside the fridge. He pulled leftover turkey out to make a sandwich.

"There's still some pumpkin and pecan," Kelvin said. "I got the last of the apple."

Winkler wanted to strangle him just for that, but held himself and his growl back. Lissa made excellent apple pie.

※

"Lissa, do you want to do something tonight?" Winkler asked me later. He tried to pull me into his arms, so I gave him a small hug and moved away from him.

"I need to go get a few things. I think I'm almost out of soap and stuff. Is there a Target close by?" I asked.

"If there isn't, I'll find one," Winkler grabbed his jacket, found a coat for me to wear and herded me out the door.

"You're using a black American Express to buy bath soap," Winkler rubbed my shoulders as I paid for my toiletries.

"Merrill wanted me to use it. I'm using it." I got my card and driver's license back from the cashier.

We walked to the car (Winkler had driven the Jaguar). The outside temperature had dropped to around forty, which was warm compared to what we'd dealt with in Michigan and Maine. "I think you need a warmer coat," Winkler said after getting me settled into the passenger seat. "We'll go to a couple of places and see if we can't find something."

A couple of places ended up being exclusive shops, where Winkler bought two coats for me while I tried to convince him they weren't needed and to put them back. One of them alone cost eighteen hundred dollars. The other was more casual and a mere six hundred. Both were cashmere, the more expensive one ankle-length with a shawl collar. Winkler threw several scarves onto the pile and found three pairs of gloves.

"Winkler, you have to stop," I tried to slap his hands but he paid no attention to me. The long coat was in a charcoal gray, the shorter one in cognac. Winkler was picky, I'll give him that. I tried on two dozen coats before he was satisfied.

He had the tags removed and dressed me in the shorter one for my trip out of the store because, in his words, the other was too dressy to wear over jeans. I just smacked his arm and gave him a nasty look. He grinned, hugged me, paid for everything and we left.

"Been shopping?" Davis eyed me, my new coat and the bags that Winkler lugged into the house.

"Is that cashmere?" Whitney came over to feel my new coat.

"They both are," Winkler announced smugly and allowed his sister to pull the other things out of the bags. The long coat was inside a nice garment bag, the scarves and gloves inside a regular paper bag with handles. You can always tell which shops have the exclusive items just by looking at the bags they hand out with a purchase. My little plastic Target bag felt like an orphan, I'm sure.

"We're leaving tomorrow morning," Winkler informed me before letting me go to my bedroom to put away my things. "You may want to pack up before you go to bed."

"I will," I said. Everything was done before I slept at dawn and I went to bed in my usual fleece outfit.

⁂

"She looks like she's sleeping," Sam helped Winkler place Lissa inside her body bag.

"She is sleeping," Winkler said. "She just isn't breathing while she's doing it," he added. He'd set the hidden alarm in Lissa's room when she went to bed, just to make sure she didn't get any more visits from uninvited guests. Kelvin was happy with what he'd done; he'd gone to bed and slept like a baby.

"It must be hard for them to trust anybody like this," Sam said, watching Winkler zip the bag.

"I don't know that many of them would allow this," Winkler said. "I don't think for a minute that Gavin would allow anyone to touch him. Lissa is still new. She doesn't like this, I know, but right now we don't have a choice."

"The Grand Master said she took down one of the Des Moines Pack and moved faster than he could see her move when she did it."

"She did. That one never knew what hit him, it happened so fast." Winkler lifted Lissa inside her bag. "Let's go get her packed in with the rest of the bags." Sam followed him out of the bedroom.

The nearest airport that wasn't too tiny to handle Winkler's jet was in Clarksburg, West Virginia. The pilots stayed there with the plane while the rest of them packed luggage into a rental and headed for Buckhannon, first.

"Look who's back among the living," Winkler was holding out a bag of blood when I woke in the seat next to him on the drive to Buckhannon.

"Just stop already," I said, nipping the top off the bag so I could drink. Merrill had arranged for my supplies to be replenished while I was in Dallas, so I was stocked up for the present.

When we drove into Buckhannon, I discovered there wasn't a lot to pick from, hotel-wise. We ended up at a rustic bed and breakfast, taking up half of it with our usual three rooms. Gavin called while I was trying to dress for dinner with Weldon and the others, in order to meet the new Packmaster.

"Honey, how are you?" I asked. I'd sent him an e-mail the day before, telling him where we were going.

"I am fine, Cara. Tell me they are treating you well."

"I'm good," I said. "Any word on Christmas?"

"I would almost believe you want to see me," he said. I could hear the smile in his voice. Actually, I did want to see him. I did miss him, as long as he wasn't making me feel like I was six.

"I do want to see you," I said. "Tell me what you want for Christmas."

"Longer hair," he said. Did Gavin just joke with me? What alien planet had kidnapped the Gavin I knew and dropped a double in his place?

"Honey, those toupees never look right," I told him. He laughed at that.

Winkler was trying to rush me around so I had to let Gavin go. I think I shocked him pretty good when I told him I loved him. Well, I did. And when he wasn't being an ass, I didn't mind telling him so.

"I think we should have rented a house so Lissa could cook for us," Kelvin grumbled when we pulled into the parking lot for Murphy's Restaurant. Winkler gave him a sharp look but didn't say anything.

Buckhannon didn't have many restaurants that stayed open late, unless you wanted fast food. The town itself was small; less than ten thousand people, I think. There was a mine disaster there not long ago and most of the miners didn't make it out again. I thought about asking Weldon if some of the werewolves worked the coalmines, but decided against it.

The Packmaster and his Second met us at the designated restaurant. Both seemed toughened by life, somehow, and sure enough, they told Winkler when he asked that they and many of their Pack worked the mines.

That had to be hard, going into a dark place, day after day. At least they have better vision in the dark than any human ever would. As for me, if I could still be in the sun, I would. Every chance I got. To me, it only made it worse that their way of existence took them away from daylight. The next two days were routine and Weldon confirmed the Packmaster.

Mill Creek was much the same, except there were only male werewolves there. The town held not a single female werewolf, and Weldon told me that the Mill Creek Pack was more than likely destined for extinction. The youngest member was over a hundred years old.

"When there's only one or two left, they may ask to join with Buckhannon or one of the other Packs and live out their lives. The females aren't being born as often as we'd like," Weldon sighed regretfully. "The wars between the two races just about did us all in." He meant the vampires and werewolves. I understood that.

The full moon was nearly on us when we arrived in Sugar Grove two nights later, and all three wolves I traveled with were getting restless. They planned to run with the Pack first and then tend to business on our second night there.

The Packmaster and his Second met us at the tiny cabin Winkler had secured for us, and clothes were being shucked and tossed aside the minute they sniffed each other, almost. I turned to mist as quickly as I could, following along behind.

The Shenandoah Mountains are probably nicer if you have time to stop and look at them. Me? I was traveling swiftly over the heads of twenty or so werewolves, who scented a bear after a while and gave chase. Weldon was running at the head of the Pack, Winkler at his shoulder. Kelvin was running somewhere behind the local Packmaster and his Second.

Kelvin. More than once, I wondered why Winkler brought him along. Glen or any one of the others might have been more suitable for guarding the Grand Master. Maybe Kelvin was the greatest werewolf oncologist ever, but I hadn't seen a lot of evidence in that direction. As far as I knew, he hadn't even looked at the bites Weldon and Winkler had gotten in Des Moines.

Maybe it was just me, but he didn't talk like a doctor when he did talk. When he'd spoken to Norwood in Des Moines, he seemed to have the same sort of knowledge that the Des Moines Second had.

Amazing what runs through your mind when you're floating over the heads of a bunch of running werewolves. When Weldon cornered the bear, I held back—I honestly didn't want to see the creature get torn to pieces and that's exactly what happened.

Everybody got a taste of the meat—at least they ate what they killed. The hunt resumed afterward, and a large buck was brought down and devoured. I hoped Winkler got full on his venison; I wasn't about to feed him when he got back.

Two hours before dawn, my three wandered toward our cabin—the Sugar Grove Pack had already gone their separate ways. I ranged ahead of Weldon, Winkler and Kelvin, reforming on the cabin porch and settling in to wait after making a few preparations.

The sight of three naked, bloody men wandering into the clearing with moonlight clouding their eyes would probably send anyone else running for their life. I just sighed and watched them walk toward me.

I'd already gathered up their discarded clothing and taken it inside the cabin—no sense making them pick it up, as bloody as they were. They all needed a bath as quickly as possible. I'd set out soap and shampoo in the bathroom, as well as laying several towels out beside the sink for the Grand Master.

"Bathroom's ready to go," I told Weldon, who came up the porch steps first. He nodded to me and went inside. Deciding that one bathroom, shared by all three werewolves probably hadn't been a good idea; I went back inside the cabin and brought out a washcloth and a pitcher of water from the kitchen.

Winkler started in with that, so I went to find a bowl of water for Kelvin, along with a kitchen towel (we were running out of washcloths). At least they had the blood pretty much gone when they walked inside the cabin. Once again, I decided that Winkler needed to pass his genes on to someone; he was put together very nicely.

Just before dawn, Winkler helped cover me up in the bed using all the quilts and blankets he could spare, and even placed my expensive coat on top of that. There were curtains at the windows, but they were thin. If I got uncovered for any reason, they'd have a pile of ash in the bed instead of a vampire, come nightfall.

※ ※

Strange scents woke me when the sun slipped below the horizon, and I wondered briefly before uncovering myself if Weldon started on the Pack thing early while still in the cabin. So far, he'd not invited any of the Packmasters into his hotel rooms.

Three werewolves greeted me when I pulled the last of the covers off my face, none of them familiar. There wasn't much difference in their appearance either; all had dark hair and light brown eyes with a weatherworn look about them. I could tell by scent they were all related. The one in charge didn't have front teeth but he did have his canines. Probably important if you were a werewolf.

"The girlie's awake," one of them said, grinning. At least his teeth were all present.

"Where's Winkler? And the Grand Master?" I demanded, angry in an instant. I had no idea what they were thinking, allowing three strangers to sit and watch me wake. That was dangerous.

"We have 'em," the gap-toothed one spoke. "And if you want to see 'em again, you'll do what we say."

"You'll do what *I* say," I laid compulsion. Two went blank-eyed but the third, the one with the missing teeth, didn't.

"That don't work with me," he cackled. "Now, take that mojo offa these two and those three that you're so fond of won't die."

I wanted to curse but I had to keep my wits with me. "I can kill you, instead." I lifted a hand, allowing my claws to extend fully.

"But if they don't hear from me on this," the werewolf held up Winkler's cell phone (I recognized it, all right), "then they'll kill your three and where will that leave you?" He was grinning his gap-toothed grin again. I did curse, then.

"Here, now, none of them words. Take your spell offa these two and let's get goin'. We got work for you. If you do it, we'll let all four of you go."

I'd gone to bed in my clothes the night before, after helping Winkler and the others get cleaned up after their run. There was barely enough time to crawl in the bed so I could be covered up.

My cell phone was in my pocket, but I didn't remember what kind of charge it had. And, while this bunch had the Grand Master and Winkler (at least I hoped they did and that they were still alive), I had to cooperate with these kidnappers and look for a chance to call someone. I had no idea who that someone should be; there wasn't anyone close enough to provide assistance quickly.

"Fine," I said, removing my compulsion from Gap's two companions. He hadn't given his name so that's what he was going to get.

"That's more like it," Gap grinned again. "Now, girlie, just come with us peaceful and don't try no funny stuff, or the Grand Master dies with those other two."

I was compelled to follow them into the yard where an old van waited. Diffused moonlight filtered through thickening clouds overhead and the air smelled of snow as I was shoved into the back of the van.

Gap crawled in beside me while the other two sat up front. We drove away from the cabin, and since the van didn't have windows on the sides, I lost track of where we were going after a while. It didn't matter; if I could turn to mist, all I had to do was float upward and get my bearings.

As it was, these three worried me. They still hadn't explained what they wanted from me and I had no idea whether the Grand Master was still alive to begin with. I shivered as we bounced along mountain roads, silently cursing my inability to wake during the day.

Gap played with Winkler's phone after a while and got somebody to answer his call. "We're comin'," he said. "Put the Grand Master on so our girlie here won't think we killed him already." He held the phone up to my ear. I didn't tell him that I could hear both sides of the conversation he'd just had quite well. It was probably better to keep my mouth shut and not tip my hand.

"Lissa?" Weldon's voice sounded rough, like he'd been beaten up or something.

"Weldon? What's going on? Are you all right?"

"I've been better," Weldon rasped. "Right now, just do what they say. Winkler's not in great shape at the moment." *Fuck.* I didn't say it out loud so I wouldn't offend Gap. I was angry, though. Very angry. I wanted to demand that Gap tell me what he wanted, but had to hold it back. Merrill would be ashamed of me if he knew I lost my temper in such a volatile situation.

"I'll do what they say, Grand Master," I said. Gap grinned and ended the call.

"Never had a use for this stuff until now." He laughed and pocketed the cell phone. If I got the opportunity, Gap was going to die first, I decided right away.

We bumped through the mountains over rough, narrow roads for the better part of two more hours before pulling into the yard of an old cabin built of logs. It couldn't come close to what Weldon had; the three-room square looked to be a much poorer, distant cousin.

Clouds had lowered and become heavy during the drive, and a few snowflakes settled on the ground around us as I was ordered out of the van and led inside the house. I suppose I expected to see the Grand Master there, but that wasn't to be.

"He's someplace else. You think we're that stupid?" Gap laughed at me. Actually, I did. That didn't mean I couldn't track Weldon down, though. I knew his scent. I wondered if any of these people knew how good my nose was. If they left me alive, I wouldn't stop hunting them until they were all dead.

"What do you want, then?" I asked sullenly.

"Our girlie's grumpy," Gap chuckled. "We have a job for you. A job only a vampire can do. You're gonna turn somebody for us."

"What?" The word was out before I could stop it.

"Yeah. My granddaughter, Lily," Gap replied. "My son got killed in a challenge. His wife was human so she took off and then my baby girl got cancer. Brain cancer and she's dyin'. You're gonna save her."

Gap didn't know anything about what turning actually meant. I was nearly as ignorant. My only experience had been my own turning and I didn't remember any of it.

"You should have found an older vampire," I snapped. "One with experience. I've only been vampire since last January and I don't know how to turn someone else. If I try, your granddaughter will most likely die from the attempt." As angry as I was, I was being as honest with him as I could be.

"You got any vampire friends? Ones that know how to do this?" Gap was angry now as well. "You can call. You get one phone call and you can tell 'em it's a matter of life 'n death. We'll be listenin' in just to make sure you're not foolin' with us and get 'em to tell you how it's done."

"Show me the girl, first," I said. I was led into the back bedroom of the cabin. The girl lay on a small bed covered in homemade quilts. She looked like she should be inside a hospital instead of where she was, and my nose told me that her death would be coming very soon—she had a few hours remaining, if that much.

Wisps of thin, pale hair clouded about her face and her eyes were closed, whether in sleep or a coma I couldn't tell. Paper-thin, translucent skin covered what might have been pretty features once. I estimated her age around fourteen but she was small for those years, painfully thin and presently unconscious. I felt for Gap, but honestly, even if she weren't female, the turning would likely kill her just as quickly as her disease would.

"Some things are worse than death," I said, leveling a glare at Gap, who gazed down at his granddaughter.

"Don't be tellin' me any of that nonsense, girlie," he said, turning light-brown eyes at me and almost growling. "I heard the stories about what you did at the Packmaster meetin'. Lily here could be just like you. I know it. You're gonna save her."

I wanted to argue with him over that. Nobody had any guarantees, even if they did turn successfully. I wanted to tell him about the two who'd turned me. What *they* were. And about Edward's sire, Nyles Abernathy, who'd almost killed Gavin. He'd murdered several humans, all innocents, just to play a game and lure Gavin in.

Vampires were no better than humans. There were good ones and bad ones. Bad vampires, though, could be infinitely more dangerous. According to Merrill, it was against vampire law to turn anyone under eighteen. He'd taught me that in one of my lessons. This was a disaster, no matter how you looked at it.

"All right," I sighed. "But just be prepared. If this one gets turned, I'll be breaking all sorts of laws to do it." I pulled the cell phone from my pocket and punched Merrill's number on speed dial. I just hoped he'd pick up.

"Lissa?" I almost heaved a sigh of relief at Merrill's voice.

"Merrill, I have a problem," I said. Likely, he read the emotions in my voice—he was very experienced at that. Anger, fear and horror warred with one another and permeated my words. "Some of the wolves here have kidnapped the Grand Master and the others and they're holding them. They did this during daylight."

I wanted Merrill to know how things had gone down without explaining too much; that could anger Gap. "Now," I went on, "they're telling me they'll kill the Grand Master if I don't turn this werewolf's human granddaughter who's dying of brain cancer. She can't be more than fourteen, and she's hours away from dying." I wanted to wail at that admission. Instead, I did my best to school my voice and my features.

I was terrified that Merrill would say *absolutely not*, the Grand Master would die and I'd have to fight my way through a small pack of werewolves to get away, risking their bites while I fought them off. My memories of the last werewolf bites I'd gotten were far from pleasant.

I heard Merrill punch a button on his phone instead and Wlodek was on the line in seconds. I now had the two oldest vampires I knew on the phone and one of them just happened to be Head of the Vampire Council. Of course Gap didn't know that and I wasn't about to tell him. I had to explain to Wlodek what was going on; Gap was listening attentively to the entire exchange.

"Lissa, we will give you permission to try this," Wlodek said. I was stunned; I never expected that. I realized quickly it was a calculated decision, in order to buy time for the Grand Master. If Weldon died, the peace treaty between vampires and werewolves could die with him.

"You must listen carefully, however," Wlodek instructed. "While you might think that the easiest method is to slash the neck, a first-time attempt at this may be fatal. Doing it in that manner requires a great deal of skill. Therefore, you must make incisions at the wrists. Open both wrists, lengthwise. Drink as much of the blood as you can hold because the turn will require your blood, once the girl is near death from blood loss. You must open one of your own wrists at that point and feed her. Once she gets the taste in her mouth, she will accept it. Allow her to drink for four minutes, Lissa. No more, no less. Otherwise, she may get too little or too much. Do you understand?"

Vampires bleed sluggishly, so I did understand. It would take that long for enough blood to pass from sire to child. "Yes," I said. I almost added *Honored One* to that but caught myself in time.

"Lissa, the shortest amount of time it will take for a complete turn is three days, and that is if the body is young and healthy. If the girl is gravely ill, it may take some days beyond that. Do you understand?"

I looked up at Gap. He nodded at me. "Yes," I replied.

"Try to get better treatment for the Grand Master during that time and inform your captors that you will require blood—not just for you but for the girl when she wakes."

Once again, I looked at Gap who nodded his understanding. "You must also watch the girl every moment that you are awake so that you may feed her, show her how to drink properly and tell her what she needs to know to survive. Do you understand?"

"Yes," I said. "Sir," I went on, "there is one here who does not submit to compulsion."

"I understand that," Wlodek said. "Do your best, Lissa. That is all we can ask under the circumstances." Wlodek and Merrill both hung up.

"Where will we get blood?" One of the other werewolves asked Gap.

"There's a cooler full of it back at the cabin," I grumbled. I hadn't eaten yet, and my skin was tightening and my stomach hurt as a result. "It needs to be kept cold. I hope you have electricity or a generator."

"We have electric," Gap huffed, insulted. "Rowdy, go get that cooler."

"Winkler has the key," I said. "And I'm not doing anything for you until you do something for them. It won't do you a bit of good if you're going to hurt them further. Your granddaughter's life is in my hands, now."

Gap punched a number on Winkler's cell and spoke to someone, telling them to make sure their guests were comfortable and fed.

"Mess up, girlie and they're all dead," Gap informed me, tapping the end call button on Winkler's cell. If I were human, I'd have been in a cold sweat. No longer human as I was, I shivered and nodded with as much dignity as I could.

Bowls were brought from the kitchen to drain excess blood from the girl's wounds; there wasn't any way I could drink more than I usually did. I also knew, just by talking with Wlodek, that he and Merrill would make a rescue attempt but they had no way of knowing exactly where I was and it could take days to find me.

Was there a GPS tracker on my phone and would it work in the back of beyond? Afterward, we'd have to find the Grand Master. Who knew where he and Winkler were being held? I didn't even think about Kelvin. Maybe I should have, but I didn't.

Rowdy came in with the cooler of blood later, and then somebody else came in with the key. That werewolf had the scent of Winkler on him, along with a bit of Winkler's blood. Winkler had likely fought with this one before handing over anything.

I almost growled at my captors as the cooler was set against a wall of the girl's bedroom. Gap almost growled back. What he didn't know was that unless it snowed quite a lot, I could follow his werewolf cousin's tracks back to Winkler if he'd made the trip on foot.

My hands shook as I made my preparations. My sire most likely should have been there with me, talking me through the ordeal, but he wasn't. "You may have to hold her while I do this," I nodded at Gap, who came and sat on the side of the bed. He gripped Lily's shoulders tightly. Allowing my claws to slide out about an inch, I set about opening her wrists.

Gap muttered the whole time I drank from his granddaughter, but if she survived, he would have to get used to this. I didn't drink much, allowing most of her blood to collect in the bowls placed beneath her wrists. Rowdy waited off to the side, watching intently.

I heard the girl's heart slow and somehow knew when the time was right. I licked both her wrists to stop the blood flow and heal up her wounds, then opened my right wrist lengthwise, just as I'd done hers, pressing the wrist to her mouth. Gap helped, pulling her jaw open.

Just as Wlodek said, the girl accepted my blood and began to drink. Gap's cousin Rowdy timed it; he had a watch with a second hand. He called time at four minutes exactly, even though the girl wanted to keep drinking.

"We have to keep her in a dark place," I said, licking my wrist to close the wound.

Gap carried Lily as he led me down heavy, hand-hewn plank steps to a cellar beneath the main floor of the house. The cellar was small and had a dirt floor with rough, split log walls all around. At least it was swept and didn't have cobwebs. Spider bites probably wouldn't hurt me, but I still didn't want stray arachnids crawling down the back of my shirt.

A cot stood in a corner of the tiny, underground room. The mattress on it was quite narrow, with room for only one person. Lily got that. I asked for a unit of blood and one was tossed down. Gap left with the half-bag of blood I passed back to him.

"Don't let any sunlight in down here," I warned him as the cellar steps creaked beneath his feet. "And I'll need more blood when night falls again." Daybreak wasn't far off; I knew that for certain. Gap left us and when daybreak came, I slumped over where I sat.

⁂

When I woke again, I pondered my dilemma as I listened to voices and footsteps overhead. At least the girl was still whole and not ash. Lily's heart and breathing had stopped the moment I'd pulled my wrist away from her lips. I had no idea what that meant or if it was natural.

Gap confiscated my cell phone before leaving me in the cellar, so I didn't even have that to try to contact anyone else. I also wanted to know how Winkler and Weldon were doing. Hunger made its presence known so I climbed up the cellar steps to the trap door, which was locked.

Punching through it might have given me some satisfaction, but I held back. Gap's cellar was a dark place to hide and sleep. I knocked on the door instead to ask for my blood. A bath would have been nice as well, but I was told I'd have to wait another day or two for that. I wanted to curse but politely asked about Weldon and the others, instead.

"Grumpy as bears. Had to tranquilize 'em. We only wake 'em up enough to eat," Gap grinned at me while walking down the steps to check on his granddaughter. She didn't have the stink of decay about her and I imagined he could smell the same thing.

He seemed satisfied with her appearance, allowed me to walk around the house for a few minutes, then sent me back to the cellar.

No sense asking him for a book to read; I hadn't seen a single one in the entire house.

Instead, I moved over to the girl's bedside and told her stories. I told her about Franklin and Greg. About Winkler and Weldon. I even told her about some of the recent books I'd read. I catnapped, too, before passing out when dawn came. The second night, I noticed minute signs of a change. Lily was transforming. Her lips were fuller, her skin held a tiny bit of color and her hair appeared thicker.

Was this how it had happened with me? Subtle changes, here and there? I'd been overweight, though, and had wakened to a much smaller size. Was the girl going to have enough mass to get through the entire thing? She'd been so thin and wasted-looking.

Her continued existence was the only thing likely to keep Weldon and Winkler alive, too, so I was grateful for that much. Even if I killed everybody upstairs, the Grand Master and Winkler could still die before I found them.

Another day passed and a few more slight changes came by nightfall. I got my blood and drank; they'd passed me two unfinished units. I emptied both and went back to watching the girl. Gap came to observe as well.

"She's lookin' prettier," he said. I nodded. I figured if she were completely gone, she'd have turned to ash by now, just as any vampire would. "How much longer do you think?" he asked. I turned an angry gaze on him.

"This is my first turn. How should I know?" What I did know was that if he and his granddaughter escaped, I'd have to hunt both of them and kill them. Wlodek would never allow the girl to live.

"All right, no need to get testy," Gap grumbled, walking up the stairs.

A fourth day passed and I woke, getting my blood and a bath, finally. Some of the werewolves wanted to watch, I could tell, but Gap chased them off and I got the bathroom mostly to myself. The door was left open, however, and my guard stood right outside.

Someone had also gone to the cabin we'd rented and emptied it, likely so the owners wouldn't think anything suspicious was going on. My bags, along with Winkler's and the others, had all been dumped inside the log house.

Having my suitcase meant I had fresh clothes to change into and I was grateful for that. The clothing I'd worn for days smelled from spilled blood, both mine and Lily's.

I wondered what the people in South Carolina were thinking, too. Weldon was scheduled to be in Summerville the day before. After I cleaned up and braided my freshly-washed hair, I was sent right back down the sturdy plank steps into the cellar. Lily still seemed to be making progress, although slowly.

I was settled in my usual corner, not far from her bed when the racket started. At first, I thought the werewolves upstairs were arguing, but that wasn't the case. When one shrieked, I knew for sure that wasn't it. The trapdoor was ripped off its hinges and Merrill's voice shouted my name.

CHAPTER 9

I climbed out of the cellar in a blink, finding Merrill, Russell, Radomir and Brock all there, surrounded by werewolf bodies. All the werewolves were dead. Gap's head lay in a corner of the cabin's main room while his body occupied the kitchen. Both spaces were splattered in blood. Merrill didn't have a hair out of place as we stood there, surveying the bodies.

"What about Weldon and Winkler?" It took an effort to gather my wits; I was still dazed from the surprise rescue and the smell of death about me.

"We split up. The other vampires are at a cabin twenty miles away. I imagine that's over with as well. Where's the girl?" Merrill asked. I led the way to the cellar.

"She's started the change," Russell sighed, eyeing the girl. "Probably a quarter of the way there, or close enough."

"Lissa, one of us can do this if you don't want to," Merrill placed an arm around my shoulders as we stared at Lily's body. It was hitting me, then. The girl could turn completely if we didn't stop her. This would be my child, if she made the turn and was permitted to live. Wlodek would never allow that. Likely, he'd instructed Merrill to dispose of her if she hadn't turned to ash already.

Merrill or one of the others was prepared to destroy Lily. If they didn't, she'd be fourteen forever. That just seemed wrong to me. All of it seemed wrong to me. I cursed her grandfather for making me do this. I cursed him again for not letting her go. For failing to understand that death is not always the enemy. I didn't realize I was doing my cursing out loud until Merrill squeezed my arm.

"Lissa, perhaps it's better if we do this."

"No." I wiped tears away. I was angry. As angry as I'd ever been, I think. And sad, too. "I'm so sorry, Lily. So very sorry. You should have gone on already." My claws were swift as they separated her head from her body. Both began to flake away. I turned and ran up the stairs.

※

"The girl had started the turn, Wlodek." Merrill's words caused Wlodek to cease signing his name between the L and the O.

"You think Lissa might make more females for us? That she has the blood gene to do it?" Wlodek's hand was still, poised over the documents that lay on his desk as he gazed at Merrill.

"Possibly. That girl was dying before Lissa got to her, no doubt about that, and wasted away as well. Any male would have lost her quickly, I believe." Merrill wanted to sigh but didn't.

"I don't believe the girl would have successfully turned; there wasn't enough body mass," Merrill went on. "She may have remained intact for two more days, but no longer than that. Lissa was quite upset over the whole thing. I am hopeful that Lissa has the gene, however. That would bode well for our future."

The Vampire race needed more females. Were desperate for them—but Lissa had been too upset over Lily's death. Merrill hoped Wlodek wouldn't force her to attempt turns after her five-year probation was over. The ten-turn rule would be ignored if the turns were all female.

"We will keep this under advisement and make a decision when the time comes," Wlodek guessed at Merrill's thoughts. "In the interim, we will not add this to the records. It is most fortunate that your friend Griffin let the information slip about the genetics. We would likely still be searching for reasons why females couldn't complete the turn."

"He says it's extremely rare, and nearly impossible to find," Merrill muttered, wondering if he shouldn't have kept the information to himself after all. At the moment, only he and Wlodek held the information, and it would remain with them.

"I expected as much," Wlodek nodded sagely and finished signing his name.

※ ※

Weldon, Winkler and Kelvin were allowed to recuperate in the Packmaster's large home located outside Charleston. Winkler was in the worst shape of all of them; the moment they'd allow him to wake from the tranquilizer darts they kept shooting into him, he'd start fighting. That meant he was beaten by six werewolves, every time. While werewolves heal notoriously fast, continued beatings will take their toll.

Robert and Albert had been in on that kill, along with Stephan. All of the vampires went home after the remnants of the Sugar Grove Pack had either been exterminated (if they knew about Gap's little indiscretion) or sent to Buckhannon if they didn't. Buckhannon got two females out of it; a father and a mate had known. Weldon had been vicious and thorough in his decisions. You don't kidnap the Grand Master and expect to live over it.

"You bought us time," Merrill hugged me before he left. "I knew you'd be somewhere in the area since you keep me updated on where you're going. It just took a little time to track you. Davis from the Dallas Pack helped; he knew where Winkler rented the cabin. The snow slowed us down a bit but we were able to find you."

Wlodek had also insisted that I call and talk to him, so Merrill dialed his number and I talked. Wlodek said he understood the pain of having to kill a child of your own making. He also said that it was likely the girl didn't have enough mass to complete the turn and her final death was an inevitability. Hoping he was being honest with me instead of lying to spare my feelings, I brushed away tears and struggled to numb myself to all of it.

Weldon sorted things out with the Summerville Packmaster while he, Winkler and Kelvin rested. It was two weeks away from Christmas and the holiday week would be spent in Dallas unless I had somewhere else to go. The call I was dreading to make after the Sugar Grove ordeal, however, was the one to Gavin. I made that call the day after we arrived in Charleston.

"Honey, it's me," I said the moment he answered. Gavin growled. He'd already heard something from somebody. Maybe one of the Enforcers. This was what I was afraid of—his anger. When he was coherent enough to talk, he let me know what he thought.

"You should have just ripped into them!" He shouted, making me hope he was underground somewhere so nobody would hear. I had to hold the cell away from my ear; his voice was so loud and painful.

"But they would have killed the Grand Master."

"Fuck the Grand Master!" I'm sure he didn't mean that in the physical sense. "What were you going to do, Lissa? Would you care to tell me that?"

"I was hoping that if the girl turned, the wolves would clear out and I could go hunt them," I said. "I wanted to take them down as quickly as I could and hoped that I could find Weldon and the others in the process."

"They wouldn't have let you live," Gavin snorted.

"Maybe. I did the best I could, Gavin. Wlodek told me to stay with the girl, and I was hoping he and Merrill would send somebody. At least to keep the Grand Master alive."

"Fuck the Grand Master."

"You said that already," I retorted. My temper was rising, now. "This was my assignment, Gavin. The Council sent me to do this."

"The Council has no business sending a youngling female out on an errand such as this with no supervision." He started cursing in French. Or maybe it was Italian. How did I know? And he'd called me a youngling female. That burned my toast. If he'd been there with me, I'd kick him for that. And then he'd more than likely pound me. So far, being engaged to a vampire sucked most of the time.

"Gavin, if you want to punch me, then you'll have to wait until we see each other," I interrupted his cursing. That made him curse even louder. Well, he was pissed, no doubt about that. Merrill hadn't said one cross word to me the whole time he'd been here. Why couldn't Gavin do that? I wondered how long it would take him to realize I'd hung up on him in mid-rant.

"This was my fault," I told Weldon later. I'd taken a tray of food into his room so he could eat dinner. He wasn't in bed; he was on the sofa in the sitting area, watching television. "Somehow, that idiot found out about me at the Packmaster's meeting last spring and decided that his granddaughter would make a good vampire, since she was dying and he wasn't willing to let her go."

"Lissa, sit down," Weldon muted the television and patted the sofa next to him. Here came the fatherly lecture. I sat down.

"Yeah. He did it because of that," Weldon acknowledged. My eyebrows shot up. "But Winkler, Kelvin and I were caught off guard and we shouldn't have been. We were all lounging around, not expecting anything of the sort when those assholes just waltzed right in with a fake story and before you know it, they had all three of us tranquilized up to our eyeballs. They hauled us out of that cabin trussed up like sheep. You can't take all the blame for this, Lissa."

"Weldon, I don't think I ever want to see you trussed up like a sheep."

"I don't want you to see me trussed up like a sheep." He grinned at me. "Bad enough you've seen us all naked."

"Don't forget covered in blood. I'm not much for hunting, but those assholes had to have testicles the size of a small planet after they saw you take down that bear."

"Saw that, huh?" Weldon put his arm around me and pulled me against his side.

"Yeah. I can mist, you know."

"Yeah. Somebody told me. Somebody also told me you did what those assholes told you just to keep the rest of us alive."

"I was prepared to do some shredding if somebody died," I said. I didn't tell him either him or Winkler. Kelvin I still didn't know about. "Did you know you were going to be thinning the herd when you started this trip?"

"Lissa, I usually do two or three confirmations a year. The most I ever had to do before was five. This time, there were more than thirty because of the attempted coup. I figured somebody would get out of line somewhere. I hope the rest will be peaceful."

"Me, too," I said.

※ ※

Three days later, we were on the jet and headed for Dallas. I woke midflight; Winkler had already pulled me from the body bag and settled me into a seat on the jet. He still looked haggard after his ordeal and hadn't spoken much about it. I got the idea that he'd never been in a situation such as that, and he didn't appreciate it one bit.

Kelvin had cooperated with the kidnappers completely, didn't mind talking about it and his bruises and swellings were the lightest as a result.

I still hadn't heard back from Gavin after I hung up on him. No telling how pissed he was now. I'd either be spending Christmas with Winkler or by myself.

Davis stood alongside a Winkler Security van, waiting to drive us to the house in Denton after we landed at the Dallas airport. At least the van held all the luggage. I asked to borrow a car after we arrived at Winkler's home, and went to do some Christmas shopping, since I'd most likely be in Dallas for the holiday.

Winkler loaned me the Cadillac, so I got to drive in style. I bought Winkler a gift card for several massages. If he got one of the girls at the massage chain, he'd probably have them talked into an after-work drink or something.

Davis got a gift card to a sporting goods store. His weight-lifting outfit was worn out; I'd washed it the last time I was there. Whitney and Sam got something from Williams-Sonoma. I hadn't gotten them a wedding present yet so it did double duty. Then I went shopping for Franklin, Greg, Merrill and Gavin.

I went back to the store where Winkler bought my coats. They had men's styles too, so I bought two. Merrill's was a nice camel color; Gavin's was black. They'd look good in them, I knew. I had the shop wrap them for me. Greg and Franklin got nice gloves and scarves—New York is cold in the winter—or so I've heard.

I called Franklin to get a mailing address for Merrill in New York; it was a post office box so I wrote that down. Somebody might have to go to a local post office for me if there wasn't another way to get things mailed.

I bought packing boxes at Walmart along with tape, Christmas cards and a felt tip pen. Gavin would have to wait for his gifts, since I didn't know where he was and I certainly didn't have his mailing address. Is that weird—that I was engaged to Gavin and I didn't even know where he lived?

I bought jewelry for Lena, intending to mail it to the address we used in London. She'd pick that up anyway.

Winkler said he'd get the packages mailed off for me the next day; some of his crew were dropping by anyway. The werewolf bunch Winkler brought in put up a tree for him while they were there. I woke the following night to a fir tree smell and winking lights.

❧ ☙

"Here's what we got on Kelvin's contact at the lab," Davis handed a folder to Winkler. "We've been tailing the woman. The others she's met up with are recorded in that folder too, along with photographs and background checks. We figure Kelvin's counterfeit medical degree came from one of those contacts; we saw her getting documents from one of them. I think we've traced most of them back to Albuquerque State University, where Tate Briggs was a student."

"Have you gotten into the school's records, yet?" Winkler flipped the folder open to read. "Looks like they were searching for something in Lissa's DNA. They ran tests on the stuff we substituted," Winkler flipped through more records inside the folder.

"We're working on the school records, now. I asked Glen to go in person; he's been in Albuquerque since noon today. Too bad the vampires didn't get information on the ones they killed in Great Britain."

"Maybe they did and didn't share," Winkler said. "In the meantime, this information stays with us. If Wlodek discovers we let them touch Lissa like that, we may not see her again."

Davis nodded. "So, it looks like Kelvin knew Tate pretty well. Possibly from college," Davis said softly as he watched Winkler go through the gathered records. "Since Kelvin is a werewolf, maybe he ran with Lester Briggs' Pack. We just don't have any records of Kelvin with Lester's bunch."

"It's an assumed name," Winkler said. "His medical degree is certainly assumed. He may have been in pre-med or the early stages of med school, but he's no doctor."

"He knew how to use that speculum," Davis muttered. "You think he's played around with that stuff before?"

"I want to kill him every time I think about it. Lissa certainly wouldn't waste any time if she knew."

"Well, Gavin would torture and then kill, if he knew," Davis said.

"Yeah. And that's why we're not handing that information over. Not only would Lissa be kept from us, but our asses could be on the line."

"Yeah. There's always that."

I spent the next couple of days e-mailing Charles, who agreed to get some Christmas presents parceled out to people that I didn't know how to reach otherwise. He had a generic post box address I could use. Russell's gift was the easiest; I sent him a framed print of dogs playing pool for his billiard room.

Will got a print of dogs playing poker; Charles told me both Enforcers lived in the same house (in separate quarters, of course). Radomir was harder to buy for, but I found a pair of cufflinks—he always wore dress shirts with cufflinks, I'd noticed.

Wlodek already had the painting, so I didn't do anything other than a holiday card for him. Who knew if he celebrated Christmas or not? Charles, on the other hand, was getting a computer game. It was something new that I thought he might smile over, called Evil Alien Bunny Invaders. The bunnies looked innocent until they decided to kill, and then they became huge and attacked. The game had several levels. I'd seen an icon on Charles's laptop for a popular auto theft game, so I hoped he'd like this one.

The last thing I sent, and I had to think about it, was a gift basket of food—to Merrill's friend, Griffin. I knew he wasn't vampire. I still didn't know what he was or how I knew his name, but he more than likely ate. I'd mulled him over in my mind, although I'd only gotten a brief whiff of his clothing the night I was so sick.

The term Wizard came to mind, but that didn't really seem to fit, either. Merrill most likely thought I'd completely missed him or forgot. I sent the gift basket to the street address in New York that Franklin had given me. A pair of cufflinks for Gavin finished up just about everything; they'd go nicely with most of his dress shirts. Now, if he'd just calm down enough so I could give them to him.

I was just getting Christmas dinner on the table for the werewolves when my cell phone rang, so I pulled it from the pocket of my jeans. The caller ID showed it was Gavin. I almost cursed, motioned for everybody to sit down, then went into the kitchen to take the call.

"Hello?" There was a definite question in my greeting.

"Lissa, pack a bag and meet me at the front gate," Gavin growled. *Fuck*. Fuck squared. He was *here*. Why didn't he warn me?

"I'll be there in a few minutes," I said and terminated the call. "Gavin's at the front gate," I told Winkler, who was helping himself to mashed potatoes. Daryl and Kathy Jo had come to spend the holiday with Weldon and they looked up at my announcement.

"Is everything all right?" Kathy Jo asked.

"Oh, sure. He'll just yell for a while," I said. "I have to go." I left them there and nearly ran to my bedroom. I tossed jeans, tops and two nice outfits into a bag, along with my toiletries, grabbed both of Gavin's boxed gifts and headed toward the front door. Winkler was right behind me.

"Call if you need somebody to come get you," he said softly.

"Merry Christmas," I said, standing on tiptoe to kiss his cheek. He still had to lean down to receive it.

"Same to you," he said. I'd left the werewolves' gifts under the tree while they weren't looking; they were planning to open them after dinner.

Gavin had a rental car—a Lincoln—parked outside Winkler's gate, so I punched in the code and let myself out. He was out of the car, a huge frown on his face and tossing my bag into the trunk in seconds while I placed the other two boxes in the back seat. Gavin came up behind me, almost dumped me onto the passenger seat, buckled my seatbelt in less time than it takes to blink and we were off.

He didn't talk and I was afraid to ask where we were going. I glanced his way a time or two, but his face was set in the usual mask. I decided to stare out the window after pulling my knees to my chest.

We ended up at a safe house in Dallas. A nice one, actually, in a better neighborhood. The ground floor was spacious and well furnished, as was the basement. Gavin carried my bag down; I brought the boxes and my purse. Once my bag was deposited in the largest bedroom right alongside his, he came and watched me place the wrapped boxes on the table. I imagine he wanted to put his hands on his hips before he started yelling.

"Why did you hang up on me?" he demanded. I sighed and slumped onto a chair at the kitchen table.

"Gavin, you were yelling. In languages I don't understand. What was I supposed to do, stand there and hope you'd start speaking English again someday? Yes, the whole thing was stupid but I didn't know what else to do. Do you think I haven't called myself all kinds of an idiot for not doing otherwise? Do you? And to top it all off, that girl was turning. She didn't die right away. I had to kill her when Merrill and the others showed up." I was wiping tears by that time. The whole incident still unsettled me and Gavin's temper wasn't helping.

Gavin just stood there for what seemed like forever, staring at me. "Here," I shoved the wrapped boxes toward him. "Your Christmas presents. I can get myself to a hotel or back to Winkler's." I sniffled as I got up to leave.

"Lissa, Cara, why is it like this? I get angry and you cry." Gavin grabbed my arm and pulled me against him. I had the front of his shirt gripped in my hands while I sobbed against his chest. I couldn't help it. Too many things had built up and the dam had finally burst.

More than likely, I was staining the snowy whiteness of his expensive Italian shirt with my amber tears, but he wasn't stopping me. In fact, he lifted me up, convinced me silently to wrap my legs around his waist and let me cry against his collar, my arms tight around his neck while he spoke softly in Latin. The only thing I got out of all of it, that I understood, anyway, was the "shhhh."

Gavin eventually carried me to the bedroom, settled me on the bed and proceeded to undress me slowly and carefully, kissing, nuzzling and stroking, until I was naked. Then he pulled his own clothing off and lowered himself over me.

The love was so gentle. So tender. Even the climax with the bite belonged when it came. I knew he wanted it, so I reciprocated. The string of words he uttered when he reached his own orgasm expressed his pleasure, no matter what the language.

※ ※

"How did you know the size?" Gavin liked his cashmere coat. He should, I'd spent nearly twenty-five hundred on it. My credit card was groaning from its Christmas burdens. Merrill was going to have to transfer some of my funds to pay for all of it. He couldn't complain that I didn't use the card anymore, though.

"I saw the sizes on some of the stuff you had when we were here before," I told him, sipping my blood. He'd worn me out, almost, in bed. "The suits and shirts you normally wear must be tailored, because those things don't carry any sizes in them."

"I have many things made," he agreed, examining his cufflinks. "These are nice—very nice. You have such good taste, Cara. You must look at yours, now."

He brought several velvet boxes from his suitcase and set them in front of me. There was a ruby and diamond necklace with matching earrings, and another set made with sapphires.

"Honey, this is way too much," I said, admiring the sapphires. Blue is my favorite color, after all.

"Tell me you will not have to go back to the werewolves until after the New Year; I wish to take you dancing," he said, drawing me into his arms.

"They're not planning on leaving until the third."

"Good. You will call them later and let them know you will be with me until then." Gavin was back to being bossy. I mentioned it to him. He nuzzled my neck.

"I have not seen you for weeks. How am I supposed to be?" He quirked an eyebrow after pulling away.

"Fine, O autocratic fiancé," I grumbled.

"Where you are concerned, I am not only autocratic but possessive and insanely jealous," he pulled me into a tighter embrace and nipped the skin on my neck.

"Yeah. Like I didn't notice," I grumbled. Gavin backed me against the wall in the tiny kitchen, grinding his hips against my belly. Gavin isn't small and his suit pants did nothing to hide his cravings. I knew right away what he really wanted for Christmas. A claw slid out on his right index finger and he slowly and casually ripped through every bit of clothing I wore, until the ragged strips of it dropped to the floor around me.

His clothes were removed in a similar fashion shortly after. Then, cupping my buttocks in his hands, he lifted and held me against the wall before settling my body over his. I was screaming Gavin's name, along with a few other things before it was over. Yep, God sure knew I was having sex that night.

Gavin's arms were around me and his body was leaning halfway over mine when I woke the evening after Christmas. Of course, we were completely naked—Gavin had seen to that. "You are such a sleepyhead," he mumbled against my hair.

"Well, why didn't you wake me up?" I turned in his arms so I could face him.

"I did try. New ones are this way," he said. "They sleep longer."

"Oh, so the big, tough, older vampires wake up quicker?"

"Yes. And go to sleep later, much of the time," he kissed me, then sucked and nibbled on my lower lip. I didn't get the shower I wanted until long after that.

"I think you did get your wish, your hair is definitely growing out," I ran my hands through it; it was nearly an inch in length, now. "Charles told me that hair grows about half an inch a year."

"For the younger ones, perhaps," he said. "Would you like to go out? We can go to the West End, if you like."

"You want to go to the West End? That's so unlike you," I smiled. "What are we wearing?"

"Casual, I think," he smiled back, his dark eyes twinkling. They should twinkle; he'd gotten sex nearly a dozen times since he'd shown up without warning. Gavin dressed in nice jeans after his shower but he still didn't have a shirt on.

I wore my short, cashmere coat over a nice top, jeans and boots when we went out. Gavin had a long sleeved dress shirt on but it was a button down in (gasp) a light blue. He also wore the leather jacket he sometimes used with a more casual outfit.

We parked where we could find a space and walked down the sidewalk. Plenty of people were out and wandering—Christmas had fallen on a Friday so this was Saturday night in Dallas. With all the time Gavin and I spent there earlier in the year, we hadn't gotten to see much of it at all.

Gavin pulled me closer to him when we saw a group of young people coming toward us. All were dressed in long, black leather coats, their hair dyed black, fingernails black, lipstick, if they wore it—black. They were harmless, only out to have some fun, I think. Gavin, in his usual, overprotective way, was making sure. I wondered if those kids would ever realize they'd walked right past an Assassin for the Vampire Council.

Nowadays, I looked at everything with different eyes. None of the vampires I'd met appeared to be anything other than human. Why would they want to stick out? That was just an indication to someone of what they might be. Vampires are hidden for a reason, Merrill said. The race had to be protected.

I'd learned the hard way just how vulnerable we were during the day—I didn't wake until nightfall and had no way of knowing how long Gap and his werewolves stood over me, waiting for sunset to come. I slid an arm around Gavin's waist at the thought and he tightened his arm about my shoulders.

We sat and had a glass of wine at a bar after a while, watching people come and go. There were all sorts there, some of them coming from the basketball game down the street. The West End isn't what it once was, but it still draws plenty of people.

The week I spent with Gavin at the safe house was almost perfect. He didn't lose his temper and he took me shopping several times, helping me choose a dress to go dancing in and then appropriate shoes. The dress was a deep blue so I could wear my sapphires.

On New Year's Eve, we crashed a party in a hotel. Gavin employed compulsion to get us in and we looked as if we belonged with that crowd, all of whom were wealthy. I think the Dallas Mayor was there, plus some state representatives or senators. It was a black tie affair and Gavin had come prepared, let me tell you. I don't know how many women stared at him over the course of the evening. Gavin was there to dance, though, and we did.

Strangely enough, we ran into Winkler and Weldon at the party. Winkler had an invite, of course. We only talked for a while. Well, I talked, Gavin glared. And then, Gavin pulled me away before Weldon or Winkler could ask me for a dance.

Winkler did tell me to be at the house the evening of the second; they were flying out the morning of the third. I must have frowned because Gavin asked me about it later.

"I think I hate that stupid body bag more than anything, even though they get me out right at sunset," I grumbled, taking off my jewelry.

"Better that than getting burned, Cara," Gavin kissed my bare shoulder. The dress had narrow straps and he'd slipped them down for better access.

Gavin kept me in bed most of the first, making love to me one last time before I had to clean up and go back to Winkler's on the second.

※ ※

We did a whirlwind trip back to the east coast; the werewolves of the now defunct Sugar Grove Pack had cost us time and several visits had to be postponed so Weldon, Winkler and Kelvin could recuperate.

Before our trip back east, Weldon carefully leaked information regarding the fact that vampires were now cooperating with werewolves. He hoped to avoid further incidents. I wasn't sure what Wlodek might think about that, but I couldn't blame Weldon. I was sick of the problems myself, and I sure didn't want a Sugar Grove repeat.

We were in Kentucky, Tennessee, Alabama, Mississippi, Missouri, Arkansas and Florida during that trip; some of those states had more than one Pack to visit. It was while we were in Florida however, that something happened to worry me and arouse my suspicions.

At his request, I'd been lending my mystery books to Kelvin after reading them. He hadn't returned any of them to me, though. Some people are very lax about that sort of thing, but I couldn't see that he was lugging books around in his bags.

Maybe he was one of those people who left things behind in hotel rooms. Maybe. One night in Sarasota Springs, after we were returning from dinner with yet another Packmaster and his human wife, Kelvin stopped at the front desk of our hotel. Handing an envelope to the desk clerk, he asked her to mail it for him.

Weldon and Winkler didn't pay it any mind, but my skin itched. I tapped Winkler on the shoulder when Kelvin wasn't looking and told him I wanted to go outside for some air. The werewolves rode the elevator to the third floor without me.

The girl at the desk handed over the envelope without protest after I placed compulsion, and I laid a second one for her to forget she saw me. Once inside the women's restroom just off the lobby, I opened the envelope. It was addressed to someone in Dallas. Inside, I found six pages from the novel I'd last loaned to Kelvin.

All right, that had me stumped. Why would he be tearing pages out of a novel and sending them to anybody? And why wasn't he telling me about this if that's what he intended to do with my books? The book itself was a best-seller, so those pages could be obtained anywhere by anybody.

I sat there in the stall for the longest time, trying to come up with an answer. When I did, the knowledge frightened me. I looked up a number on my cell and made a call to a local bookstore that stayed open late.

The desk clerk might have wondered why I was telling her to rip six pages from a paperback I hadn't read yet, stuff them inside Kelvin's envelope and then re-seal it, but she was under compulsion and didn't ask. Once again, I instructed her to forget the whole thing. The envelope was placed into the outgoing mail pile, the girl nodded at me and I went on my way.

"Did you get enough air?" Winkler teased when I walked inside Weldon's suite—he was there watching the late news with the Grand Master.

"Yeah. The view is nicely bland from the rooftop," I lied. Kelvin was puttering around in Weldon's bathroom when I arrived, but left quickly to go to his own room. I went inside the bathroom afterward and sniffed around.

Kelvin had touched Weldon's deodorant and his shaving cream. He hadn't tampered with them further than that (not that I could tell, anyway). Kelvin was now on my list and would get as much of my attention as possible from now on.

We were in Arcadia, Florida, which is near the center of the state, the following evening. The Packmaster owned farmland and allowed his pack to run on some of it. Unfortunately, we didn't get to visit the beach while we were in the state; there wasn't any time. I kept my eyes and ears open around Kelvin, though, and I overheard one phone conversation, saying there was more coming. *More coming.* Well, things were getting interesting. I did notice that Kelvin didn't ask for any more books. Maybe he had as much from me as he wanted.

"I don't know how she knew your name," Merrill passed the gift basket over to Griffin. "Franklin kept this in the fridge for you since some of it was perishable."

Griffin smiled and lifted the basket. "Lissa's different," he said.

CHAPTER 10

We made our way west of the Mississippi, landing in Kansas City just after nightfall. Winkler was rubbing my neck when I woke on the jet and handing my unit of blood to me when my eyes unglued. Winkler has a great smile, no doubt about that.

Weldon also informed us on the way to our hotel that he was changing plans—he'd decided to go to the west coast next, which meant Oregon and California.

Then, he intended to swing back through Arizona and New Mexico, before doing Colorado last. He'd fly to North Dakota after Denver, and I'd be on the Council's jet back to England. The changes were fine with me. I'd never been to Oregon before and I was looking forward to it; Weldon had a confirmation and a wedding there.

Kansas City had to be taken care of first, however. The new Packmaster in the Kansas City area lived in Overland Park and we went to dinner not far from a Barnes and Noble in Leawood.

Winkler knew I wanted to go; I'd given a little moan of desire when we'd passed it while driving to the restaurant. I also had a whopping huge gift card in my purse for Barnes and Noble—my Christmas gift from Winkler. Honestly, no disrespect to Gavin or anything, but the way to my heart might lie through a bookstore.

Weldon and Winkler had coffee in the café at the bookstore and Kelvin walked around outside while I shopped. That told me right then he hadn't been reading any of the books I'd loaned him. If you read and you're next to a bookstore, you're going to look. It can't be helped.

Since I didn't want to donate any more to Kelvin than I could get away with, I only bought three books and Weldon and Winkler were happy to leave. Kelvin was snapping his cell phone shut when we walked out the door.

Weldon confirmed the Packmaster in Overland Park the following evening and then we flew to Wichita. This was where Lester Briggs' biggest supporter, Bart Orford, had been Packmaster. My skin itched the moment Winkler unzipped my body bag on the jet that night.

"Winkler," I grabbed his arm and practically hauled him off the jet. Desperate to find a spot where we could talk without being overheard, I walked as far away from the plane as I could, dragging him along. "There's something going on here, I just feel it," I whispered.

"Lissa, we know this was Bart's Pack," Winkler attempted to soothe me.

"I know that too, but I have a really bad feeling about this." How else could I tell him? I just had a feeling.

This was almost like standing in front of the Council, telling them how I felt when Weldon was walking into a trap. Well, running as a werewolf into a trap might be a better description.

"How are your pilot and co-pilot on protection?" I asked. They were werewolves too; I just didn't know what they could do as far as guarding or fighting went.

"You think we need them?" Winkler was running hands through his hair.

"Yeah. Feel free to make fun of me all you want if nothing happens, Winkler. But I'm telling you, my skin is crawling."

"Lissa, I don't think Weldon will pull these guys away from their job," Winkler sighed. "Just be on guard, all right? We'll get through this." He put a hand on my shoulder and gave me a lop-sided grin.

"I sure as hell hope you're right," I said as we walked back to the jet.

We made it through dinner with the Packmaster. It was boring, to be honest. I was beginning to think Winkler was right and I was only jumping at shadows as I sat on the sofa in Weldon's suite later. The Grand Master snored softly in his bed only a few feet away.

One of my new novels was in my hand and I was reading when I heard footsteps walking down the hallway outside. People come and go inside hotels all the time, but it was three in the morning so I set my book aside, just in case. Winkler's connecting door was open, too—he usually left it that way.

Truthfully, I expected the footsteps to walk right past on their way to another room on the same floor. They didn't. What shocked me most was the knock on the door with the accompanying, "Police. Open up."

"Fuck," I muttered, tossing my book aside. Weldon was out of the bed like a shot, as was Winkler next door. They were both pulling pants on while Weldon told me to answer the door and to be careful when I did it.

Two officers stood outside, their guns drawn when I pulled the door open. "Is there a problem?" I asked, visibly shivering. I had no idea what was going on. I'd been shot before and survived it, but had no idea how badly Winkler or Weldon might be wounded if they were hit.

How did werewolves react to gunshot wounds? Were silver bullets required, like in the movies? I had no idea. Compulsion also came to mind, but if these guys had been sent to our room for a reason, then more would come.

"Back up, put your hands against the wall there and spread 'em," one of the officers barked. Both still had their guns trained on me.

"What's the meaning of this?" Weldon stood behind me now, with Winkler right behind him.

"You're all under arrest," the second officer said. "On suspicion of murder."

"You will tell me now just exactly why you think we murdered someone," I placed compulsion, then. No way was I going to stand there and let them put their hands all over us. We hadn't done anything. Not in the last couple of weeks, anyway, and these were Wichita cops. "And put those guns down, too."

Both cops lowered their weapons. "There are two dead hotel employees downstairs and somebody placed a phone call saying you three did it," one of the officers said.

"We didn't do it, we've been asleep," Winkler asserted. "Besides, what proof do you have?"

"We have the murder weapons," the other officer said.

"You'll not find our fingerprints on them," Weldon scoffed.

"Oh, lord," I muttered. "How quickly will somebody else be up here to check on you two?" I asked the officers, placing yet another compulsion for them to answer my questions only with the truth.

"About five minutes," one said. We had a dark-haired officer and a nearly bald officer. Baldy was the one who spoke.

"Winkler, get on your cell phone," I ordered, thinking as fast as I could. "Call Tony Hancock. *Now*. If you don't have a direct number, I do." I still remembered the number he'd given me; it wasn't the one on his card. Somehow, I knew he'd answer the one I had when he might not answer anything else.

"Here," Winkler handed his cell phone to me. I dialed as fast as I could.

"Winkler, what the hell do you want and how did you get this number?" It was an hour later on the east coast but still too early to be calling anyone. Tony's voice was rough from being wakened from a sound sleep.

"Tony, it's not Winkler." I knew he'd recognize my voice.

"Lissa? Baby, where have you been?" Tony was wide-awake now.

"Tony, I don't have time to chat. We've got real trouble here. I'm in Wichita, Kansas right now and somebody is trying to frame me, Winkler and another man. I only figured out recently that they've been collecting our fingerprints and now the cops are here, telling us that somebody was murdered in our hotel and they have the murder weapons. I'm giving good odds right now on whose fingerprints will show up on whatever it was they used to kill those people."

"Which hotel?" Tony was up and getting dressed, I could hear that plainly.

"The Saint James," I told him. "I only have a minute or two before more cops show up. They'll arrest Winkler and someone named Weldon Harper."

"Is there some way I can get in touch with you?" Tony asked. I gave him my cell number. "Got it," he said.

"Call me during night hours only," I said and hung up.

"Weldon, your little shithead Kelvin has been collecting our fingerprints," I said, turning to mist. "I'm sorry, but I can't go to jail with you guys. For obvious reasons. I'll take the blood and my phone charger with me."

Weldon and Winkler nodded, so I waited until I was nearly mist to take my present compulsion off the cops and to place a new one: "You never saw me, I wasn't here," I said and disappeared.

Winkler and Weldon both growled but allowed the cops to search and handcuff them. I'd given Winkler's cell phone back to him before changing and they took that. The cooler of blood was now with me, along with my purse and cell phone charger.

At the last minute, I floated into Winkler's room and pulled out the envelope of cash I'd stuffed inside my suitcase, turning my laptop case to mist along with it. I waited until the werewolves were herded toward the elevator before I left as well; the forensics team had shown up, ready to take our hotel rooms apart.

Misting inside Kelvin's room, I found that the little shit had left, taking his bags and other belongings with him. It was probably a good thing, too—the cops would've had a third murder on their hands if I'd found him.

Compulsion is a wonderful thing. It got me a room at a nearby hotel with cash, no credit card and an assumed name. Once inside the room, I called Merrill in New York and brought him up to speed. It was too late to call Wlodek or Charles; it was day in Great Britain and they'd be sleeping. It was nearly daylight in New York, too, so I had to hurry and give Merrill the information I had.

Charles got an e-mail as well—a rather lengthy one, as I explained the current situation with Winkler, the Grand Master and me. I also called the hotel desk clerk, informed him that I was a day sleeper and hung the *Do Not Disturb* sign on my door. No sense in tempting fate any more than I had to.

The last thing I did was call Davis. Thankfully, he kept his cell phone by his bed so I told him what was happening. He said he'd have Winkler's lawyers out in force in no time and he would be on the next flight up. I thanked him, told him to call if he needed something and barely ended the call before I conked out with the sunrise.

❧ ☙

"Lissa?" It was Merrill's voice on my cell. He'd been trying to get me to wake for several minutes already.

"Merrill?" My voice and my head were still thick with sleep.

"Lissa, sweetheart, we have a safe house set up for you. There are two vampires on their way to escort you there," he said. "Get your things together. Is there any incriminating evidence inside the other hotel room? Anything that might raise suspicions?" He was asking if anything would point to my being vampire.

"No, I don't think so. I got the blood and my laptop out."

"Thank goodness." Merrill heaved a sigh of relief.

"I don't have any clothes, though, other than what I'm wearing," I said.

"I understand. The two who are coming will help with that."

"Do you know who they are?"

"No. This is someone that Charles and Wlodek were able to get. They just happened to be in the area. They're not local."

"All right," I said. It didn't matter, I'd know by their scent they were vampires.

"Lissa, Wlodek notified Gavin. He may be calling."

"Merrill, you know he's only going to yell," I muttered. Of course, Merrill heard.

"I know." Merrill didn't sound happy about it either.

"Tell Franklin I'm okay for now," I said. I didn't want him worrying.

"I may have to lay compulsion on my human child and I don't like doing that," Merrill said.

"Don't let him fret," I said. "Tell him I love him."

"I will." Merrill hung up.

I had to break the lock on the cooler, since Winkler still had the key. I had just finished drinking my blood and placing the portion I couldn't finish back inside when the knock came on my hotel room door. Answering cautiously, I was relieved to find two vampires standing there. One was at least six-six with white-blond hair cut short; the other was around six feet or so with darker hair.

"Dalroy," the white-haired one introduced himself. He had a slight Texas accent. "This is Rhett," he nodded at the other vampire. I shook hands with both of them; they didn't seem to mind. Rhett took the cooler while Dalroy grabbed my laptop. All I had to carry was my purse; the envelope of cash was now inside my laptop case.

They had a rental car waiting outside for us and I caught up with them after checking out of my room. More compulsion was necessary, of course. I crawled into the back seat of the Cadillac they had, breathing out a relieved sigh. "We hear this could turn into a right mess," Dalroy said over the back of the passenger seat. Rhett was driving and nodding his agreement to Dalroy's words.

"You don't know the half of it," I muttered angrily. "Any word on Winkler and the Grand Master?"

"We've only been up a short while ourselves. We were intending to check the newscasts and the online stuff when we get back to the safe house. Don't worry; we'll get you out of here safely if we have to." Dalroy gave me an encouraging smile.

"I don't intend to leave until Winkler and Weldon are free and cleared of charges," I said.

"The Council might disagree with you on that," Dalroy pointed out. "Personally, I'm with you. Somebody is behind this, I think, and they want to take werewolves and vampires down. Or at least expose all of us," he added grimly.

"Yeah," I said. "I get that idea, too." Dalroy had a ruggedly handsome face, but looked as if he'd seen a lot of life, both human and vampire. He smelled about the same age as Charles, though.

Rhett was slightly younger than Dalroy, and I knew by the scent that Dalroy had made him. There was enough of a difference in their ages, though, that I knew Dalroy hadn't broken any rules to make his vampire child.

We pulled up to the safe house after half an hour of driving, and Rhett and Dalroy carried my things inside. Rhett offered to go out and buy clothing for me so I handed over a list. "Are you sure this isn't going to embarrass you?" I asked. There were bras and underwear on the list.

"I'll be okay," he grinned and took off. He'd been gone an hour and a half when my phone rang.

"Lissa, this is Tony," he said. At first, I thought it might be Gavin calling but the number was unfamiliar and the ID was blocked.

"Tony, how are you?" I asked brightly. It was nice to hear his voice.

"I'm fine. Actually, I'm on a plane headed your way," he said. "We'll be landing in about half an hour. Is there someplace I can meet with you?"

"Tony, why are you using your cell phone when the common herd gets slapped on the head if we even look at our cell phones on a commercial flight?"

That made him laugh. "I'm special," he replied.

"Honey, we all think we're special. That doesn't mean we get to use our phones on airplanes." I know, I was teasing him and I was smiling while I did it.

"Stop beating around the bush and tell me where I can find you."

"There's a Barnes and Noble on Rock Road," I said. I'd scoped it out on my computer the night before. One of the books I bought in Overland Park was the first in a series and now I wanted the others.

"That's good enough," he said. "Don't keep me waiting." He hung up.

"Who was that?" Dalroy asked.

"Dalroy, it's better if you don't know," I said. "I need to meet this guy alone. He doesn't need to see me with you or Rhett. I'm just trying to get Winkler and the Grand Master out of this the best way I can. If you have to report this to Wlodek, go ahead. He may lift my head from my shoulders as a result, but this is what I know to do."

"You don't know much about how the Council looks at the American vamps, do you?" Dalroy asked softly. "We're upstarts to them. None of us old enough to know anything. I'm surprised they thought to contact Rhett and me, instead of flying their own bunch in here. If you don't have a foreign accent, you're too young to have any sense at all. There's not a single American on the Council and no American Enforcers."

"Yeah, I get that too," I grumbled. That's exactly how Gavin treated me most of the time.

"So, how long have you been vampire?" he asked.

"Just over a year," I said.

"And they're sending you out to do this?" Dalroy didn't know what to think.

"I'm a mister," I said. "And I can mindspeak." That caught Dalroy's attention.

"That how you got out of the hotel without anybody seeing you?" There was a light in his eyes.

"Yeah. That's how I got out." Rhett walked in carrying bags of clothing. I could have kissed him. I took the fastest shower I could, dressed in jeans that had been pre-washed while I silently thanked Rhett, a top that wasn't too bad, my athletic shoes (I hadn't asked him to buy shoes), and borrowed the keys to the Cadillac. Dalroy said they'd see about getting a second car when I walked out the door.

The Barnes and Noble wasn't far from the safe house and I was only ten minutes late to meet Tony. He was sitting in the café, having a latte and flipping through a magazine.

"Lissa," his eyes and his kiss were both warm when he stood and greeted me. We sat down. "Winkler's lawyers are as busy as ants, right now," he said, first thing. "I spoke with Winkler this afternoon and the FBI is talking to the local authorities. We know neither he nor the other man are involved in this. We have camera footage, showing who actually did commit the murders. What we're trying to figure out now is how they got the fingerprints all over the guns."

"They used more than one? Why?" I couldn't believe this.

"No idea; both employees were killed in the same room. But one set of fingerprints was on each weapon—one belonging to the Harper man, the other to you."

"Tony, I didn't kill those people."

"I know you didn't." He reached over and took my hand in his. "Unfortunately, the local authorities ran both sets of fingerprints through the nationwide databases. They got a hit on yours. Care to tell me how you're here instead of in Oklahoma City where they reported you missing over a year ago? Also how you manage to look like you do now instead of like the photographs I was given?"

He took his hand away and drew a copy of the photo they'd used for my ID badge at the courthouse from his jacket pocket. That's where they'd gotten my fingerprint records, too; the courthouse fingerprinted all the employees and the records were kept in a database by the Sheriff's department. *Fuck.*

My skin was quivering so badly, I didn't know what to do. I twisted my fingers together to keep Tony from seeing how much they were shaking. "Tony, all I'm asking is for you to get Winkler and Weldon out of this mess," I begged. "And then let me walk away from you tomorrow morning, right at daybreak. I promise you won't have to worry about me past that."

My eyes met his and I was pleading silently with him to do this. I could have placed compulsion, but without a doubt, there was back-up for Tony somewhere. In fact, there was probably a crowd of people there at the bookstore, waiting for big, bad Lissa to do something untoward and they'd come blasting their way in, guns blazing.

"And what will happen if you walk away from me at daybreak?" Tony asked softly, his eyes searching my face for information I couldn't give.

"Why don't you try it and see?" I asked, hugging myself and hunching my shoulders in fear. I kept telling myself that walking into the sun was the best thing, now. Doubtless, this was what Kelvin and whoever he was in league with were planning all along. Expose Lissa and Weldon.

The only thing that we had in common was the successful defense against Lester Briggs, Bart Orford and their horde of henchwolves. Most likely, Tate Briggs and Kelvin Morgan, if that was his real name, had somehow planned this together. Too bad Tate had gotten his in London.

I wondered if Kelvin would have included Winkler in his plot for revenge if he'd known that Winkler executed Tate. Plus, with the information he had, Tony could now uncover the vampires and the werewolves with very little effort.

If Kelvin had been anywhere around at the moment, I would have killed him right in front of Tony and then allowed him to arrest me and haul me in. If they tried to move me anywhere in daylight, they wouldn't have anything except ash to show for their efforts.

Tony wasn't saying anything; he just kept staring at me, his fingers still on the photograph of me at my frumpiest best—overweight and graying slightly. "How many people are here in the store with you, Tony?" I asked. "How many have guns, ready to shoot me if I make a wrong move?"

"You told me to contact you at night for a reason, didn't you?" Tony's face was showing disbelief. "You always worked nights and slept days before, didn't you?" *Christ.* He was putting it together, right in front of my eyes. "And now," he went on, "you want me to let you walk into sunlight. What will happen, Lissa? Why won't I have to worry about you after that?" His gray-blue eyes held a hint of steel as he questioned me.

"You'll just have to trust me, won't you?" I mumbled, dropping my eyes. "What are you going to do about Winkler and Weldon? Anything?"

"Winkler is very important to us. You know why—you suggested he come to me in the first place," Tony said. "He's the one who can upgrade the software. He knows all about it, Lissa. The man is a genius. We have the footage of the shooter; he looks young, about five-ten or so, dark hair."

"If it's who I think it is, he's been going by the name of Kelvin Morgan, but I don't think that's his real name." I turned my head; I didn't want to look at this man any longer. He was trying to trap me.

Sure, I could tell him everything, and the vampires would find me afterward. They wouldn't hold back from killing me a second time if I exposed the race. Better to walk into the sun. That would be my decision.

"If I hazarded a guess at what you are, Lissa, what would happen?"

Still not looking at him, I mumbled, "I'd be dead. Very, very dead."

Tony's cell phone buzzed; he had it on vibrate but I heard it clearly. He looked at the ID and answered. "Yes?" he said.

"We have the shooter," the voice on the other end replied.

"Good. Where did you find him?"

"One of the detainee's friends tracked him down and handed him over. Some guy named Davis Stone."

If I could have, I'd have given Davis a huge kiss. As it was, I wasn't likely to see him again.

"Where?" Tony asked. A location in Overland Park was given. I had no idea where that was. "We'll be there in a few," Tony said and ended the call. "Well, Lissa, I'd like to bring you with me for this. Am I going to have to handcuff you to do it?"

"No." My voice was sullen. Tony took my arm and led me out of the store. Three men detached themselves from whatever it was they were doing and followed us out. I kid you not; two of them wore sunglasses.

A van waited outside and I was loaded into the back seat. One of the three men scooted in beside me. I sniffed him; he was human enough, as were the others. He also wore a gun in a shoulder holster—he'd opened his suit coat and pulled it back so I could see the weapon.

I wondered what he'd do if I told him I'd been shot in the back three times and lived over it, even after Gavin had dug around to get the bullets out without the benefit of anesthetic. Now I wondered if anesthesia would even have an effect on me. Alcohol didn't unless it was mixed with blood or my donor happened to be drunk.

We drove along for fifteen minutes before pulling into an underground garage beneath a red brick building. The agent or whatever he was that sat beside me opened the door and motioned for me to get out. Did he think I was going to jump him? So far, he hadn't done anything to warrant that.

Tony was already walking swiftly toward the bank of elevators located in a corner of the well-lit parking garage. Two other vehicles were parked there—another van and a dark sedan.

The whole place was low ceilinged and claustrophobically concrete, interrupted by rows of thick columns holding everything up. There were no signs anywhere to tell me where I was and our footsteps echoed as we followed Tony toward the elevators. An elevator answered Tony's call after he inserted an ID card in a slot and we all loaded in. The doors closed, Tony hit the button for the third floor and up we went.

A long, carpeted hallway stretched out before us as Tony led the way again. One agent was behind him, two others were behind me. If they left me inside a room, I wondered if I'd have enough time to turn to mist before they saw it on a monitor somewhere.

Tony pulled the card out of his pocket again, swiped it through a reader outside a door and we followed him inside an interrogation room.

Kelvin sat at a wide table, handcuffs on his wrists, his expression sullen and angry. Two other agents were already in the room, sitting at the table opposite the prisoner.

Kelvin was staring at the tabletop, but the moment he got a whiff of my scent, he drew in a huge breath and stiffened, his dark eyes wide as he lifted them to stare at me. I almost growled at him but held myself in check. No need to show everybody there just what it was I was trying so hard to hide.

"You're afraid of her," Tony said softly to Kelvin, looking from him to me.

"Hmmph," Kelvin lied.

"He's lying," one of the two men at the table looked up at me. I got a good whiff of that agent and the one who was sitting next to him.

"As are you," I said.

"You three, out." Tony gestured to the three who'd been at the bookstore. They left immediately. After the door closed behind them, Tony turned to me. "What do you know?" he said softly.

"You think I'd tell you anything?" I scoffed. "How many cameras do you have in this room, Tony?"

"There aren't any in this room," the agent I'd accused of lying said.

"Yeah, like I'd believe that," I grumbled.

"We're part of the FBI—special agents," the other one said. Well, that was a new one on me. "We know of Weldon Harper," that one continued. "And we're now trying to uncover what this one knows." He jerked his head toward Kelvin. "Our division is cooperating with Hancock's here to try and keep everything stable. We don't need the population turning on itself in fear, now do we?" He gave me a grin. For a werewolf, he had a nice smile. I wondered what his wolf looked like.

"Are you crazy?" I stared at Tony. The werewolf's partner was a vampire. FBI special agents? Puhleeze.

"They say they can tell by the scent," Tony said. "They knew right away that a werewolf pulled the trigger and it wasn't anybody that had been in those two hotel rooms where Winkler and Harper were staying. This one's room had the stink all over it, though." Tony grinned at me.

"Boss," the vampire said to Tony, "I probably shouldn't be telling you this, but I'm sure you've already figured out that our little girl there is a vampire. What you don't know, however, is how rare the female vampires are. There may be a handful, if that, in existence. This one I haven't heard of, so she's new."

"Little more than a year," Tony nodded. At that point, I sure as hell hoped there weren't any cameras or bugs in the room. These guys were spilling secrets left and right.

"What have you got so far?" Tony asked, nodding toward Kelvin, who was sweating.

"A list of names," vampire agent said.

"And a promise to be a good boy and never do this again," werewolf agent added.

I was growling by that time. "How are you connected to Tate Briggs?" I said to Kelvin, looking him right in the eye and putting the strongest compulsion I had into my voice.

Kelvin whimpered and nearly collapsed on himself. "I can't tell you," he sniffed. That spelled out one thing to me—another vampire had placed compulsion and he was a stronger vampire. An *older* vampire. I looked over at vampire agent, who looked up at me. "You try," I said. I'd scented him; he was nearly as old as Charles.

"Tell us your connection to Tate Briggs," vampire agent tried his compulsion, only he met with the same results.

"What does that mean?" Tony looked from me to the vampire agent.

"It means an older, stronger vampire placed compulsion for him not to tell," vampire agent sighed.

"Do you remember that?" I asked Kelvin. "Do you remember having someone place compulsion on you?"

Kelvin growled softly. "He said you'd ask. He told me to tell you if you asked that Saxom may be dead but his children are alive and well." After that statement, Kelvin passed out, banging his head on the table as he folded up like a bad hand of cards.

Well, his words didn't mean anything to me and the vampire agent was also shaking his head—he didn't know either.

"Do you have a trace on my cell phone?" I asked, studying Tony's face.

"Not yet," Tony replied enigmatically. Likely, he just hadn't had time to order somebody to do it.

"I don't know whether to trust you or not," I said.

"Use mine, then, it's untraceable," Tony handed his cell over to me. I had no idea if Merrill would answer or not. He certainly wouldn't recognize the number. I still stared at Tony, unsure about all of it.

"It's as he says," vampire agent told me.

"Yeah. Like I trust you, too," I grumbled. I tapped Tony's cell and dialed Merrill's number from memory. Things like that came so easily to me now.

"Hello?" Merrill wasn't sure about the call either.

"Um, hi. This is Lissa."

"Lissa, where have you been? The two who came to get you are nearly frantic."

"Um, can't discuss that, right now," I said. "I have a question and it may be an important one," I added. "Do you know who Saxom was?"

The silence was so long on the other end I was afraid the call had dropped. Finally, after what seemed a very long time, Merrill sighed. "Yes. I know who Saxom was. I assume you cannot mention names at the moment or tell me where you are?"

"No," I said. "But the one who actually killed those employees at the hotel says that a vampire placed compulsion on him and told him that if anybody asked about it, to say that Saxom may be dead but his children are alive and well."

More silence. "This is the worst of news," Merrill said eventually. "Are you safe for the moment?"

"I suppose," I said. "As safe as I can be anywhere, I guess. Tell the two that I'll try to get with them soon."

"I'll pass that on. Lissa, your fiancé is about to have a fit."

"Well, tell him to join the club."

"I will not attempt to contact you," Merrill went on. "I will wait to hear from you, instead."

"I hope you do," I told him and hung up.

Handing the cell back to Tony, I said, "He wasn't happy with that news and knew better than to say anything. Besides, these two could probably hear both sides of the conversation." I nodded to the vamp and werewolf agents.

"You guys can do that?" Tony looked at the special agents. The werewolf just shrugged.

Kelvin was struggling to wake again. "What happened?" he asked, sitting up.

"You fainted," werewolf agent snorted.

I was narrowing my eyes at Kelvin. "What kind of idiot would murder two people and not check for security cameras?" I asked. "Was Tate the one who approached the vampire? Tell me." Compulsion was back in my voice.

Apparently, if you ask the right questions, you can get around many compulsions. Kelvin was instructed not to reveal his connections to Tate. This, though, he hadn't been instructed not to reveal. "Tate met him on campus, one night," Kelvin said. "The vampire knew what he was, of course. Tate's father had just been killed; it was listed in the newspapers as an auto accident with the body mangled beyond recognition so it was a closed casket. The vampire recognized Tate."

"More than likely went looking for him," I muttered. Kelvin stared up at me in shock.

"You think so?" he asked.

"Duh," I said. "Let me guess, the vampire told Tate that he knew Lester had gotten killed in a challenge. Isn't that right?"

"Well, yeah."

"And then he offered to help Tate get revenge."

"Yeah."

"By exposing the vampires because he had an ax to grind, too."

"Yeah." Kelvin couldn't believe I knew all this. Actually, any idiot would have known all that. He should have read some of those mysteries I'd loaned him instead of sending the pages off to be fingerprinted.

"Well, idiot boy," I said, "he intended to expose your race, too. Imagine what would happen if you were locked in a cell come the full moon?"

"Oh." *Now* Kelvin was getting the bigger picture.

"The campus you mentioned, is that here in Kansas?"

"No." We were back to sullen answers. I wondered how old Kelvin actually was, and had Winkler truly been fooled by all this? I couldn't imagine that he'd be that stupid.

"Then it's New Mexico," I said. "Tate was from Santa Fe, as nearly as I remember."

"You said Tate Briggs?" The werewolf asked as he pulled out his cell phone and hit a button. "Delgado, Renfro here," he said. "I need any records pulled up on Tate Briggs, a student at any college in New Mexico." He waited; apparently, somebody was checking.

"Albuquerque State University," I heard the voice on the other end of the call quite clearly. "Majoring in sports medicine."

"Check for Kelvin Morgan," Renfro said. I knew the werewolf's last name, now.

"No Kelvin Morgan. There's a Kevin Miller, enrolled in the same program," the voice said.

"Is that your name? Kevin Miller?" I asked Kelvin. He blinked stupidly at me. He'd been told not to answer but I think I'd gotten answer enough.

"Any fingerprints on Kevin Miller?" Renfro passed the message along.

"Not required by the school," the voice said. Renfro had called him Delgado. I wondered if he were furred or fanged.

"Where are Winkler and Weldon now?" I asked Tony as Delgado was looking for other records on Kevin Miller.

"They're out of jail and the media are being told that they were arrested by mistake—that we are currently seeking the real suspect or suspects," he said.

"And just how do you intend to deal with that?" I flung a hand toward Kelvin/Kevin. It would be just as I'd said. When the full moon came, he'd turn. No way to prevent it that I knew of. Tony just shrugged. He had something planned, I just knew it, and there wasn't any way he'd be telling me.

"Am I under arrest?" I asked him instead.

"No."

"Can I walk out of here?"

"I was hoping you'd come out to dinner with me so we could talk." His gray eyes were begging me to say yes.

"You used to be one of my good memories, Tony Hancock," I said bluntly.

"And I'm not now?" He actually looked disappointed.

"Now you're just like all the other males I know." I stalked out of the room. He followed me for a bit and when the three who'd been in the bookstore tried to block my way, Tony told them to let me go.

Figuring that I'd be followed once I left the building, I caught scent of my tracker. He wasn't furred or fanged, so I started running, turning to mist as I ran. The poor schmuck lost me after three blocks. Tony still had my cell number, though, so I was going to have to fix that.

I came back to myself about two miles away and asked a nice young man outside a bar if I could borrow his cell phone. He was more than happy to, handing it over with a grin. I called Winkler.

"Where are you now?" he asked.

"Funny, that's what I was about to ask you," I said. "I need another cell phone. I don't need Tony tracing my number."

"We'll get you one tomorrow. Weldon is talking to the new Packmaster tomorrow evening and we're hopping the jet immediately after."

"We've got lots to talk about," I said.

"Same here," he said. "We're at the Marriott hotel. Weldon wanted to shake the dust of the Saint James off his feet; they offered us free rooms since we were wrongly accused, but we respectfully declined."

"I have to catch up with a couple of people to let them know I'm okay," I said. "I'll be there before the night is over."

"Good," Winkler sighed. I hung up, thanked the young man and then placed compulsion to forget about me.

Rhett and Dalroy were about to have a fit when I wandered into the safe house. "You probably need to get rid of the Cadillac," I said, first thing. "And rent something else, just in case."

"Already got something, it's in the garage," Dalroy told me with a grin. I'd misted inside the place; there are cracks just about everywhere. "Where's the Cadillac?"

"In the parking lot about two blocks from the Barnes and Noble on Rock Road," I said. "I didn't want to take any chances, and I still don't. They probably didn't connect me with the car but you never know."

"I'll go get it," Rhett offered. I handed the keys over to him; they'd been in my pocket the whole time.

"I need to get back with Weldon and Winkler, they're expecting me," I said. "I need to take the cooler with me, too."

"Take this one, it has a lock on it," Dalroy pulled a replacement out of a broom closet. A set of keys were taped to the top of it. Vampires were prepared, looked like. And, since there were two keys, Winkler and I could both have one.

"Where do you need to go? I'll drop you off," Dalroy offered.

"The Marriott."

"I know where that is." We loaded up the clothing that Rhett bought for me and I tried to pay him for it.

"Nope. The Council said they'd reimburse me." He was smiling. "It was worth it, even if we didn't get to see you for more than a little bit," he said. "Neither one of us have ever seen a female vampire before."

"Well, that's too bad," I said. "I hope I get to see you again."

They both gave me cell phone numbers and I gave out my e-mail address. "Don't be afraid to e-mail me," I said. "I like hearing from my friends."

We loaded up into the second Cadillac. Dalroy dropped Rhett off about a block away from the other car before making our way to the Marriott. I hugged Rhett, too, before he trotted off to collect the Cadillac. I leaned over and kissed Dalroy on the cheek before getting out in front of the Marriott, and told him thanks.

He helped me get the cooler out of the car; this one had wheels and a handle so I dragged it behind me as I walked into the hotel. Winkler had given me room numbers so I carried my bags of clothing, my purse, my laptop and dragged my cooler down to Winkler's suite and knocked on the door. Winkler looked through the peephole before letting me in. Yeah, I didn't blame him a bit.

"Come on, you'll miss it," he said, nearly dragging me inside his room and closing the door. Weldon was there, glued to the images displayed on Winkler's flat screen television.

There was the usual media circus surrounding a residential area, with cameras rolling, journalists talking and all of them being held back by the police. A reporter announced the breaking news with glee: the suspect in the Saint James hotel murders had barricaded himself inside a house and exchanged gunfire with the police. Things were now silent and the authorities were cautiously moving in.

"That didn't take long," I muttered.

"Davis said they picked him up earlier," Weldon muttered. Eventually, a body was hauled away from the house. I wondered if Kelvin/Kevin had died before or after he'd arrived in the first place.

"Were either of you aware that there are werewolf FBI agents?" I had my hands on my hips. Weldon had the good grace to look guilty.

"You did. I may smack you myself," I snapped.

My cell phone rang roughly an hour later. It was four in the morning and Winkler and Weldon had gone to bed. I always put my cell on vibrate during that time so they wouldn't be wakened. The call was from Tony.

I walked into the hall to take it. "What do you want?" I asked. Yeah, I was grumpy.

"Lissa, I still want to talk to you."

"Tell me why."

"What did you mean earlier when you said I was like all the other males, now?" Why was he worried over what I thought? He knew I was vampire. He really ought to let it go.

"Tony, every male I know is manipulative and controlling," I sighed as I explained. He waited patiently while I'd gone silent, wondering whether I should answer or not. "You joined their ranks tonight. Congratulations."

"Even Winkler?"

That deserved a snort. "Even Winkler," I said. I wasn't about to go into detail about that—how Winkler blackmailed me and the Council declared me rogue—all when I was newly made.

"Renfro said he heard the word fiancé over the phone."

"Yeah. How about that? Not that the huge diamond on my hand was a giveaway or anything," I grumped.

"Lissa, I don't know what to think about all this. Do you love this man? *Is* he a man?" That thought just hit him, I think.

"Not in the ordinary sense, no," I said. He knew what I meant.

"Is this someone I might meet, sometime?"

"No. Not if you want to stay in one piece," I said.

"Ah."

"Yeah."

"Lissa, we could make this work."

"No. Don't even go there."

"What if I need your help sometime?"

"You can try. I'll be honest with you; they keep me on a short leash because I'm young. My kind doesn't get to just run around and do as they please until after they're a certain age. That won't be for a while, yet. Feel free to e-mail me, though, if you have a problem."

He took my e-mail address. "You're dumping your phone, aren't you?" he asked. "What if I promise not to have it traced?"

"No deal."

"Is this just because you don't want me to know where to find you or because of your associates?" He was digging for information.

"The latter, I assure you. It's safer for both of us that way."

"They wouldn't harm you."

"Yes they would. Trust me on that," I said.

"The other agent tonight, Townsend?" Tony was giving me the vampire agent's name.

"Yeah?"

"He said to tell you he was the one who tipped off the Council about the rogue in Florida a few months back."

"Tell him thanks," I said.

"You know about that?"

"Tony, I killed the fucker." There was silence on the other end for a minute.

"You still there?" he asked finally.

"Yes."

"Lissa, why do I have the feeling that you took out the terrorists that attacked Winkler's house in Texas?"

"You'll have to stew over that one. I admit nothing."

"You did. I know you did."

"You'll never hear me admit it. If somebody ever comes and tells me you told them that, I will call you a liar."

"Lissa."

"Don't Lissa me, Tony. Even the little bit of information you have could get me killed. You don't have any idea what my life is like. None at all."

"What happened to the Tate kid?"

"Same thing that happened to the Miller kid."

"Did you have anything to do with that?"

"No."

"I still want to see you, Lissa. Townsend tried to tell me what a rarity you are. I can't believe that. Is it true?"

"As true as anything can ever be," I told him. "Stop talking and go to bed, Tony. You have to be tired."

"I'd feel better if you were here with me."

"Yeah. I get that a lot," I said. "What would you do with me, Tony? How would you feed me? Deal with my sleeping habits? Keep me safe when I do sleep? How?"

"Townsend says there are ways."

"Yeah. Forget about that, Tony. My fiancé doesn't take kindly to advances by others."

"How did you get engaged to him in the first place? I get the idea that this isn't a love match."

"Tony, stop digging. We get along okay. Forget it, all right?"

"Lissa, I had more fun with you on three dates than I've ever had with anyone before, and we didn't even sleep together."

"And that's for the best, I assure you," I said. "There can't ever be a you and me, Tony. Not ever."

"I'm not going to trace your phones. Not officially. But that doesn't mean I might not call you now and then."

"Then try not to call when my fiancé is around. That could get me pounded."

"Now I'm worried about you."

"Don't be. I'm a lot tougher than I look. And tell those schmucks who were with you tonight to stop wearing sunglasses inside a bookstore, for cripe's sake. That's not a giveaway or anything."

"More than likely, they were blinded by the printed word. I don't think they read at all."

"Go out and hire somebody who reads, then. Are you the boss or not?"

"Lissa, you should know those aren't the questions we ask in interviews."

"Yeah? I can hear it now. When's the last time you maimed somebody? Yesterday? Good. How about breaking bones? What's the best way to crack a skull or bust a kneecap? The one who revealed his shoulder holster tonight? That was just showing off."

Tony laughed. "I haven't asked those questions yet but I'll consider it next time."

"See that you do. Otherwise you may get an inferior kneecap buster."

"You still like me, admit it," Tony teased.

"Tony, part of me will always like you. I'll always have fond memories of those three dates. You made me laugh when I desperately needed to laugh. That's why I sent Winkler to you in the first place. I thought you'd be the one to take his software and treat him fairly over it. I thought you were a good guy. Don't make me revise that opinion."

"I'll work hard to keep that good opinion you have of me. I won't have your phones traced for the department. But, like I said, that won't prevent me from trying to call you from time to time. You could call me, too, baby. And not just when you need help."

"Tony, no offense, but I hope I don't need your help again. Ever."

"Now, is that any way to be?"

"You weren't the one who had the gun in your face when the police came to make arrests."

"Someday, you're going to have to tell me how you got out of that."

"Fat chance. Go to bed, Tony. If you're lucky, you might still get a couple hours sleep."

"What if I have cracker crumbs in my bed?"

"Then you deserve to wake up with salty crumbs stuck to your skin," I huffed. "Didn't anybody teach you not to do that?"

"No, I was raised by wolves," he said. That hit me like a slap in the face. Why hadn't I thought of that before? Why? Werewolves had human mates at times and they produced human children. That didn't keep those human children from knowing what their werewolf parent was.

"You could have saved me a lot of worry if you'd mentioned that early on," I muttered.

"See, Lissa, we're not so far-fetched," he said. "That's how I knew about all those things. That's how I convinced the FBI to create an entire department for those races. We need them, Lissa. They can do things the other guys can't."

"That still doesn't mean we could have anything close to a relationship. I wish I could explain all this to you, but I can't. Suffice it to say I have a fiancé, and he's not going to let me go. That's that. Good night, Tony."

"I really won't have your phone traced."

"I'll think about keeping it, then."

"Good," he sighed. "Should I say pleasant dreams?"

"You'd be wasting your breath," I said and hung up.

CHAPTER 11

The note I left for Winkler said not to bother with a new phone. He got me one anyway. "How was the sojourn in the pokey?" I asked, ruffling his hair after I woke. I handed over the second key to the cooler of blood as I sipped my dinner. I was heading into the bathroom to clean up when Winkler answered.

"It smelled awful," he said. "Too bad Kelvin's dead; I'd kill him all over again." That was all the local news was talking about—how the police had a standoff with the shooter and killed him.

"Kevin. Kevin Miller," I stuck my head out the bathroom door to remind him. "And this isn't over yet, I don't think." I wanted to call Merrill—ask him who Saxom was and why his children were going to be a problem. Merrill was as unhappy with that information as I'd ever known him to be. "Did Weldon get a copy of the names that Tony got from the kid?"

"We got it but it's pretty much the same list that Davis and Glen put together." That statement had me marching right back out of the bathroom.

"William Wayne Winkler, do you mean to sit there and tell me you guys were already suspecting this idiot and you didn't think to mention it to me?" I shook my toothbrush at him.

"We didn't know what he was doing," Winkler tried to pull me into his arms. He was sitting on the end of his bed, a sad puppy look on his face. "We knew his credentials were bogus, but we were waiting to see what the reason was. Besides, you knew he was collecting fingerprints and you didn't tell us."

"If you'd let me know to begin with I would have, rather than waiting to see what the fuck his problem was." I tossed a hand in the air and headed back toward the bathroom.

"Lissa, baby, don't be upset." Winkler was in the bathroom right behind me and he managed to get his arms around me and kiss me on the shoulder before I could get away.

"Winkler, go put two socks on that match," I pointed to his feet. The white tile in the bathroom floor played up the one navy blue sock and one black sock.

"Well, will you look at that," Winkler grinned at me.

"Out," I pointed toward the door. "I have to clean up." He went reluctantly.

⇜ ⇝

The confirmation later was uneventful. Weldon interviewed most of the Wichita Pack and all of them expressed dissatisfaction with Bart Orford; he'd had a heavy hand and didn't like it if anyone expressed an opinion that disagreed with his. He'd killed two Seconds who challenged him because they didn't like his beliefs.

The new Packmaster seemed competent and he was nice on top of that. He had a human wife who really was excited to meet me. "I just never met somebody like you before," she gushed. "Don't worry; I know how to keep a secret."

I desperately hoped she could keep a secret, but I didn't tell her that. We just talked about this or that. She was the one who let it slip that werewolves were possessive in bed. Like I wanted to hear that. "They just wrap you up and if you move, they nip a little," she giggled. As information goes, that was something I could have done without.

Then, to make my evening complete, Gavin called. Of course, he was furious.

"Gavin, honey, please speak English," I said after a while. The English that came out of his mouth was still punctuated with cursing—in Italian, I think.

"Lissa, I truly want to take you over my knee," he shouted. I'd gone back into the hallway so Winkler couldn't hear but he may have heard some of Gavin's rant anyway, it was so loud. "Merrill said he gave you the message that I wanted to hear from you and what do you do? Of course you do not call!"

That was followed by another spate of Italian. No, I hadn't called him. I'd sent him e-mail with my new phone number and told him what happened. Of course, that wasn't enough. Merrill and Franklin had both gotten e-mails, as had Charles. *They* weren't complaining or cursing in foreign languages.

The diatribe went on for twenty minutes, at least. I wanted to hang up on him again but thought better of it. When he started cursing in French, I did the next best thing. "Of course, honey," I said when he took a breath. "You're right, sweetie-pants," I said the next time. "Absolutely, booby-kins," I agreed during the following minuscule pause.

"Lissa, what the hell are you saying?" That was after the booby-kins remark.

"I'd like to ask you the same thing," I said. "Except that you'd probably answer me in yet another foreign language. Do you know Swahili? Maybe Setswana? That's the language they speak in Botswana. At least that's what I hear."

"Lissa, why are you so far away from me right now?"

"I don't know, honey. Am I far away from you?"

"Yes. I am prevented from telling you where, but I am."

"Then be careful, all right?"

"I am always that," he sighed.

Oregon was beautiful. I only wished I could see it in daylight. Yes, I see very well at night but the moon doesn't sparkle on the water like the sun does and the sky looks a deep blue instead of the sunny blue I remembered.

It was raining when we landed, the water running across the tarmac as we taxied to a stop. The little rack squeaked a bit as I collected postcards at a twenty-four hour pharmacy in Portland while Winkler bought shaving cream and shampoo. Weldon was foraging through the snack aisle and loading up a hand basket.

I thought about calling Tony and asking him if he was still sleeping in cracker crumbs but thought better of it. He'd take it the wrong way and all I wanted was a non-judgmental friend with whom I could laugh.

Daryl, Weldon's son, was handling some of what Weldon would normally deal with while in North Dakota—disputes over running grounds and the like. Some of the larger cities had more than one Pack, Weldon informed me, and if your Pack was over forty members it was harder to control.

Weldon had been on the phone most of the night, helping his real Second with problems that had cropped up. I couldn't blame the Grand Master for having the munchies now; worry always did that to me when I'd been human.

The cashier didn't bat an eyelash when I handed over at least twenty postcards, all with scenes photographed in daylight. I couldn't take the photographs myself so this was the next best option.

We were spending the night in Portland, but the Pack Weldon was scheduled to visit was just outside Tillamook. We'd be driving there the following day with me in my body bag, of course. They were planning to start the drive in the afternoon. Winkler figured I'd wake somewhere along the way.

There was a guest laundry inside the hotel after our trip to the pharmacy, although it consisted of two coin washers and dryers. I gathered up all the laundry and headed down to the second floor of the hotel to put it in. The pharmacy carried laundry soap and dryer sheets, thank goodness.

The window inside the tiny laundry room allowed me to watch the rain pound the parking lot outside; Winkler's pilots had problems landing the jet at the airport earlier, because of the storm. The local news was all about the record snowstorm only two weeks before and now the rains that were currently hitting the Oregon coast. Several rivers were swollen and flood and landslide warnings had been issued. Of course, Tillamook was right in the middle of all *that*.

The laundry was all done and nicely folded, waiting to be packed into suitcases when Winkler got up and I slipped into his bed. Winkler appreciates clean clothes as well as anyone—he just doesn't like the process of getting them clean. He gave me a warm kiss when I crawled in bed to lie down, and he covered me up before I passed out with the sun's rising.

"They're evacuating parts of the area because of the flooding," the desk clerk informed Winkler later as he checked out. Weldon was outside, watching the bellman load up the luggage into the rented SUV, including Lissa's bag. Weldon just shook his head as the man tossed her bag right in on top of the other luggage.

"We may have to change hotels when we get there," Winkler grumbled, folding up the printed receipt the desk clerk had given him. "There's a lot of flooding in the area."

"No surprise," Weldon nodded, climbing in on the passenger side. Winkler was driving the first leg. "Is the rain supposed to let up at all?" Weldon leaned over so he could look out his window at the heavy gray clouds overhead.

"Doesn't look like it; the weather service says it may clear in a day or two."

"The run is going to be a wet one, then."

"Yeah."

The full moon would occur their second night in Tillamook, the dinner the third night and the confirmation would be held the fourth night. There was also a wedding scheduled and they'd waited until the Grand Master could perform the werewolf portion; a local clergyman had already done the normal ceremony. Weldon hoped the weather would clear up for that, at least.

"Hancock left a message—said he picked up Kelvin's female collaborator in Dallas for questioning," Winkler said. "Funny, don't you think, that he was working on parts of this from the opposite end?"

"I think he has information he's not handing over, that's what I think," Weldon grumped.

"Possible," Winkler agreed. He and Weldon drove through pouring rain in silence for a while afterward.

Rain was still coming down when Winkler's watch went off and he traded driving duty with Weldon, who would finish the drive into Tillamook. Winkler pulled Lissa's bag into the back seat and sat there with her, waiting for the sun to go down completely before getting her out.

※ ※

"Is it still raining?" I stretched and yawned in the back seat of the vehicle.

"At least you haven't been driving through it," Winkler grumbled at my side. He handed me a unit of blood so I nipped the top off and drank.

"Did Mr. Fuzzy get wet?" I gave him a smile.

"Mr. Fuzzy has been dry for a while." Winkler was still grumbling. Okay, he and I weren't talking about the same thing.

We were driving westward on the Wilson River Highway, and when we caught glimpses of the river, it was easy to see that it was overflowing its banks. Not a good sign by my way of thinking, and the werewolves would be running in the wet during full moon the following evening.

I'd never seen them go on a hunt in the rain. This was going to be interesting and possibly not in a good way. We arrived in Tillamook without incident (other than the pouring rain), and then headed north on the Oregon Coast Highway, where we ran into trouble. Not only was the road flooded at one point—we couldn't go any farther north—but there were two cars nearly covered in water ahead of us.

Three other cars were there; two of the drivers had already called the police but the water was rising too rapidly. The driver of one flooded car was already on top of his vehicle; the other driver was climbing out, a baby in her arms.

"Holy fuck," I muttered. "We have to do something."

Weldon was nodding and taking his shirt off when I grabbed his arm. "No, let me take care of this," I said. "You and Winkler be ready on the sidelines." My change to mist that night broke all records. Less than two minutes it took, even as the water rose faster.

The other spectators were screaming; they didn't have ropes or anything else to facilitate a rescue. Winkler was trying to keep them calmed down and prevent them from jumping into the water. Weldon was the one blocking me from their view so I could change.

I have no idea what those people were going through, other than feeling the stark terror of impending drowning when they all turned to mist after I touched them. I learned that I could carry multiple people that way, picking up the woman and her baby first and then heading toward the man who was just about to be swept off the roof of his car. They became solid again the moment they were dropped on the very edge of the water, where it was lapping the tires of Winkler's SUV. Now I had to turn back to myself and lay compulsion.

"The man saved the woman and her baby," I told the three watchers who nodded obediently. Then I went to the man and the woman and told them the same thing—that the man had leapt into the water and let the current carry him to the woman's car where he managed to rescue her and her baby. He'd gotten them to the edge of the water where Winkler and Weldon managed to pull them to safety. That was good enough.

The police had arrived by then and wrapped all three of them tightly in blankets before handing them over to a waiting ambulance. The hospital would check them over and make sure everything was all right. They also took witness statements. The compulsion worked without a hitch, with input from Winkler and Weldon, of course.

I was more than thankful that none of the witnesses had a recording of the event on their cell phones or anything, or taken pictures. That would have required even more compulsion, along with Winkler's skills to get rid of the evidence. My phone had a camera but I'd never learned to use it; Winkler was the gadget-oriented one.

We were forced to find another hotel since the highway leading to ours was flooded. It might not have been as nice as the one we'd originally reserved, but it was dry inside and away from the river, which was fine.

My fear, the entire time I'd been going after those people, was that the woman and her child would be swept away before I could get to them. The water was nearly to the woman's waist when I arrived, and I had no idea what would happen to my mist if I actually dived into water myself.

⁂

Winkler was waving a newspaper in my face when I woke the following evening; it held an account of the incident—modified of course—and everyone was calling the rescued man a hero. He was also interviewed by several nationwide television crews. *Fuck.*

I hoped the compulsion held since he was going to be recounting that story for a while, it seemed. Winkler and Weldon were mentioned as two travelers who'd happened by and helped pull victims the final feet to safety. Good. We didn't need Winkler's name in the news one week for getting arrested on a bogus murder charge and then called a hero the next for saving flood victims.

The rain was lighter at least when we headed toward the forested area where the local Pack was meeting to run. Both Winkler and Weldon were itching to get started; I could see that while we drove. I thought Winkler was going to start yipping and howling before we could park the SUV in a muddy field where several other vehicles were already sitting.

Most of the werewolves were already turned; they were only waiting for the Grand Master and his temporary Second. Clothes were flung aside and Weldon and Winkler both changed on the run. I gathered up the clothing, placed it on the hood of the truck and turned to mist as fast as I could, satisfied with the knowledge that the more I turned, the faster I was getting. It might become something of a weapon after all.

I misted over the Pack as they ran. The wolves scared up two deer and gave chase. Nothing on four legs gets away from werewolves, I discovered. They ran those deer into exhaustion before they felled them and all twenty-six werewolves fed. I held back from that, watching from a distance in case Weldon or Winkler needed me. They went hunting again, bringing down one more deer before the wee hours.

Weldon, Winkler and the others wandered back to their vehicles afterward and I waited while they dressed. What surprised me, however, was the female who followed Winkler.

"Here, drive her car back," Winkler plucked the woman's car keys from her hand and tossed them to me. Okay, at least this wasn't a bar. That didn't keep her from being a floozie in my eyes. Yeah, I shouldn't be judgmental, I know. Maybe this was the *One*. How was I to know?

Also, I should know better than to feel jealous. That didn't keep me from feeling a slight twinge, anyway. Winkler wasn't for me. Wasn't ever meant to be. I knew that. That didn't keep me from feeling like crap as I drove her little import to the hotel, trailing behind Winkler and the Grand Master.

The connecting door was closed between the rooms afterward, but Weldon and I were chased out of his room because we could hear every bit of what was going on. Winkler's guest wasn't quiet, let me tell you. Weldon got an early cup of coffee and we talked for about forty minutes before I had to go back upstairs to sleep—in Weldon's room, this time.

"So, what happened to Daryl's mother?" I asked.

"She moved on after Daryl was born," he said. "Female werewolves back then weren't obligated to give their mates two children. She married somebody from one of the Chicago area Packs. Daryl has two step-brothers."

"Has he met them?"

"Hell, I've met them," Weldon grumbled. "I'm the Grand Master, remember?"

"Yeah. So, did you change the rule or whatever about having two?"

"Yes I did, at one of the meetings. The females, if they go to a male, have to produce two children from that union before they can go to someone else. As you've likely noticed, most werewolf matches are arranged and love isn't involved all that much until those first two kids are produced."

"Yeah. I figured that out with Whitney and Daryl," I said. "I took three bullets over that one."

"And Daryl and Whitney are both grateful, as are their mates," Weldon nodded.

"So, what about you?" I asked. "Surely there's a female out there for you."

"I have one, only she's not Pack," he said. "She doesn't know what I am and is quite surprised that I care for her," Weldon went on. "She's in her early forties, still looks pretty good, isn't as thin as a stick, puts up with me in the sack and I love her as much as I can love anybody."

"Looks like you're happy with that," I said. "Does she live in Grand Forks, or something?"

"Just outside town. Owns a ranch there. We see each other two or three times a month if I'm lucky. She's busy, I'm busy. I'll be glad to get back, though."

"Yeah," I said. The trip was beginning to wear on me, too. "I have to go to bed soon and if I don't go now, I won't have time to get my bath or brush my teeth."

"At least you won't have to listen to Winkler having a good time," Weldon grumbled. His empty paper coffee cup was tossed into the trash and we went back upstairs.

There was still noise going on, making me wonder how long Winkler could go on before reaching exhaustion. Well, none of my business. I was clean and my teeth brushed when Weldon covered me up on one side of the bed. He crawled in on the other side and I briefly thought it awkward that I was to sleep with the Grand Master before my eyes shut with the dawn and it didn't matter anyway.

⁂

The woman was still there in Winkler's room when I rose, only she'd gone out to pick up some clothing from somewhere. "I'm Kellee, with two E's," she informed me perkily. Well, I was dumbfounded, with three D's. I shook her hand when she held it out, informing me she was there for the wedding, acting as bridesmaid to the bride. Whether I wanted to know or not, Kellee told me all about the dresses, flowers and every tiny detail of the wedding. I wanted to yawn in her face.

We went to dinner later with the new Packmaster and his Second, along with Kellee, of course. I was getting pretty good at gauging werewolf ages, too. Since I'd known Daryl and Winkler's ages, plus Whitney's, I knew Kellee was in her early twenties.

My mother would have described her as *not having a lick of sense*. She was giving Winkler an ego boost, though, making him out to be the big, tough werewolf and he was eating it up. More power to her, I guess.

I wondered why she hadn't been forced to mate or marry or whatever they called it, but learned that her father was a Packmaster and whatever his little girl wanted, she got. It looked like she wanted Winkler. She was also doing a lot of talking during the meal. I just sat on Weldon's other side so Kellee wouldn't get upset if Winkler was sitting between two females.

More noise came from Winkler's room that night. I don't know how Weldon managed to sleep during the whole thing—he must have been really tired. The wedding and confirmation took place the following evening and Kellee was turning and smiling at Winkler the whole time she stood up with her friend.

Weldon performed the ceremony, accepting the girl from her former Pack and turning her over to her new husband's Pack. I had to put all of it out of my mind and play nice with the two older werewolf women who sat beside me and asked personal questions. Eventually I told them I wasn't allowed to say how vampires had sex, just because I don't like answering those kinds of questions and the whole thing pissed me off.

Gavin called later, too, wanting to talk. I took my conversation outside Weldon's room so he wouldn't be disturbed. I also sent out e-mails to Merrill, Franklin and Charles and even checked in with Dalroy and Rhett, just to say hello.

"Is Kellee going to be traveling with us?" I asked Weldon the following night as I tossed clothing into my suitcase. We were driving back to Portland and would be flying to California the next day. I don't think Winkler and I had spoken two words to each other since Kellee had come along.

"She'll be with us for the rest of the trip," Weldon grumbled. He wasn't getting Winkler's attention, either.

"Maybe you should send him to Dallas and ask Davis to replace him," I said, zipping my bag.

"That's not a bad idea," Weldon considered the suggestion. "Davis certainly helped us out with the arrests and such. He got Winkler's attorneys out in force and sniffed out Kelvin so he could be picked up."

"Yeah." I'd called Davis to start with to get the ball rolling but I was used to not getting credit for anything.

Weldon presented the idea to Winkler later, and to say Winkler and Kellee didn't like the idea would have been an understatement. "I'll send for Glen; Kellee wants to see California and New Mexico," Winkler grumbled, pulling out his cell to make the call.

I wanted to mimic that statement behind his back but I didn't. I went to the roof of the hotel for the first time in a long time instead. Glen met up with us in San Francisco; Kellee and Winkler left the Grand Master with Glen and went shopping. If Winkler ended up with Kellee, Whitney was going to have a shopping buddy, at least.

Glen had caught the first flight out of Dallas and took over what Winkler had been doing up until that time. I made sure I got the key to my cooler back from Winkler and kept both of them.

Weldon had a dinner meeting with the San Francisco Packmaster while we were there. He wasn't new; he was a good friend of Weldon's and a big supporter. He was also one of the few gay Packmasters. There were other gays in the werewolf world, male and female I learned, but they seldom went after the Packmaster position.

Glen went with Weldon and that allowed me to explore San Francisco on my own. It felt like freedom to me as I wandered along Fisherman's Wharf, rode a cable car and generally had a good time. It was foggy, so I didn't get to see the Golden Gate or Alcatraz through the mist, which was a shame. I'd never been to the city before and might not get to come back for a while, if ever.

A man tried to pick me up while I sipped a glass of wine in a bar along the wharf. He wasn't going to give up easily, so an apology and a little compulsion turned his attention elsewhere. Tony called me while I was sitting there, finishing my wine. He'd tracked me on my new phone. Big surprise.

"So, how's San Francisco?" he asked.

"It's fine," I said. "Mostly foggy so I can't see the bridge, but it's nice otherwise. How did you know where I am?"

"Winkler's pilots have to file a flight plan," I could hear the grin in his voice. Yeah, the man knew too much for his own good and I told him that. He laughed.

"So, what's up?" I asked.

"I got some info on that Saxom guy." That made me stop for a minute. Merrill had evaded the question every time I asked and I discovered quickly that the topic wasn't up for discussion. Nobody wanted me to know.

I'd even asked Gavin about it. At first, he'd ignored my e-mail questions but finally told me that it was confidential information and he wasn't allowed to give it out. Yet here Tony was, calling with information. I wanted to hear this. "What did you find out?" I asked, my voice nearly breathless.

"He was a member of the Vampire Council who went bad," he said. "The information I got says the whole thing was hushed up, somehow. They didn't know about the children thing until that Kevin Miller kid spilled the beans."

"Just lovely," I said. "So they're hiding this. Why?"

"Don't know. Didn't get any information on what the guy did or anything that would cause the Council to declare him rogue. Or what happened to him. He's dead; at least that's what the kid said."

"Yeah. But if he was bad, how bad are his kids?" We were talking in generalities in case anyone was listening in. Another thought hit me. The vampire laws said you could turn up to ten, but if Saxom ignored that law like the two who'd turned me, how many could be out there now? They weren't registered with the Council; they'd have been aware of them if they were. "Did your source say how old he was?"

"Didn't get that info," Tony said. "They guard that closer than they guard the crown jewels."

I had a story about some of those crown jewels and I could never tell it. Too bad; Tony might find most of it amusing. "So, save the country and all that lately?" I asked instead.

"Every day," he teased.

"Man, you must be exhausted," I said. "What does your dry cleaner say when you take that super hero outfit in to get washed?"

"The last time they yelled because I got mustard on it," he replied.

"Yeah, save the world with one hand, eat a hotdog with the other," I teased.

"Exactly. We have to eat on the fly, you know."

"Very funny, mustard boy," I taunted.

"Damn, now my alter ego is out of the closet."

"I'm gonna post it on the internet," I said. "Along with one of those police artist sketches. That way they'll never be able to tell who it is."

"Hey, now, are you knocking police artists?"

"Yes."

"Just so I know where we stand."

"I'm standing in San Francisco. You're standing in your bedroom dressed in your mustard man costume that still has a stain on it that won't come out," I laughed.

"I wish I was there," he said.

"You know, I wish you were, too." I ended the call.

❦

Our caravan stopped next in San Jose and did a confirmation with no problems. That one wasn't one of Lester's screw-ups. Our next stop was Sacramento, where Thomas Williams Jr. was waiting to be confirmed. I wanted to meet him. I'd watched his father die, helping to protect the Grand Master when Lester Briggs and his cronies attempted their coup. I'd sent him a note about it and he'd replied. His name was also signed on the bottom of the certificate naming me *Pack*. He had other family and I wondered if I'd get to meet them.

Kellee and Winkler were the first ones to meet Thomas and his brother and sister at dinner, but Thomas gave them the barest of civilities and came straight to me. He even kissed my hand and no other Packmaster had done that, outside Martin Walters.

"I can't tell you how glad I am to meet you," I said, smiling at him. He was handsome—around six feet tall, as was his brother who was his twin. I wondered how often twin werewolves occurred but didn't ask.

His brother, born a few minutes after Thomas, was named Theodore but he went by Teddy. Their sister, Leigh, gave me a hug. I was happy to hug her back. Thomas Williams Sr. had died with honor and courage and I told them that.

Kellee had the oddest look on her face while I talked with the family of werewolves. Glen's eyebrows were raised as well. Leigh asked me what happened to my salad after I ate it and I told her. I'd only ordered the salad and a glass of wine. Somehow, the wine made it easier to get rid of everything later. Go figure.

"Of course you only should do something like that if you're what I am," I said. I didn't want to give anybody else ideas on what to do with their dinner and I certainly wasn't promoting eating disorders. Leigh laughed as I explained that.

Kellee, for some reason, rubbed against Winkler throughout the entire meal, feeding him bits of her dinner and that sort of thing. If she was jealous, she needn't be. I was getting over it. I'd even told Gavin the last time he'd called that Winkler had found himself a lady wolf and I'd used the term *lady* loosely. Gavin seemed quite happy about it. If he knew I'd talked to Tony, he'd probably go back to cursing in multiple languages.

Leigh asked about my ring, too. She'd been admiring it. "Is that an engagement ring?" she asked.

"Yes," I nodded.

"What's his name?"

"Gavin. And if you added up the ages of everybody at this table, you still wouldn't come close to hitting his numbers," I said. Winkler almost choked on that.

"What's that like?" Leigh was smiling.

"Uncomfortable at times," I admitted. "He speaks several languages and I can't understand him half the time."

I thought Kellee was going to have a fit when Leigh invited me to go out with her after dinner, "to have a drink or two," she'd said. Kellee wasn't invited to go along. I went after Weldon said he didn't need me; Glen was enough protection.

Honestly, Winkler would have been better off with Leigh than the airhead he was towing around but that wasn't my choice to make. Another werewolf joined us at the bar and I could tell Leigh liked him a lot. His name was Brady and he watched over Leigh while she had a couple of beers. Now *that* was love.

Leigh wanted to sing Karaoke when they got that started. That's how I was dragged up on stage, and Leigh and I did *Dancing Queen*. I hadn't sung anything since I'd been turned but it came back and I was able to hold my breaths better, for some reason.

Yeah, I used to sing once in a while. I sang at my mother's church growing up. I turned down a music scholarship when I graduated from high school so I could stay home and commute to school at OU. I took the art scholarship instead. Leigh and I got some applause when we finished.

"Do something else," Leigh begged, so I looked through the options and chose *Take a Bow*.

Leigh's brothers, Weldon, Glen, Winkler and Kellee all came in shortly after the song started. I ignored them and went on. Leigh was back when that one was done, asking me to do one for her father. I did *To Where You Are* for Thomas Williams Sr. If I'd had a piano there, I would have provided the music too, but the bar didn't have one. There was a standing ovation when I finished that song. I left the stage afterward.

"I wish I'd known you could do that," Winkler muttered in my ear.

"We don't always get to know everything, do we?" I said and walked out of the bar with Leigh and Brady.

They dropped me off at the hotel as I asked and I went walking after that. I even called Gavin. "Lissa?" he sounded so surprised. I suppose he should be.

"Hi, honey," I said. "I just wanted to see how you were."

"I am well," he replied. Yeah. I was homesick. I didn't think that was possible, but it was. And Winkler's defection for bubblehead hurt, too. I knew I should make the call short and sweet before I embarrassed myself. "I am home for the moment," he went on, "but they will most likely send me out again."

"Always a problem, huh?" I asked. "Honey, do they ever let you take a vacation?"

"I could request time," he said. "Would you like that cara?"

"Yeah. I think I would," I replied. "All this traveling is wearing me down, I think."

"When you return, we will plan something."

"That sounds good, honey. I should go. I love you."

"And I you, cara mia." I snapped the phone shut before I started blubbering like a fool.

※ ※

Thomas' confirmation went very well and Weldon handed over a framed certificate afterward, along with a photograph of his father's gravesite on his North Dakota property. The certificate was similar to mine only it denoted the service that Thomas Williams Sr. had rendered to the Grand Master and the werewolf race as a whole.

Thomas and his entire family hugged me before we left, including his mother, who apologized for crying. I told her that her tears were an honor and worthy of her husband. She hugged me again.

Kellee and Winkler had their first fight that night; I could hear it even though Weldon and I were two rooms away. Glen must have been going crazy since he was right next to them. The sex afterward was almost as noisy. I just shook my head. Weldon covered his head with a pillow and turned over in an agitated manner.

We stopped in Fresno briefly so Weldon could pass a second certificate off to Martin Walters. It was nice to see him again and he smiled and took my hand. His wife was there so a hug was probably out of the question. Too bad he couldn't receive mindspeech; I'd have told him he looked nice and asked about his two children.

Another stop in the Los Angeles area followed and it went without a hitch. We went on to Arizona after that and it was fine. Kellee and Winkler were still at it hot and heavy, either sex or fights. I wondered why they didn't just head on to Dallas. Weldon did his best to ignore them, most of the time. Glen rolled his eyes every chance he got when Winkler wasn't looking. I just kept my mouth shut. New Mexico was next and that was the one I was worried over.

CHAPTER 12

There were three confirmations in New Mexico: Albuquerque, Taos and Santa Fe. Lester's Pack was in Santa Fe and I had no idea who had taken it over. Weldon wasn't sharing that information, either.

Albuquerque was our first stop; we landed there and would take cars or SUVs to the other locations. At least my skin wasn't itching; that was a good sign as far as I was concerned. We arrived late enough that Weldon wouldn't be doing anything until the following evening. I knew the trip was wearing on me so it had to be wearing on him. I walked up beside him as we headed toward the two SUVs and slipped my arm through his.

"Are you holding up, Grand Master?"

Weldon stopped, pulled his arm away and placed it around my shoulders instead. "I've been better," he said. I knew then that he wasn't looking forward to dealing with New Mexico any more than I was.

"We'll get through this," I said and leaned my cheek against his shoulder.

"We will," he nodded and we walked on.

Kellee was already whining when we arrived at the hotel. Thankfully, she and Winkler drove their own SUV so Weldon, Glen and I were spared at least that much. The werewolves were all hungry too, so we dropped off our bags and trooped out to a restaurant to find something to eat.

It turned out to be a twenty-four hour diner that the truckers liked, just off I-40. Winkler growled at a trucker who leered at Kellee on the way in. Kellee was a werewolf; she could have put that poor man through one of the plate glass windows lining the restaurant. Kellee—all six feet of her—simpered for Winkler's benefit I'm sure.

Yes, she was pretty and she knew it, with long, straight, almost black hair. She had dark eyes, too, but she wore colored contacts, not because she needed them but to change the color of her eyes. I'd never seen a werewolf that needed glasses. Her eyes were a gray-blue with the contacts.

She could have been a model if she wanted but she'd gone into her father's business. He was an attorney in Boise and the Packmaster on top of that. Kellee hadn't gone to law school; she was a paralegal and happily told anybody and everybody. I'm sure daddy paid her well or still supported her; a pair of her least expensive shoes would feed a family of six for two weeks. I think Glen hated her already.

Winkler ordered two stacks of pancakes with extra bacon and sausage. Kellee only ordered two pancakes and two strips of bacon and then proceeded to eat off Winkler's plate. Weldon noticed and just shook his head. I'm sure he was with Glen all the way on this one. Everybody always said love was blind. They just didn't say anything about it being deaf and dumb, too.

Merrill inspected the Enforcers and Assassins that lined the wall of the warehouse. Wlodek had even considered coming for this but he'd been convinced to stay behind. "No sense losing both of us if that's what comes to pass," Merrill said and Wlodek eventually nodded his head in agreement.

The information was kept from most of the Council. Flavio knew and he was there now, the only Council member that had come.

Radomir had also come, as had Russell and Will. Robert and Albert, the mindspeakers were there, along with Henri, one of the misters.

Gavin would have come if Wlodek asked, but this involved Lissa and he didn't want Gavin anywhere close since Lissa might guess at his nearness. They didn't want her to know; they wanted her out of the way while they attempted to take care of the situation. All they needed was for Saxom's brood to get their hands on her.

Saxom was very old when he'd been killed. Adam Chessman, the former Chief of Enforcers had taken Saxom down before his own swift and subsequent disappearance. Saxom never registered any turns with the Council so these vampires could be many and quite old as well.

Dalroy and Rhett walked in while Merrill was turning these thoughts over in his mind. Merrill hadn't met them before so they introduced themselves. He'd had never had a problem with American vampires; in fact, all his living children were American. He nodded briefly at these two.

Dalroy's records indicated he was a Texas Ranger when he'd been turned; he'd been severely wounded in a battle on the Texas-Mexican border. Rhett was slightly younger, turned by Dalroy fifty years later after being shot outside a bar in New Mexico.

Originally, Rhett was from Philadelphia and a medical student at the time. His father, a physician, had given permission for his son to explore the Wild West before returning to school. His exploration had cost him his human life.

"Some of you know why we're here," Merrill said after they'd gathered together. "This is what you don't know."

❧ ❧

We had dinner with the new Packmaster and his wife the evening of February eleventh. It was a Thursday night and we weren't fighting weekend crowds but the restaurant was busy anyway. Kellee made sure she gushed and complimented the Packmaster's wife when we were introduced. Didn't matter to me; I didn't have history with this woman. She was embarrassed over it, I could tell.

When Kellee asked if she wanted to do something after dinner, the woman was too polite to say no. That meant that Kellee, Lewis and Marian Gilliam (Packmaster and wife) and Winkler all went to see a movie after they finished eating. I hoped they liked Kellee's kind of movies, because that's what they were surely going to get.

Glen growled as he watched Kellee and Winkler climb into the Packmaster's car. Lewis said he'd drop them off at the hotel afterward. Glen turned to me, then, and said something that I will always remember.

"Lissa," he said. "I had my doubts when Winkler brought a vampire into the house. I'm old school and remember when the vamps and the wolves used to tear each other apart. I have to tell you, though, that I would pay money to work alongside you any day rather than spend one day at extra pay with what Winkler's out with right now."

Glen always operated in Phil's shadow. When I'd been hired by Winkler, Phil was Winkler's Second and had turned on him the moment Winkler completed his security software. Someone had offered Phil a lot of money and the Dallas Pack.

After Phil's death, Glen slid farther into the background and Davis had taken over the Second's spot. I blinked up into Glen's dark blue eyes for a moment after he made his announcement.

"The feeling is mutual," I said, offering him my hand. He took it and shook firmly. Weldon witnessed the entire thing; he was smiling as we walked toward our SUV.

Lewis was a good pick for the Albuquerque Pack; the Packmembers respected him and the confirmation on Friday night went without any problems. We spent Saturday night in Albuquerque, so I located a laundry near the hotel and did laundry for everybody except Winkler and Kellee.

When she found that out on Sunday, she stewed about it all day until I woke Sunday evening on our way to Taos. I was riding in the

SUV with Weldon and Glen. Glen unzips my bag but he doesn't take me out of it like Winkler does. I think he was afraid of offending me. I was discovering that Glen was a gentleman. Kellee borrowed Winkler's cell phone and called me from the other car.

"Well, it was certainly *nice* of you to ask if we had any laundry that needed doing," she spat, right after I said hello. Yeah, I should have asked—that would have been polite—but miss lily-white could do her own laundry as far as I was concerned. I wasn't getting paid for this trip. Not that I knew of, anyway. I was Pack and had been requested by the Grand Master. The Council had agreed so here I was.

"Hello, Kellee, how are you?" I asked tiredly, instead of responding to her accusation. Glen was driving and he and Weldon were listening in on the conversation.

"All you had to do was ask. I have a bunch of things that need to be washed," Kellee was still spilling acid over the phone.

"Kellee, I didn't want to interrupt you and Winkler," I said, being as tactfully sarcastic as I could. Glen snickered.

"You could have phoned us, I'd have been glad to leave our things outside the door for you."

All right, that pissed me off. Really. Even Weldon drew in a breath at the insult. I was nothing more than hired help to Kellee and I'm sorry to say I let my temper run away with me.

"You know what, Kellee, if you'd get off your back once in a while, you could actually do some of these things for yourself. And if Winkler would stop thinking with his smaller brain for a few minutes, he could help. When are you going to tell him, Kellee? When are you going to tell him you're pregnant?"

The instant it left my mouth, I slapped a hand over it, but it was already too late; I'd spilled what I'd known for two days. My sensitive nose had told me and now Winkler was going to pay through his own nose, whether he married her or not. At least he'd get a child out of it. I hoped Kellee wouldn't teach it to hold his father and the rest of the world in contempt like she did.

Glen had swerved the car and Weldon had his eyes glued on me over the back of his seat at the news. No doubt Winkler had been listening in on the whole conversation, his hearing was still fine as far as I could tell. "You don't know that!" Kellee shouted over the phone. "How can you possibly know that? You're lying!"

"Nope, not lying," I said and terminated the call. Someday, maybe I'd learn to control myself—develop that stone face that every other vampire wore. *Someday.*

Weldon's phone rang in seconds—it was Winkler calling. He wanted to pull over at the next available spot. We were coming up on a truck stop so both vehicles whipped into the parking lot. Kellee was crying when she got out of the car, Winkler was cursing and there I was, the cause of it all. No, I didn't get Kellee pregnant but I'd certainly spilled the beans.

Weldon took charge of the situation, thank goodness. We trooped inside the truck stop after Weldon told Winkler to calm down and stop yelling. After finding an empty table in a corner, we sat down and ordered coffee.

"Now, Kellee, were you aware you were pregnant?" Weldon looked at her.

"I was only a few days late," she sniffed. She might get sympathy from Winkler and the others, but I wasn't going to offer any. Winkler had probably done the deed when he laid her the first time.

He wasn't even looking at me, which was fine, I guess. I hadn't been the one to tell him to screw her. I'd just driven her rental car to our hotel like an obedient little servant so he could take her with him in the SUV.

"Let's go buy a pregnancy test," Glen suggested. Weldon nodded. I had no idea what this meant in the werewolf world. Glen asked our waitress where the nearest pharmacy would be that stayed open late and she told us there was something in Española, only a few miles down the road. We paid for our coffee and left.

Winkler was fidgeting and growling whenever Weldon wasn't looking as we waited outside the pharmacy restroom. Kellee came out with the little plastic thing in her hand, and she was crying again. Winkler looked at it and said, "*Fuck.*" I kept my mouth shut this time and didn't point out that the word he'd just said was why he was in this fix to begin with.

"I'll contact her father tomorrow and make arrangements," Weldon said.

"Does this mean a shotgun wedding?" I asked Glen quietly a little later. Kellee was going up and down the brightly lit aisles of the pharmacy, buying an armload of tissues and other things. Winkler was frowning the entire time he followed her around and then paid for everything, of course.

"In a manner of speaking, yes," Glen whispered back. "If her father had anyone picked out for her, there's compensation to be made. And now, because of the law, we'll have to put up with her until she has the second one." Glen wasn't looking forward to that, I could tell. I just patted his back in sympathy and headed toward the car. I didn't get any more phone calls during the rest of the trip into Taos, which was fine with me. I felt bad enough as it was.

"How did you know?" Weldon asked me later while he was preparing for bed.

"The smell," I said. "I knew Kathy Jo was pregnant, too, when she got married."

"You knew that," Weldon was turning it over in his mind. "We can smell it after a while, but it takes a little longer than this." He raked fingers through his hair.

I didn't tell him about the other things my nose told me. That I could tell who somebody's parent or parents were, whether they were human, vampire or werewolf. That I could sniff out their age, too. I had Weldon pegged around eighty or ninety. No wonder he liked that forty year-old woman. She was more than likely half his age. More power to her, in my opinion. Where do people get off telling others that love is only for the young and pretty? Everybody needs it. *Everybody.*

Kellee had a conversation with her father, as had Weldon. Kellee's dad was probably hopping with glee when he found out who'd gotten his little girl pregnant. Her dad was an important man in Boise, but Winkler was important everywhere. Kellee was in a better mood when we went to dinner with the new Packmaster and his Second, that night. Winkler, on the other hand, hardly spoke at all. He came to find me later after Kellee was asleep.

"I shouldn't have let her call you," he said when we sat down in the hotel hallway outside Weldon's room with our backs to the wall. My knees were pulled up to my chest and I was leaning my chin on them.

"You'd have found out sooner or later," I said.

"Go ahead, call me an idiot," he sighed.

"No sense telling somebody something they already know," I muttered.

"Now we have to have two children, Lissa. I don't know if I can survive that. I was ready to send her home, she was getting so bitchy, and now this happens."

"Winkler, she would have been the last person I'd have picked for you," I said. "Leigh Williams would have been a great match for you. She was in love with somebody else but I get the idea that he's not the one she's going to get."

"Yeah. Maybe I fucked this up all the way around. If Kellee hadn't been there, well…" he didn't finish his sentence.

"Kellee is a bit on the imperious side, and it will only get worse, I can almost guarantee it. I hope you find some way to love her—something to love about her—because you're stuck now."

"I know. Lissa, in a perfect world, you and I," he left it hanging.

"We don't live in anything close to a perfect world, Winkler, remember?" I elbowed him in the ribs. "Gavin isn't going to let me get away. That's all there is to it." I straightened up, then, and fiddled with my engagement ring. It had probably cost a fortune; I couldn't find anything like it on the internet and the diamonds alone would be really expensive. I'd seen Kellee eyeing it on more than one occasion.

There were times, especially when Gavin started cursing over the phone, that I would have gladly handed it off to her and walked away if I could. I couldn't. The Council would just declare me rogue again, hunt me down again and this time I would die. No question about that.

We talked a while longer in the hallway before Winkler went back to Kellee. I was grateful I didn't have to see her sprawled all over his bed. I sighed, let myself into the Grand Master's room, picked up the novel I'd been reading (I can read just fine with little or no light at all) and resumed my guard duty.

᪥ ᪥

Taos went like clockwork. Kellee even got to go skiing with the Packmaster and his wife. Winkler went too, during the day of course. Weldon and Glen begged off. Glen was developing a sense of humor, too, teasing me while I drank my meal after waking. "Gotta get those corpuscles," he'd say. I just swatted at him, put the blood I couldn't finish back in the cooler and went to clean up.

Kellee still wasn't speaking to me, which was great as far as I was concerned. But if she caught Winkler looking anywhere near my direction, she made sure she got his attention, one way or the other.

We headed toward Santa Fe on Wednesday and my skin was already itching the minute they unzipped my bag on the way. What shocked me most, however, was what waited for me at the hotel. Merrill was there when we arrived.

He, Weldon and I went to the hotel restaurant where Merrill and I both ordered an obligatory meal. Merrill explained that he and the Council weren't taking any chances and that I would be left behind while Merrill performed vampire guard duty for the Grand Master during his stay in Santa Fe.

To me, that meant they might be expecting trouble. I didn't care that Merrill had come to protect the Grand Master through this one because it worried me, too. And Merrill could put up with Kellee's pettiness while he was at it.

Merrill had a room on another floor, but I was still keeping watch over the Grand Master at night for some reason. During the dinner and confirmation, Merrill would be there instead of me.

I leafed through pamphlets and tourist brochures while they went to dinner Thursday evening, wishing I had time to go out and visit some of the landmarks nearby. An old Adobe church had caught my eye, as had a few other things. Time had gotten away from me, too, and I realized (with a bit of shock) that it was February eighteenth, a month and a half after the anniversary of my turning and my husband Don's death.

I didn't know what to think at first, before going to my laptop and powering it up, thinking I might be able to order flowers and arrange to have them delivered to Don's grave. There is actually a service that will do just that for you. Go figure.

I ordered an arrangement, paid with my credit card and then answered e-mail. Franklin had sent something so I wrote a quick answer and sent it. Then I amused myself, watching television and reading until they all came back from dinner. Don't get me wrong, my skin still itched; I just didn't know what to do about it.

"Stay inside the hotel," Merrill told me as they prepared to leave for the confirmation the following evening. I nodded, even though there wasn't compulsion with that order. "You may not follow us," he added, compulsion heavy in his voice. I blinked at him. And then blinked again.

The compulsion slid right off my brain like a raindrop on a window. Merrill's compulsion was struggling to stay with me; it just couldn't, flying away from my mind like an exhaled breath. No way was I going to tell him about it. Not right then, anyway, since they were all loaded up and ready to go.

I just nodded like a good girl and waved as they took off. Was it because I was older, now, as a vampire? I had no idea why it hadn't worked and Merrill's compulsions were stronger than anyone else's I'd encountered, including Wlodek's commands.

Walking back to Weldon's hotel room, I pondered the situation, considering what it might mean and how it might affect my future. The whole thing was truly strange and I was about to call Gavin to ask him about it, but other things drew my attention first.

My cell phone was in my hand when the door to the hotel room was kicked in, causing me to leap to my feet immediately. I hadn't been paying attention; people had been walking up and down the hall all evening.

Three women stood in my doorway; two were werewolves, one was human. The human woman? I knew right away she was Tate's mother. One of the werewolves? Kelvin's mother. Well Kevin's mother, I should say. Tate's mother held a Taser. Did she think that was going to stop me? What the hell did they want, anyway?

"Look what we have here," Tate's mother gave me a nasty smile.

"Hello, ladies," I said, nodding at them. "What can I do for you?"

"You can't do anything for them," the vampire came up behind them; he'd been off to the side, hiding himself at first. "But you will come with me quietly. I have a use for you." He smiled.

The compulsion was dark and heavy in his voice and I almost laughed with relief when it slid away easier than Merrill's had. He was old; I could tell that right off. Older than Wlodek, actually, and he had a stink about him; something that I hadn't smelled from any other vampire. Nyles Abernathy had something similar when I'd scented him in Florida, but this was overwhelming. If evil had a smell, this guy had it bad.

"I don't think I'll go anywhere with you, but thanks for asking," I said, backing up. The women were advancing into the room, the vampire right behind them. The vampire drew in a breath when he discovered his compulsion didn't work. Now, I was either going to have to go out the window behind me or fight my way out. Concentrating on turning to mist while I considered this, I headed straight for the window.

It was a new record, I know; seconds it took me, not minutes, and instead of breaking through the window once my mist particles hit the glass, that portion of it turned to mist with me and solidified again once I was through it and on the other side. That was a shock, let me tell you, and I wasted precious seconds bringing myself back to reality while my would-be kidnappers shouted inside the hotel room.

Realizing quickly that this was only one arm of an attack on all of us, I zipped through the air, high over the lighted parking lot of our Santa Fe hotel. Winkler said the confirmation would be held at some Packmember's business, but what was it? I was racking my brain; it was still addled at the attempted attack.

I saw the vampire and the three women fly through the hotel door and rush toward a vehicle in the parking lot. Ten to one they'd be headed in the right direction as soon as they got the thing started. I decided to go along for the ride. Somewhere along the way, while I was flying over the top of their car, I gently lowered myself onto the top and rematerialized.

Hanging on with one hand, I pulled my cell phone out of my pocket with the other. I tried to get Merrill first but it went to his voice mail. Same with Winkler, Weldon and Glen. Fuck. *Fuck cubed.* I had a feeling Mr. Bad Vamp sitting in the passenger seat below was one of Saxom's get and still nobody had explained just who or what Saxom truly was. Now what was I supposed to do? I called Tony.

"Lissa?" He sounded as if he were doing something else while he talked to me on the phone.

"Hi, hon," I said. "I don't suppose you have any agents in the Santa Fe area armed with flamethrowers, do you?"

There was a moment of silence before he answered. "No flamethrowers, no," he said. "Do we need some?"

"You might unless you have some folks who can move mighty fast, armed with wood stakes," I said.

"Where?" he asked.

"That's what I don't know," I told him. "I'm on top of a car right now and they're headed in the right direction I'm sure, I just don't know what direction that is."

"I don't have time to get triangulation on your phone," he muttered.

"Wait," I said, "we're pulling into a parking lot. The sign says Galloway Recycling. Gotta go." I ended the call and turned to mist again. Mr. Vampire was sure to hear me once the road noise quieted.

I floated off the car—far above it, in fact. The vampire's scent offended my nose more as time went along. He and the three women parked the car and raced toward the building. The business was a single-story brick with high, narrow windows and looked a bit like a warehouse with plenty of fluorescent lights burning brightly inside.

The confirmation was probably in progress if it hadn't been interrupted already. What scared me as I floated closer (and would have made me shiver horribly if I'd been in a corporeal state), was the seventeen vampires and the twenty-six werewolves clustered against a brick wall adjacent to the front door.

They all looked ready for battle; most of the werewolves were naked and ready to turn. And their numbers were being increased by Mr. Vampy and his three bitch companions. What were they hoping to gain from all this?

I had no idea.

Merrill? I sent. *Merrill, if you can hear me, there are eighteen vampires, twenty-eight werewolves and one human outside, just waiting to come crashing in, I think.*

What was I supposed to do now? I'd tried to send Merrill mindspeech once before and he hadn't heard me then. He wasn't hearing me now, either. Would those people inside the building even have a chance when the army outside burst through the door?

I misted toward the front and peeked in through a high window. They were in there, all right and it looked like the ceremony was going on as it normally would. Merrill was standing off to the side, completely oblivious.

I misted to the opposite end of the building, watching as at least twenty people were sneaking along and crawling up a deep ravine on that side. They all were moving silently, rifles strapped to backs. If those were regular guns, good luck on getting those to work against the vamps.

I misted lower and discovered that a few among those crawling along, scattered here and there, were vampires and werewolves. Those guys might have a chance against what waited on the other side of the building. I smelled Townsend and Renfro among them and then, well, I smelled *Tony*.

He was here. Somehow, the information he'd gotten from Kevin or somebody had tipped him off, I guess. He was here, now, but I had no idea what his chances were against the ones on the other side of the building. I misted down beside him; he was crawling up the ravine, just like the rest of them.

Tony was dressed completely in dark clothing. A gun strapped to a wide belt was around his waist and a rifle was at his back with lots of bullet clips to go with it. What the hell had this guy done before he started doing what he was doing now? I had to admit to myself that my brain wasn't functioning at its best at the moment; it was mist particles, as it were.

Taking a huge chance, I solidified next to him. I had to put a hand over his mouth; he was so shocked at my sudden appearance he gasped. How was I going to tell him what was on the other side of the building? *Tony?* I sent. Hell, it was all I had.

Lissa? What the hell are you doing here, Lissa? What the hell are you, *Lissa?* His silent words were coming in loud and clear as he stared at me with those beautiful, gray-blue eyes.

Tony, there are eighteen vampires, twenty-eight werewolves and one human on the other side of this building, I replied, blinking at him as earnestly as I could. He flipped out some sort of communication device and sent something like a text message, I guess. All the other guys crawling in front of us whipped out their little communicators and got the message. *Holy crap.*

Lissa, you were supposed to stay at the hotel, Tony grumbled inside my head.

And I would have stayed there if it hadn't been for the visit from Mr. Vampy and his three bitches, I returned snippily. We were still crawling up the ravine as we mindspoke each other.

We need to get inside that door over there, Tony nodded toward a side door in the building—we'd gotten to the top of the ravine while having our mental conversation. *It's locked, though,* Tony went on, *and it'll make noise if we knock it down.* It would make noise, all right—the thing was made of steel.

I'll get it, I said and turned to mist right in front of his face. He looked quite shocked when I disappeared and flew over the heads of his advancing army to the space beneath the door.

I unlocked all three deadbolts, and hoping the door didn't creak when I opened it, cautiously cracked it open. It only creaked slightly, so I opened it as wide as it would go, finding a concrete block sitting next to the wall. Evidently, somebody else had used the cinderblock for that purpose before. I grabbed it to prop the door open. The army was nearly at the door, still crawling along. I ducked inside so they couldn't see and turned back to mist.

The minute the first of Tony's troops slipped through the side door, the rogue vampire/werewolf army crashed through the front. Chaos wasn't the term. Chaos to the tenth power might come close. People were screaming, growling, hissing and fighting.

I was still mist and having trouble sorting out who were the good guys and who were the bad guys for a bit until I finally relied on my nose. The bad vamps were my first targets, but I was shocked to see Radomir, Russell, Robert and Flavio, all fighting alongside Merrill. Dalroy, Rhett, and a couple of other vampires I didn't recognize were also fighting.

I knew they were good, plus they didn't have the taint like Mr. Vampy did. Weldon, Winkler and Glen were all fighting too, while Tony's troops were doing their best to shoot the bad wolves. Some of them were already inside the building during the confirmation, I think. They'd just waited for their cronies outside to come crashing in before attacking.

Claws were formed on my hands that materialized out of thin air, taking the head from Mr. Vampy, first thing. He was the one I wanted to die first, so I tracked him down. Then came Tate's mother, Kevin's mother and the female werewolf that had been with them.

They were quite surprised; there was definitely shock in their eyes when they saw claws form from nothing and take their heads. Swift. Clean. Too bad I didn't have time to question them, but they threatened too many others.

Winkler was fighting beside Glen and he was shouting at Glen to go back and protect Kellee, who was cowering in a corner. Glen didn't want to stop fighting but he did as he was told and went back to Kellee. I followed to see what I could do in that area, swiping off a couple of vamp heads while I was at it.

The shrieking started when some of the bad vamps and werewolves pulled out crossbows loaded with wooden arrows and started shooting. There were six bad vamps left, but I wasn't sure how many rogue werewolves remained. Most had turned to werewolf, but those from the inside were still in human form. Tony's men were having quite a bit of success in that area, at least. And Merrill? Wherever he was, it was like a tornado had been loosed in the place—he and Flavio both. Those older vamps had some moves, let me tell you.

Right about that time, I noticed we had a mister with us. The Council must have sent one of them; he was off to the side, rematerializing slowly so he could help out I'm sure. In slow motion, almost, I saw two of the remaining bad vamps take aim with crossbows loaded with wooden arrows—one at the mister, the other at Glen. I was between both of them at the moment and time stood still for me right then. I could save one but not the other.

Glen was too far away to do anything other than stand in front of Kellee, who was whimpering and cowering behind his back. The mister was solid enough to take a hit but not completely solidified. I had a choice to make and I prayed it was the right one; an arrow in Glen's torso might not have as devastating an effect as one to the mister.

Both bolts were shot at nearly the same moment, so I streamed toward the mister, my hands materializing out of thin air as I knocked the wooden shaft away. It had been aimed right at the center of the vampire's chest and would have killed him I think, if I hadn't deflected it. The one aimed at Glen? If I had known, my choice might have been different, I think.

What do you do in that small moment? When time stands still and you find yourself transfixed while the train wreck happens before your eyes and you're helpless to do anything other than cry out? That image plays in your mind at times, for the rest of your life. Glen took the arrow in his left eye and he was dead before he hit the floor.

That infuriated me past anything I had ever felt as a vampire. The mister was shocked, I'm sure, when I materialized fully in front of him in less than two seconds, wading into the fray and slashing heads off anything unfriendly.

I had the scent of Saxom's get in my nose that night, and anything that smelled like that died; they couldn't move fast enough. I'm sure I was shouting something as I killed, I just didn't know what it was. The rogue werewolves? Same thing. If I knew they were bad, they died.

When I finally ran out of something to kill, I think I knocked out the front of the building. It blasted out in front of me, I know that much, and I was still enraged. I stood on the empty sidewalk in front of Galloway Recycling, screaming my lungs out in fury. The owners might have some recycling of their own to do if I took down the entire building.

After my lengthy scream ended, I paused a moment just to catch my breath. That's when Merrill and Flavio came to stand nearby, one on either side of me.

"That was impressive," Flavio observed calmly. "But you disobeyed your sire. There will be consequences." As first words spoken after a battle go, those sucked.

"Lovely," I said, turning swiftly to go back inside the building, both vampires following behind. Merrill still hadn't said anything to me. Quite possibly, he was seething or something and didn't trust himself to say something until he had his temper under control. How did I know?

Winkler was already kneeling beside Glen and I went to join him. I wanted to hurl curses at Kellee, who was weeping fake tears against the far wall, but neither her tears nor my anger would bring Glen back. He and I had just started liking each other, teasing each other and having actual conversations.

"Glen, honey, I'm so sorry," I was crying, now that reality was setting in. "I had the choice to make and I made the wrong one. I went to protect the mister thinking you might have a better chance at surviving. I was wrong." I reached out and touched his hand; it was already going cold.

"Lissa, he can't hear you," Winkler said softly. I turned on him.

"How the fuck do you know?" I shouted, wiping tears away. "What the fuck do any of you know?" I stood up and turned to mist right there in front of everybody in the space of a blink. I heard some muttering around the wide warehouse, but I didn't care.

There were other dead scattered around the room, some of them werewolves. The vampires had already turned to ash. I saw Tony off to the side with his men; they were collecting their own dead into a corner. This had been a cooperative effort between the vampires, werewolves and Tony's department. They'd planned this and left me completely out of it.

If Mr. Vampy hadn't come to the hotel with his bitch contingent, I still might not have known. My skin would have continued to itch and I would have known after the fact, if at all. Yeah, I was young as a vampire but that didn't make me worthless or stupid. They were going to treat me that way, though. And Flavio said there would be consequences for disobeying my sire. Well, swell. I had to go back before they took it upon themselves to declare me rogue again.

Merrill was standing near Winkler and Weldon while bodies were carted away. I noticed that the trucks that had come were unmarked. That spelled Tony to me. Flavio and Radomir were also there and they were discussing something with the Grand Master. When I misted closer, I discovered they were talking about me.

"Where do you think she might go?" Flavio asked. "We have already checked the hotel. She isn't there."

"Like I had time to get there," I made myself solid. I wanted to say duh, but that probably wouldn't be a good idea. Flavio was on the Council, after all. Plus, Wlodek was his sire. That was trouble to the twelfth power.

"Lissa," Merrill gripped my arm, "you may not leave my sight unless I say so, do you hear me?" That compulsion sounded like the voice of God and it still slid right off my brain. I wasn't about to tell him that, though. Somehow, I got the feeling that if he knew and if Flavio knew right then, things might go very badly for me. I nodded instead. That information was about to stay with me. *Permanently.*

જી જી

I sat on the bed in what was once Glen's room, wondering if he had any family while I listened to the argument going on next door. Weldon was shouting at times and I sure hoped there wasn't anybody human within hearing distance. Merrill had left me in Glen's room, told me not to go anywhere and then went with Flavio to do verbal battle with Weldon and Winkler.

Weldon didn't mince words. "Do you know how many of those fuckers she took out?" I could see him in my mind, he gestured wildly when he was that angry; I'd seen it before.

"We are aware of what she did," Flavio calmly replied and there was knowledge of the good and the bad that I'd committed in his words. The bad being my disobedience, I suppose, and then allowing everybody to see me turn to mist. I'll bet there was a lot of compulsion surrounding that one.

"I still expect her to finish out the tour," Weldon snarled.

"Out of the question," Merrill said. "She will be returning with us immediately. We are assigning Dalroy and Rhett to you; they will protect you just as well."

Weldon wasn't convinced and said so, along with the fact that he trusted me and not some strange vampires foisted off on him.

"The Council is insisting," Flavio said. Yeah. He was on the Council so of course they were insisting. And, since he was Wlodek's vampire child, what Flavio knew, Wlodek would know. If he didn't already, he would very soon.

I had no idea where the other vampires went; I'd been hustled right out of the building by Merrill and Flavio and driven straight to the hotel. I might have wanted to talk to Tony but didn't have the chance and Merrill had taken my cell phone away. If the Council wanted, they wouldn't hold somebody back from killing me this time. Maybe it was for the best.

CHAPTER 13

All of Glen's things were neatly packed up in his suitcases by the time the argument was over and I'd tidied his room. My things were still in Weldon's room and I couldn't get to them while the conversation had taken place.

Merrill walked in, ordered me to go get all my things and stood against Weldon's wall while I did it. Flavio had left already; he might have been pissed but he wasn't showing it to the wolves. Oh, no. He wore the mask just as well as any of the rest of them.

When I had all my things packed up, including my laptop, Merrill pointed me in the direction of his room and I had to go. I figured the lecture was coming and I wasn't wrong. "Now, Lissa, you will explain to me why you left the hotel and how you found us." He was angry.

I had to tell him about the vampire and the three women who'd come for me, explaining that I'd managed to get away from them and then followed them out to the parking lot. I hadn't disobeyed Merrill's compulsion—I hadn't followed him and Weldon. I had followed Mr. Vampy and his companions instead, knowing they were most likely headed to the confirmation. I didn't know whether help or a warning was needed and I attempted to explain that to Merrill.

He listened, stone-faced, to my story. I was truthful when I told him that I had no idea the other vampires and the soldiers or whatever they were would be there, too. He nodded at that—nobody had told me anything.

He also asked if I'd been telling the truth about whether to protect Glen or the mister. I wiped away tears when I said yes. There was no comfort from Merrill and I didn't expect any. If Gavin was ordered to remove my head this time, I figured he'd just close his eyes and do it.

Vampires were a strange lot and I still didn't feel I belonged to their race. Truly, I had no idea what I was, not being human any longer and feeling like an outsider as a vampire. What I realized, however, was that I was now stuck in vampire limbo until the vampires who ruled the race decided my fate again. After all, Wlodek told me the first time that if I found myself before the Council a second time, it was likely the death penalty would be levied.

Dutifully I answered all of Merrill's questions, my head bowed as I pondered my fate. After going over my story multiple times, searching for cracks or discrepancies, Merrill fed me half a bag of blood shortly before dawn. I was thirsty and exhausted; I'd used up a lot of energy, after all. The rest of the bag was returned to the cooler and I covered myself up in one of two queen beds, turning my back on Merrill and falling asleep with the dawn.

We stopped in New York on our way home, but since we were in the Council's jet, I didn't get to see Merrill's apartment. Franklin had already left for London; Merrill told me that at least but little else. Flavio, Radomir and Russell were on the flight with us but the others had already gone on to other assignments or back to ones already started.

More than once, I wondered what the Council was going to do to me and got the shivers every single time. The trip to London was longer, of course, and we landed with little time to spare. I discovered I was to be kept in a building on the outskirts of London rather than going back to Merrill's manor. It was a larger cell than the first one I'd had but it was still a cell, holding only a small bed, a tiny table and nothing else.

The Council didn't see me for six days and Merrill didn't come to see me, either. Gavin might have dropped off the face of the earth for all I knew, or perhaps I wasn't allowed visitors. What I knew and they didn't, though, was that I could have turned to mist at any time and just slipped through a crack. I didn't.

Their compulsion didn't work when they told me to stay silent and not escape. I had no intention of breaking either of those commands. They'd kill me for sure and maybe that wasn't a bad thing. Too many things had happened to me during the past three months—some of them awful things.

Maybe this was karma for killing Lily. Even if she'd made the turn, I just couldn't let her live like that—a half-life, hidden and requiring blood to sustain herself. The Council wouldn't have let her live anyway; she was too young. Her death at my hands had been swift while she was between death and vampire. No, that didn't make me feel good about it. Not in any sense of the word.

Radomir came for me on the sixth night and we didn't talk as he placed the usual silver alloy chains on my wrists and asked me to walk before him out of the building. I was blindfolded when we reached the park I remembered from before and he led me for quite a while. I knew when we passed the two vampires at the entrance to the cave—Russell and Stephan, this time, I could tell by the scent. We didn't say anything to each other. I'd made a choice and now I was about to pay for it.

The blindfold was removed and I found myself facing Wlodek and the Council, just as before. Charles had a deep frown on his face as he tapped away on his computer. I scented the room and could have described everyone there, including Merrill and Gavin. They were both present.

Wlodek was toying with his gold pen. Perhaps that was his way of dealing with things that irked him. He pulled out the pen and twirled it or flipped it in his fingers. There certainly wasn't any expression on his face to give anything away. Charles didn't meet Wlodek's eyes when he nodded to him. Wlodek cleared his throat.

"Lissa Beth Huston, formerly known as Lissa Beth Workman, it has been reported to the Council that you disobeyed your sire. Is this true?"

"Of course it is," I said, handing him a level look. It was probably on the vampire version of Youtube or MySpace. Besides, how many witnesses were there? More than enough to convict me, that's for sure. I shivered.

"Explain, please." I did. I told him exactly what I'd told Merrill. My recall was almost perfect. It must have been a side effect of becoming vampire but Merrill and I had never covered that in our lessons. Those were likely over, now. I didn't expect to walk out of the Council chamber.

"So, you took it upon yourself to leave the hotel after you knew the ones who'd come to kidnap you were leaving?"

"Yes." He asked me to explain, so I did. He looked at his papers. He didn't ask me to explain how I'd gotten away from my attackers at the hotel or how I'd managed to kill at least ten of the bad vamps along with several werewolves. He did ask me about the incident where I'd saved the mister rather than the werewolf.

"And you considered this werewolf your friend?"

"Yes." I did, there at the last.

"Very well. The Council has already reached a decision in this case; we only wished to hear you answer the pertinent questions. It is all as reported previously." He touched the papers under his hands. Great. *They'd reached a decision.* "Lissa Beth Huston, punishment is always meted out when a child disobeys his sire," Wlodek went on. "In your case, we have unanimously decided to administer a beating. Twenty strokes. Sebastian." I went cold at Wlodek's words. *A beating.* Just the thought brought back horrible memories. No, those had to be pushed down. I couldn't show my fear. I couldn't. My skin was quivering so violently I wanted to curl into a ball.

That wasn't an option.

A vampire I didn't know came forward and stood before me, holding what looked to be a long nightstick in his hands. I had to clamp my fingers together; they were shaking so badly. Had to get through this. *Had to.* Was he going to hit me in the head? Had to squash that thought. "Remove your clothing," Sebastian ordered. *Oh, God.*

When I wasn't doing it fast enough to suit him, he ripped my clothes away instead with shortened claws that appeared on his fingers. I wanted to moan when he tore away my bra and underwear. I stood there before the Council and all the others inside the cave, shivering so hard they couldn't help but notice. I was completely naked and about to receive my beating.

The first stroke came so swiftly I almost didn't see it coming. Sebastian hit my shoulders. The club was some sort of hard rubber. If it had been steel, he would have broken bones on the first stroke. He was putting vampire strength into his blows anyway, which caused indescribable pain.

He broke my left wrist on the sixth blow. I whimpered and bent over, but tried my best to straighten up quickly. Three ribs went with another blow; the crack was audible as they snapped. I received a glancing blow to the head; he'd aimed for my shoulders again on the seventeenth stroke.

Someone off to the side counted the blows as the fell. Sebastian knocked me down completely on the eighteenth blow and then shouted for me to get up so the last two could be delivered.

I got up. It was slow but I got up, my chains rattling. They were still around my wrists and the manacle on the left was causing horrible pain. I took the nineteenth blow to the back, the twentieth, and I'm sure he did it on purpose, right to the head. Blessed darkness descended.

※ ※

"Sebastian, you were told not to hit her in the head." Wlodek growled. Sebastian the Assassin turned to face the Head of the Vampire Council.

"As you say, Honored One," he bowed slightly.

"I will consider your punishment now," Wlodek sighed, looking behind Sebastian at Lissa, who lay in a small heap on the cave floor. "Derlin, please come forward and check on the girl." He motioned the vampire forward. Derlin held several medical degrees and was attached to the Council as their official physician.

"Broken wrist," Derlin said, feeling his way over Lissa's body. "Cracked skull. Three broken ribs. Multiple contusions." He laid Lissa flat on her back on the floor and looked up at Wlodek.

"She must be more fragile than the males," Sebastian shrugged. "I've never beaten a female before." Gavin, off to the side, curled his fingers in to hide the claws that were threatening to grow.

"I believe I'll allow Gavin to deliver one blow, as punishment," Wlodek said, leaning back in his chair. Gavin came forward and took the baton from Sebastian, who stood at the ready in front of Wlodek. "Gavin," Wlodek nodded. Gavin delivered the blow, right to the back of Sebastian's neck, knocking him unconscious to the floor and cracking several vertebrae in the process. He tossed the baton onto Sebastian's back when he was finished and walked back to his spot.

"That was enlightening," Wlodek nodded. "Derlin, perhaps you should go with the girl and make sure the bones are in the proper position to heal while she sleeps. Is there any further business?" Nobody said anything. "Very well. The meeting is adjourned."

"You'll have to be careful; if she wakes while you're carrying her, the pain will be quite intense," Derlin gave Merrill and Gavin instruction. Merrill removed his coat and covered Lissa with it; Gavin lifted her in his arms. Lissa didn't show any signs of waking. None at all.

※ ※

"You let them beat her." It was a statement and not a question as Griffin looked at Merrill across Merrill's desk.

"What was I supposed to do?" Merrill rubbed his face and looked out the window at the darkness beyond. The view during daylight was quite spectacular but his night vision was nearly as good.

"I don't know. Argue harder?" Griffin wasn't happy and Merrill knew it. "And who let that thug beat her to begin with?"

"None of the others wanted the job."

"So, of course the one who wants it is going to do his worst," Griffin grumbled. "I've had enough of this place for a while. Try not to get her killed, all right?" Griffin vanished before Merrill's eyes.

※ ※

"Don't move her, the bones are set," Derlin warned Gavin as he watched the vampire physician closely. "Don't even sit on the bed; the ribs and the wrist are fragile right now and the slightest movement will cause them to come out of alignment." Dawn was close, so Derlin planned to stay for the day, as did Gavin, just to make sure Lissa didn't move before she went into the rejuvenating sleep. Derlin went to the bedroom Merrill had given him at the last possible moment. Gavin slept in Lissa's room on the sofa.

※ ※

There was still pain when I woke on Saturday, February twenty-seventh. I moaned as I moved. My entire body ached, but my wrist, ribs and head were the worst. "Don't move, cara, if it hurts I will bring the physician." Just the sound of his voice had me off the bed and crouching across the room, claws out. "Cara, it is only me," Gavin walked toward me. Well, he needed to stay away. Far, far away.

"Get the hell away from me," I threatened, my claws still out. My rush to get off the bed hadn't helped my aches any. Gavin stopped in his tracks a few feet away.

"What's going on?" Merrill and another vampire I didn't recognize rushed into the room. I knew the strange vampire's scent from the night before, however. He'd been there to witness the whole thing. He drew back swiftly when he saw my claws. "Lissa put those claws away!" Merrill ordered. Yeah. Right. They stayed out.

"Stay away from me. All of you," I hissed. Right then, they needed to get as far away from me as they could go. I wanted nothing to do with vampires. I hated vampires. I'd never wanted to be a vampire in the first place. Didn't want to be one now. Nothing but pain had come of it. I think I was shouting that at them before I realized what I was saying. "Get out!" I yelled as loudly as I could. "Get the fuck out!"

"Lissa! Stop that this instant!" Merrill's words held compulsion again and not a weak one, either. Would they beat me again or kill me if they found out compulsion no longer worked? I hung my head and wept while I retracted my claws.

"You will allow the physician to examine you," Merrill ordered. The strange vampire knelt next to me and ran his hands over my body, beginning with my skull and then going to my wrist and ribs. I was still naked and I didn't like his hands on me. I didn't want another vampire to touch me. Ever. I shuddered.

"The bones are healed; I expect that she still aches but that will go away with one or two more sleeps," he said and stood. I remained huddled on the floor. I wanted to tell him to fuck off. I wanted to tell Merrill to fuck off. And Gavin.

"Lissa, clean up, get dressed and eat, I want you in my study in an hour," Merrill said as he forced Gavin and the other vampire away from my room. I did all those things as ordered, crying most of the time before making my way to Merrill's study just under the wire. I had a pocket full of tissues with me, too. I couldn't stop the tears. I hadn't put any shoes on so my knees were up to my chest in my favorite chair.

Merrill had his back turned to me, staring out the window. At least my nose didn't run any more when I wept. Not worth becoming vampire over, I assure you. Merrill didn't turn around when he spoke.

"The Council has to maintain order, Lissa," he began. "They have to be fair in their dealings with all vampires. If a rule is broken then punishment is given. It's as simple as that."

Good for them. I'm sure they never made a mistake. I wanted to say it out loud, but I didn't. So far, too, I hadn't been on the receiving end of too much fairness, I don't think. From the idiots who'd turned me to Gavin hunting me down, preparing to eliminate me the moment the Council gave the word. And now this. No good deed truly goes unpunished.

"You should be thankful they didn't require your life," Merrill went on.

If they'd killed me, it would have been quicker and less painful and it would save me from listening to this crap now. I remained silent, wiping tears away with a tissue. Yeah. See if I ever put any effort into saving their worthless hides again.

They reminded me of a bunch of stuffed parrots. The kind you can pull the string on and get one of a handful of pre-recorded words and sayings. Had I cared for Merrill? That wouldn't happen again.

"Lissa, you should make every effort to follow the rules from this point forward," Merrill went on. "You have two strikes against you. I can only imagine what one more will do."

As lectures go, this one was sucking just as much as most others I'd gotten. I wondered if we were anywhere close to being done. Merrill had come around his desk and knelt beside my chair. He reached out to touch my cheek and I jerked away from him.

"Don't touch me," I said sullenly. He pulled his hand back and stood. If someone beat me, that didn't mean I had to love them. If they watched while someone else beat me, it didn't mean I loved them for that, either. And they certainly weren't going to put their hands on me afterward like everything was all right and nothing had happened.

"Gavin wants to see you," Merrill sighed.

"I don't want to see him," I muttered. "Ever."

"Lissa, please."

"Don't make me talk to him. Or to you. Or any other vampire on this God-forsaken planet."

"Very well. Go to your room," Merrill ordered. "I am keeping your cell phone and your computer for the time being." I almost laughed at his words. I wanted to tell him what he could do with my laptop and cell phone, but I didn't. I just got up from my seat, walked out of his study and went straight to my room.

Gavin passed my bedroom several times before he stopped. I didn't want to see him. Truly. I couldn't think of a single soul I'd met since becoming vampire that I would have welcomed right then. They'd all sold me down the river in one way or another.

I huddled on my sofa, watching television for a while, listening to the news concerning the usual rapes, murders, stabbings, child abuse, domestic violence—the entire gamut of human mistreatment, one for the other. Too bad there wasn't vampire television; I'm sure my beating would have been televised as a warning to others.

Half an hour before dawn, I went to my bedside table and pulled Gavin's ring from my finger, setting it down where he could find it. Then I turned to mist and made my way out the barest of cracks around the window, floating up to the roof. Dawn was too near for the stars to be visible except for one or two, far off.

Carefully, I undressed and folded my clothes. Even with the absence of ash as a telltale sign, my clothing would let them know they needn't come looking for me. There wasn't any concrete around the manor to stand on. Nothing else, either, that might prevent me from digging my way into the soil in case the pain became unbearable.

The rooftop was the next best thing. I knew the moment the sun peeked over the horizon, although my eyes were closed. My skin burned, and then blackened and began to boil as dawn broke over tranquil, English fields.

※

"Lissa!" Merrill's shout could be heard from one end of the manor to the other. He fled to the rooftop as fast as he could, the sun warm on his skin as he flew. "Lissa!" Merrill was crying her name as he found her, her skin completely blackened and flaking away. She toppled over as he rushed toward her. Wrapping Lissa's body in his arms, Merrill pulled her from the rooftop and sped toward a window.

The End

ABOUT THE AUTHOR:

Connie Suttle lives in Oklahoma with her patient, long-suffering husband and three cats (the cats are not long-suffering and are certainly not patient). Connie adores fantasy of all kinds and loves vampires, werewolves and most other things one might bump into in the night. When she isn't reading, she's writing (except when the cats are hungry). For information on forthcoming titles, please visit her website at www.subtledemon.com, her blog at subtledemon.blogspot.com or follow @subtledemon on twitter or Connie Suttle Author on Facebook.

Made in the USA
Charleston, SC
28 June 2014